Unfinished Business

Mia Kerick

Dreamspinner Press

Published by
Dreamspinner Press
5032 Capital Circle SW
Ste 2, PMB# 279
Tallahassee, FL 32305-7886
USA
http://www.dreamspinnerpress.com/

Unfinished Business
Copyright © 2013 by Mia Kerick

Cover Art by Catt Ford

ISBN: 978-1-62380-509-8
Digital ISBN: 978-1-62380-510-4

Printed in the United States of America
First Edition
March 2013

To my mother, who inspires me.

August 25, 2007
Cory

I'VE never lived a particularly conventional lifestyle; why start now?

I glanced around at all of the preppy coeds, accompanied by their equally preppy siblings and, if possible, even preppier parents. (Let me tell you, that added up to one heck of a lot of Madras and seersucker, and there was no shortage of those little ponies in the vicinity, either.) Clearly, it was an inherited gene, one that had completely bypassed my family tree. And like a J. Crew fall fashion show, parading up and down the staircase of my new apartment building, they carried floral Lilly Pulitzer garment bags, Lands' End totes, and groceries from Trader Joe's, not to mention that what looked like professional moving men cautiously lifted their brand new L.L.Bean furniture.

Now, I could appreciate the simplicity and timelessness of classic preppy décor. Really, I could. But at that particular moment, I didn't have much time to debate the merits of sailboat striped canvas vs. full-grain, hand-sanded leather couch fabric, as I was perched rather precariously midway up the first flight of stairs, opposite my wild-haired and even wilder-eyed boyfriend, wrestling with a queen-size mattress. And losing. Badly.

Hard to believe that the very same Cory Butana, who had never really belonged anywhere, was moving to live as male partners with his boyfriend of one month (or four years and one month, depending upon how you looked at it) into a tiny studio in the three-story brick apartment building just across the street from the Leighton University campus. Once again, not even slightly typical. And I certainly didn't give a hoot; I wouldn't switch places with a single one of those soon-to-be-yuppies who were swarming past me sporting Brooks Brothers chinos.

Just then, the unlikely pair that we must have made, struggling for dominance over a queen-size mattress, caught the eye of a discerning underclassman. The dude stepped out of the doorway of his apartment, hair rather tousled, looking more as if he'd just stepped off a sailboat, and stared down at us in a clear attempt to surmise just exactly how the unpolished bad boy and the unassuming schoolboy fit together as roommates at L.U. But it didn't take long for the gawker to snap out of his musings, readjust the sweater he wore loosely tied around his popped-up collar, and return his attention to the rolling Ralph Lauren duffel bag waiting for him in the hall, and most probably whom he was going to get to buy beer for him that night.

"Well, dear, the scenery around here certainly deserves a five-star rating." All right, I was already accustomed to the appreciative glances Brett received from the female student population. But a middle-aged *mother* had actually just snagged her daughter's arm and nodded less-than-subtly in Brett's direction. "If you like that rough-around-the-edges type."

Her daughter was a very agreeable girl. "Mom, all he really needs is a Kennedy-ish haircut and an IZOD shirt, and he'd be good to go."

Well, I wasn't blind; I could admit it: the woman and her acquiescent spawn were correct in their appraisals. Brett Taylor was freaking gorgeous. And when he stopped briefly on the landing to rip off his sweaty T-shirt in a single inelegant stroke, exposing six foot three inches of solid, sculpted male muscle, that cougar nearly dropped her blender.

But neither was I particularly worried. Brett was now, and had always been, completely devoted to me. There was a lot to be said for "unconventional," I supposed. So now, if all of those middle-aged moms and their pretty daughters would just pick their jaws up off of the dusty floor of the staircase, extricate their eyeballs from my boyfriend's spectacular pecs, and put one boat-shoed foot in front of another, we could all get on with moving day.

"Hey, kid, yer real quiet up there. This thing ain't too heavy for ya, is it?" Brett's sexy drawl rose up from beneath the mattress, a few steps below.

"No, I've got it. Just a couple more steps, and I'll be on the second floor." I felt the mattress jerk and then practically lift up out of my hands. As usual Brett was overcompensating for my lack of— "Okay, okay, Brett, I'm here!"

The two of us turned the mattress sideways to wedge it down the narrow hallway that led to our apartment. I pushed open the door with my backside and directed our burden to the center of the floor.

"Well, that's everything from the truck, baby." Brett tipped the mattress until it dropped down on the floor. Then we flopped down on it flat on our backs, our chests heaving from exertion. Grabbing my sweaty palm with his own and squeezing, Brett turned on his side to focus his green eyes on me. "Welcome home, kid."

I squeezed right back. "I'm starving. How about we order a couple of pizzas to celebrate?"

"Sure thing. I wonder if they make a decent Greek pie anywhere 'round here?"

August 26, 2007
Cory

"GOTTA say, I fuckin' love that Walmart Super Store—the place ain't nothin' short of a miracle!" Brett was unpacking groceries in our little kitchenette. I could hear the cabinets snapping open and closed. "We got us our sheets, towels, pots, furniture, an' groceries all in one stop, and mostly on sale, they all was!"

Yes, we were indeed bargain shoppers, but it couldn't be denied: our studio apartment was little more than a cubby hole, but we had set it up so it looked really cute, like a miniature home. I glanced around our new place from where I stood by the bed. The rather large bed. The focal point of our apartment, actually, as it took up at least half of the floor space. And I was sort of proud of the fact that I had found this shiny purple comforter in the very bottom of the sale bin, underneath a couple of outdated *Barney & Friends* beanbag chairs, in the bed and bath section of Walmart. Maybe it looked very gay, but it was still so pretty, and after I'd put on crisp new sheets, I'd draped my prize over the bed.

"What do you think?" I pointed with pride at my handiwork.

"Uh… that there's real nice. It looks super, uh, super invitin'." Every time Brett so much as looked at that bed, I would swear that the man blushed like he was the schoolboy. And I had to admit that I probably turned an interesting shade of pink, myself, each time I considered exactly how close the two of us would someday become on that very surface.

Time to open a window; it's getting hot in here.

Other than our enormous bed, we'd managed to squeeze in a reclining chair, a tall bureau, and a nightstand on the three sides of the bed, a slim futon folded into the shape of a couch, and a small white table with two matching chairs in the kitchen area. And all of that didn't break the bank. *Yeah, Brett is right—thank you, Super Walmart!*

"Hey, buddy! Catch this!" Brett tossed a single matching purple throw pillow, the only one that'd been left in the 75-percent-off bin, across the room into my waiting hands.

Propping it carefully on the bed next to the stuffed bear my father had given me as a "good luck at school" gift, I said rather suggestively, "Come here, Brett."

Brett took a few seconds to snap the cabinets shut and a few more to drag all of the empty plastic bags into a single pile, and then he very slowly crossed the room, tugging awkwardly at his shaggy blond curls as he walked.

"Ta da! Our bed—want to try it out?" Now I was sure of it; Brett was blushing like a schoolboy. "What's the matter? Scared of a shiny purple comforter? It's not gonna bite you!"

Before I knew it, I'd been playfully tackled onto my back on that silky bedspread and was gazing up into laughing emerald eyes. "This fluffy purple cloud might not bite *me*, but *I* might just take a bite outta *you*!" Brett's nose playfully nuzzled into the hollow of my neck, his teeth grazing my throat.

A bite outta me?

Well, that thought certainly brought me back to less jovial times, didn't it? Last summer's assault on me by the rather legendary (especially in his own mind) rock drummer, Steven Percy, was never very far from the front of my brain. But I managed to shrug away the disturbing memories as I angled my neck in such a way that Brett's shiny teeth could nip me in that sensitive place behind my ear. Nothing was going to ruin this moment for us. I wouldn't let it.

September 26, 2007
Brett

LOOKED like Cory'd got himself a bodyguard. A full-time one, at that. And it looked like I had got myself a second full-time job. But don't think I was complainin' none, 'cause I wasn't. No, sir. This here arrangement 'tween me and Cory'd got set up just exactly the way I wanted it. More'n that, it was the way I fuckin' *needed* it.

Turnin' down the main hallway in Welch Hall, Leighton University's largest academic buildin', I glanced at my watch and felt a smile creepin' onto my lips. Cory'd be in his biology lecture and then his lab for the next three hours. Nice 'n' safe. If I jogged back to the Bar and Grill across campus, I'd have more'n two hours to place food, linen, and glassware orders before I had to head back to pick up Cory and walk him to the library. Yes, sir. Sounded like a plan.

The very second I pushed through the restaurant's front door, my assistant, Barry Janek, spotted me and waved me over to the bar where he was countin' glasses. "You placing an order today, Boss? We seem to be down about eleven beer glasses."

"Shit! Eleven glasses in a week?" I slipped behind the bar and popped open the cash register drawer. "Yeah, I gotta put glasses on the list fer sure. How busy was the lunch rush after I left?" I picked up the pile of twenties to count 'em.

"It eased up as soon as you were out the door. And that's already done. I counted the cash and wrote the totals on a sticky note—it's on your desk."

"Mr. Get-'er-done, huh? You's gonna put me outta a job if I ain't careful." I winked so's he knew I was just givin' him a ration o' shit.

See, Barry was a great dude. A Business and Management major at L.U., Barry spent as much time workin' at the B&G as he did in his classes and studyin' at the library put together. I personally thought he liked the live action at the bar much more than the readin' and writin' and memorizin' kinda action he got in the classroom. And he'd do anythin' that needed to get done; he was a hands-on sorta guy. Kinda reminded me of the way it'd been 'tween me and Brian Deacon at the Downtown Pub back in Belton. Yup, Brian'd taught me how to be his right-hand man when I'd worked at the pub. In fact, the man'd taught me everythin' that I knew 'bout how to run a restaurant and bar. Plus Brian's excellent recommendation'd led me right to landin' the job I got now. And life sure was good up here at Leighton University.

Christ, I sound like one of them touristy T-shirts. Life is good, huh?

"What's your schedule look like for the rest of today, Boss?"

Rinsin' off my hands in the little sink behind the bar, I barely even had to stop and think. "Well, Cory's got class 'til four, and then I'm gonna bring him over to the library 'til after the dinner rush."

"Are you bringing him here to eat afterwards? I wouldn't mind seeing him; it's been a while since he's hung out here."

"Yeah, after dinnertime, I'm gonna go get him at the library and bring 'im over here so's he can eat, an' then we'll be off to the Sports Complex. We's gonna work out tonight." I suddenly had a vision of my baby wearin' them slippery joggin' shorts, runnin' laps 'round the weight-liftin' equipment on the indoor track. Some nights it was alls I could do to keep my brain on pumpin' iron and not on what it'd be like to be pumpin' on Cory's cute little ass, which teased me without no friggin' mercy each and every time the kid ran by.

Sure hope I ain't droolin' none.

"Sounds good, man. Where do you want me?" Barry nodded, his long dark red bangs fallin' into his eyes.

Didn't take me too much thought to answer that question, neither. "How's about you stay at the bar 'til dinner starts an' then head out back to help with the cookin' 'til supper's done? One of them work-study fry cooks called in sick for tonight."

"Consider it done." Barry turned back to where he'd been hangin' glasses without no comments or complaints. "And tell Cory to come say hello when he gets here, okay?"

"Will do." Come to think of it, Barry never questioned the way I ran around helter-skelter 'tween the academic buildin's, the library, and the Bar and Grill, escortin' my boyfriend every place he needed to be so's that he didn't never have to walk nowhere alone. And I sure appreciated my employee's closed mouth about that shit, as well as the way Barry could be counted on to cover for me whenever I hadta take off without no notice. Number one employee, for goddamned sure, Barry was.

So it looked like them T-shirts had it right. With friends like Barry and a boyfriend like Cory, life surely *was* good.

September 28, 2012
Brett

IT WAS fuckin' late, and I was more'n ready to hit the hay. And before noddin' off to sleep, I'd get me a chance to visit heaven, or, in plainer words, I'd get to hold my baby tight in my arms in our big purple bed. So's I didn't have no worries at all, did I?

Usually on weekend nights, Cory'd come to the B&G and hang out while I worked late, but this week he'd got swamped with homework, so's he'd stayed home to study. Gotta say, I'd sorely missed him. I wondered if I'd find Cory all tucked up snug in our bed, or if he'd be bent over the kitchen table, nose still stuck in them books.

Well, as folks say, wonders never cease, or somethin' on that line, 'cause the instant my key touched the lock, that there door flung wide open as if by magic. Seemed that the kid'd been hoverin' by the door, waitin' for his man to come home from work. And that there was a real nice ego boost, ain't gonna deny it.

Cory stood in the doorway. Silky-smooth bare chest with them perfect little muscles and just a tiny bit of scattered dark hair leadin' my wanderin' eyes downward, narrow waist and slim hips, and legs with a runner's definition, well-shaped arms in the perfect proportion and—

Oh, man.

I surely hadn't never seen my baby wearin' them silky royal-blue boxer shorts before. Snug, shiny, beggin' to be touched, them things was. Real nice.

What the hell is my boy up to?

"Uh, I'd better go hop in the shower, Cory. Gotta scrub off all o' the beer stickiness on me, y'know?"

Cory licked his lips kinda slow, and he just stood there gazin' at me, not sayin' nothin'.

Lickety-split, and I was in the shower, streams of hot water shootin' at the back of my head. Had to bend down a bit so's I could soak my whole mop of hair. Sometimes it seemed like everythin' in our studio was undersized, like this here shower. (And even Cory.) Everythin' but me. Uh-huh, once in a while I even felt like I was starrin' in a real-life *Gulliver's Travels* when I was in our apartment. Whatever. The warm spray of water still felt good but not nearly as good as Cory and them silky shorts was gonna feel pressed up against me in our bed.

Blue. Silky. Boxers.

Blue. Silky. Boxers.

So's maybe I didn't completely rinse all o' the suds from outta my hair.

That there ain't no crime, far as I know.

And it didn't take more'n a minute to scrub down there where the sun don't shine. Then I was done. Clean as a whistle.

Blue silky boxers, here I come.

Emergin' from the bathroom with nothin' but a towel wrapped around my middle, I glanced over toward the bed to see if Cory was waitin' on it for me. And he was. Oh Jesus, was he ever.

Draped like some kinda fallen angel over a puffy purple cloud was my baby. Cory's arms was flung out wide on that there shiny bedspread, and his legs was spread just enough, and the look in his eyes was more'n a little bit naughty. Had *come and get me* written all over him, head to toe, he sure did. And so's I just stood there gawkin' at the picture-perfect gift on the bed that was my Cory, my fingers tinglin' with a fierce need to touch.

"Come here, Brett."

I can do that. Ain't no problem whatsoever.

Climbin' over the foot of the bed, I kinda lost my towel, but that was okay. And the closer I moved to Cory, the better it got, 'cause the kid smelled like he'd soaked himself in a big tub o' peach iced tea. He just smelled so damn good. Downright temptin', yes, sir.

I s'posed it was well past time that my hands got busy. So's in one swift move, I dropped down beside Cory and pulled the kid right on top of me, so's we was belly-to-belly, my palms drawn like magnets to that there silk-covered ass. Then my lips found Cory's neck real quick and my nose pressed into them sweet, silky locks of hair; uh-huh, my senses got overloaded, yes, sir, they did. In a good way.

Wanna be insida him.

I pulled Cory's head down so's my mouth could meet with them pouty lips; alls I could manage to do was get a quick taste of that wiggly little tongue 'fore it wriggled outta my reach. So's I pulled that there tongue 'tween my teeth to keep it still, and I sucked on it 'til my boy couldn't keep still no more. And then before either of us even had a chance to blink, I'd seemed to've already flipped Cory underneath me, yanked them pretty boxers down his legs, and slipped 'em right offa his feet. Bare-naked, the two of us was soon grindin' our privates together without no shame. Only problem was that tonight I wanted more'n that.

Wanna get inside.

"Gettin' real tough for me to hold back." Them words slipped out like some kinda guilty confession. "Just wanna be insida ya so bad."

Soft, blue eyes lifted up and met my own lovin' gaze, not even a speck of fear to be seen there. "Then don't hold back."

In order for me to see my baby's whole face, which was super important to me just then, I pushed up offa the bed a measure, suspendin' myself over Cory without nothin' but the strength in my forearms. See, more'n almost anythin' in the whole entire world, I wanted to take what Cory'd just offered, but it just wasn't that damned simple. "You been through so much, y'know, when that bastard nearly raped ya over the summer, and, well… well, the truth is—baby, I can't hurt you and live with myself afterwards."

Like always, Cory's hands found the sides of my face underneath my mop of curls that was hangin' down. He looked right up at me and said, "The first time is always a little bit uncomfortable, Brett. I'm not afraid of that."

But I still remembered the bloody water I'd seen drippin' down the backs of Cory's legs in the shower after Steven Percy'd hurt him in July. That there memory had me sorta slumpin' offa Cory; I fell to my boy's side on the bed, my burnin' hot fire of passion all cooled down. "I ain't never gonna hurt you. I'm s'posed to be here to protect you from pain, see?"

This here ain't no joke: it almost sounded like Cory'd giggled at me a little. "But I know that you'd never *try* to hurt me—that's why it would be different." And then the kid smiled so bright, well, them blue eyes pretty much glowed. "And so what? Maybe it'll hurt a bit in the beginning, but making love will bring us closer than we've ever been." Cory's soft fingers pushed against my chin so's I'd turn my head and look at him. "I want us to make love. Please… please, Brett."

Now, I didn't *need* to have sex with Cory to be satisfied; I was already as happy as a man could ever be by just lovin' the kid with my whole heart and soul. But it sounded like maybe Cory had some needs of his own. "I *do* wanna… I wanna make love to you too." I sorta panted a coupla times 'cause I was scared of what I was gonna say next. "All o' the time I dream o' being joined up with you." Finally, I let my eyes meet Cory's.

Shimmerin' and hopeful and filled up with love, them blue eyes was. "I'm already joined with you, Brett. We eat, sleep, and do about everything else together. I just want to feel you inside me."

Before Cory's lovin' words could carry me away, I made my brain remember the real important shit. In fact, the most important shit of all. I pushed myself up so's I was sittin', which made Cory look kinda confused, along with a touch disappointed. "Sex. Well, it ain't no small step to take, you know, Cory. Ya see, it ain't just about our bodies feelin' good."

I could tell that Cory had absolutely no idea where I was goin' with this here little speech, and who the fuck could blame him? So's

I got offa the bed, helped Cory up too, and led him to the foot of the bed in front of that there futon-couch where there was a little space to stand. "Stay here for a second." I scrambled over to the bureau and pulled open my underwear drawer, and after riflin' around a bit, my hand popped out clutchin' a small black velvet box.

Yeah, you heard that right—a velvet box.

When I returned to Cory, I dropped right down onto one knee. My boyfriend's baby blues got real wide.

"Before we make love to each other, I wanna get somethin' straight 'tween us, 'kay?"

Them eyes grew wider. But I was pretty sure Cory nodded, if only just a hair.

Lookin' up at Cory, with all of the hope I held in my heart written plain right there on my face, I said these words: "I wanna offer you a commitment."

Them eyes got still even wider, they did. And the kid's head'd tilted a measure.

"Wanna give you my whole future and wanna ask for the same outta you."

Now them real wide eyes got kinda wet.

At this point, I couldn't do nothin' but pray, so's that's just exactly what I did. Didn't know just exactly who I was prayin' to, but that there wasn't the point.

Cory banged his forehead with his hand a coupla times as if he was tryin' to knock some cobwebs outta his brain. But on the good side, he didn't look disgusted at all. He spoke real quiet. "What *exactly* are you asking me, Brett?"

I figured that the best way to answer would most probably be to just go ahead and open up the damned box. So's that's what I did. A thin gold band studded with four tiny chips of sapphire and emerald (kinda reminded me of Cory's blue eyes and my green ones all lined up in a row) sparkled up at Cory. "Cory, I wanna keep you forever. I'm asking for ya to say you'll… that you'll, uh, you'll m-marry me."

Truth be told, I hadn't never seen eyes so wide and wet as Cory's was at that very moment. (Betcha mine was pretty wide and wet right then too.)

"W-wear my ring." Had me some trouble talkin'; couldn't breathe too good, neither.

The kid just gawked at me. And not likin' the sound of silence that was settin' in around us one bit, I decided it might be best to keep on explainin'. "See, it's like this: once we make love, it's gonna be like we already gone and took our vows."

Cory nodded. A real small nod, but I s'posed that I was makin' progress.

"When our bodies get joined up, so will our whole entire lives, honey, and we'll be married."

One tiny teardrop spilled outta Cory's left eye and rolled slowly down his check, kinda detourin' around that scar that Percy had left there. (Which totally pissed me off, but I pushed them feelin's aside for the moment.)

"So's, uh, what do ya say, baby?"

Cory cleared his throat. "I say my future is already yours."

"Once I make love to you, you'll be my husband?" My voice sounded like I was askin' a question, but really I was more givin' a warnin'. 'Cause truth was, folks shouldna be engagin' in sex acts unless they had forever in their hearts, y'see? And forever was sure as shit fillin' up my whole heart.

"I know."

"And so I'll be your husband, huh? Partners forever. I want this so fuckin' bad, can't hardly even think of nothin' else lately."

Oops. Was that there too much information?

"Yes." Cory looked down at the floor a bit.

"Yes?" So's I bent right on down so that I could search Cory's face for signs of truth. When I was satisfied that Cory's "yes" was for real, I lifted my boy's left hand super gentle-like and slid the sparkly jeweled band onto his ring finger. (Stopped for a moment and kinda stared at Cory's hand with my ring on it, I did. Wanted to burn that there awesome sight into my mind real good.) "Gonna have to tell everybody else that we got us engaged and we's gonna get hitched this summer. And we can have us a big fancy wedding ceremony then. But just you and me'll know the real truth: that us two got married tonight."

Cory looked kinda flustered at this point, but it didn't change things none. I stood up and grasped both of Cory's shakin' hands in mine. "After tonight, there ain't no goin' back."

Cory didn't try to pull his hands away. "Who s-said anything about going back?"

That there reply made me smile wide. "I love you, Cory."

"I love you too… and we'll be husbands tonight."

And so's our promise got sealed with a simple kiss.

"I GOT me some condoms, just in case, y'know? Think we oughta use 'em?" Naked as the day we was born, the two of us climbed over the futon onto the foot of the bed and then crawled into the center.

"I don't think so. It's the first time for both of us." Cory was still actin' real serious, super quiet, and was fiddlin' with his new ring like a kid with his first necktie. "I don't want anything between us. Just you… inside me."

Goose bumps popped up all over my scarred forearms. If Cory kept talkin' like that, well, it could all be over 'fore it even started, if ya catch my meanin'. Just sayin'. So's I leaned across Cory to grab a tube of lotion that I'd stuck in the drawer of the nightstand. "You ready to get this here show on the road, baby?"

Christ, could I've said somethin' less romantic if I'd tried?

Shit! Ain't no smile on that there pretty face now.

"I've been ready, Brett, for a long while now."

Oh.

"Well, alright then...." Nervous as a rat in a corner at being wholly intimate with this person I'd pretty much worshipped for forever, my arms wasn't none too steady when I pulled Cory against me.

Then that sweet soft voice rose up from beneath me. "Don't worry, Brett. This is gonna be beautiful—because it's us."

Them lovin' words bolstered up my confidence enough so that I could make my move. And as always, just kissin' my baby made me feel like I was the closest to heaven I was ever gonna get. When I bent my head and pressed my hungry lips to Cory's sweet-smellin' neck and then slid my lips down to his smooth chest, well, I was lost.

Finally, I reached around behind and readied Cory's private place with gentle lubed-up fingers, that just so happened to be as fuckin' nervous as the whole rest o' me. Alls I heard outta my boy was a coupla staggered gasps and maybe a teensy whimper, but when I put 'em all together, I was pretty sure them little sounds spelled out:

D-O-N-T S-T-O-P.

WELL, a gentleman don't spill all o' the details, and to be sure, I ain't braggin' none, but I'd have to say that our lovemakin' was fuckin' unreal. Sunk deep in my brand new husband's body, I'd felt so fuckin' right. Like I was really and truly home, y'know? And an added bonus: the whole time I was doin' my thing (sexually speakin', that is), I could feel them fragile little fingers, one of 'em now wearin' *my* ring, tenderly strokin' the skin of my back, my shoulders, my ass. And sometimes, them hands'd got to clutchin' at me and the kid's breath was raspin' in my ear, like maybe it hurt some, but then a second later, I'd heard a murmured, "Please don't stop." So's I didn't stop.

Lookin' down at Cory during our lovemakin', his head throwed back and that there silky dark hair spilled out all over our bargain-bin, purple throw pillow, I knew that the kid was as lost as me. (In a super good way.) Them misty eyes of my lover'd got all glazed over, but still they was locked right onto mine. And in them eyes, I could see my whole future.

Love and trust and friendship and desire and forever all wrapped up in a beautiful shade of blue. Yes, sir, that's just what I seen.

Thinkin' back on it, even though I was pretty much swimmin' around in a pool of total ecstasy, and for that matter barely keepin' my head above water, I'd just hadta speak right then. "Mine, Cory. Now, you's all mine. Gonna love ya for the rest of my life."

And if I'da thought I'd visited heaven with Cory before, well, I musta been mistaken, 'cause that there particular moment, my body all joined up with Cory's and his manhood tight against my palm, both of us reachin' our peaks together was—well shit, it was kinda like meetin' God. In plainer words? That there perfect moment'd been the cherry on top of our whole relationship—all o' the friendship and the love and the desire that we'd built over the past four years. The friggin' cherry on top.

Okay, so's what I *did* expect was pure physical ecstasy when I was buried deep insida my lover's body. And there wasn't no surprises in that department. No, sir. What I *did not* expect, though, was the expression on Cory's face as he'd clung onto me, all lost in passion. How to put it into words, huh? How 'bout "200 percent pleasure-filled"? Nah, that there made it sound kinda like I was talkin' about a stick o' chewin' gum. Or maybe the way to say it was "blissed-out." Tough to stick a label on the look on my baby's face when I'd been lovin' him, it surely was. And maybe our lovin'd started out with Cory doin' some jaw clenchin' and eye squintin', which mighta indicated pain (truth be told, that nearly had me pullin' my part right the hell outta my boy), but it didn't take long for things to change and for sheer fuckin' joy to take over.

And lookin' beside me now at Cory—who was busy sighin' like a cat at a cream bowl, stretchin' out his legs and then relaxin' them over and over again, twistin' his fingers all lazy-like in my hair—I was fairly sure that the kid showed all the signs of being satisfied. Had I done that to Cory with my untried body and all of its clumsy moves? Sure as shit looked that way.

"I really liked that."

Huh? Come again? Guess I'd been lost in my thoughts for a long while now. I turned on my side so as to study my lover's flushed face.

"I mean, I *really, really* liked it."

And before I could even blink, the kid was bawlin'.

Shit on a shingle—my boy's crying!

To put it plain, right about then I couldn't barely fuckin' breathe. I'd been pattin' myself on the back like I was some kinda sexual superhero, and clearly I'd hurt Cory. I was actually more like a sexual arch-fuckin'-villain! "Hey, hey, baby, did I hurt you or somethin'?"

Them sobs kept barrelin' outta that there slight chest, and now, Cory was also shakin' his head back and forth.

What the fu—?

"You gotta talk to me, baby. Tell me what the hell I done wrong! I'll fix it for ya. I'll fix it right up!" Not a good time to vomit, no, sir, so's I battled down my urge to barf.

Sniffin' real loud, Cory wiped at his drippin' eyes with the insides of his wrists. "I'm not sad, and I'm not hurt." The kid gulped, or maybe it was more of a hiccup.

"Tell. Me. What's. Wrong."

Them sobs started up again, as fuckin' ginormous as ever. "I'm crying 'cause… I'm crying 'cause it was *soooo* perfect!"

I felt my chest let out all o' the air it was holdin' in a huge whoosh of relief and then puff right back up again with pure pride, 'cause I'd made my boy cry tears of joy. I somehow managed to grin at my little buddy. "So's makin' love's somethin' you might wanna do again, y'know, sometime?"

Cory nodded, suddenly all quiet and shy. "Only with my husband, of course."

I got me everythin'.

Sure did look like I had everythin' that I'd never expected in life—and everythin' that I ever coulda dreamed of, but hadn't never let myself. Got me a life partner, a regular paycheck, a home, a coupla friends, and even a measure of respect.

Pulling the peach-smellin' bundle of boneless, satisfied man beside me into my arms, I sighed real deep and uttered, "Yup. You's all mine."

SMALL hands gently shakin' my shoulders woke me up in what musta been the super early hours of the mornin'. A spike of fear speared right up my spine, 'cause mostly when I got woke up in the middle of the night it was on account of me havin' just had a horrifyin' fuckin' nightmare. Not the case tonight. "Cory, everythin' okay, kid?"

Oh. Them small hands wasn't shakin' my shoulders no more. 'Cause now they was sinkin' down lower, underneath the blanket. *Oh.*

"Things are better than okay." A coupla Cory's fingers'd found their way to my privates. *Hmmm.* "But I woke up, and I can't get back to sleep."

In the dim light of early mornin', alls I could see was them tiny twin glows of reflected light shinin' outta Cory's eyes. I stifled a yawn. "Roll on over an' I'll rub your back; that might help ya catch some more Zs."

"I had a different idea."

Shit! I hoped like hell his butt wasn't hurtin' none on account o' what we'd done last night. "Well... uh, sure. Tell me what you want me to do."

Cory suddenly sat up so's the light comin' in the window lit up his whole face. And he sure didn't look like he was hurtin' none. No, sir. But I *did* recognize that expression—I usually called it Cory's "kid who's goin' to Disneyland" face.

"Well, Brett... I wanted to know that... or if...."

Huh?

"What d'you want, kid? Tell me and it's yours!"

Glancin' outta the window in this fuckin' adorable Bambi-like way, Cory spoke again, but it was quiet. In fact, it was too quiet.

"Speak up; can't hear ya real good."

The kid sucked in a big breath. "I wanted to know if you might wanna do it again? You know, make love… again… with me?"

Silence ruled, and that there's a fact.

Cory shrugged and then continued. "As in, *right now*?" Them soft hands that I knew so well grabbed onto one of my big mitts and squeezed. "I *really* liked it."

If a simple smile coulda took over a room, then my fuckin' huge grin coulda prob'ly conquered the entire planet!

"*Well?*" Impatient. My baby couldn't hardly wait for more o' my lovin'.

Pullin' Cory back down so's he was beside me, I finally found the right words. "There ain't nothin' I'd rather do right now than make love to my beautiful husband." And takin' Cory in my now steady arms, I set out to show him just how fuckin' deep my love ran.

October 3, 2007
Brett

THE Leighton University Bar and Grill was definitely the place on campus to see and be seen, so to speak. Not that I gave a crap about that kinda shit. The establishment made its home on the entire first floor of the Food Services Buildin', which was conveniently located smack-dab in the middle of the six sorta squareish brick academic buildin's.

Now, the B&G certainly wasn't no hole-in-the-wall bar. It's two square-shaped rooms: the pub with the ginormous oak bar all surrounded by high tables and stools, air hockey games, one hell of a nice pool table, and a coupla wide-screen televisions, and the classy dinin' area full o' sturdy tables and old-fashioned chairs; took me most of a full minute to walk from end to end. Behind them two public rooms was what got called a *state-of-the-art* (but personally, I kinda thought of it more as *fancy-assed)* kitchen and my own personal cozy office, which I gotta come clean about; I fuckin' loved it.

But right now I wasn't sittin' on my ass on my comfy leather chair in my quiet office, no, sir. See, earlier in the week the Food Services Department's head honcho (aka, my big boss, Ralph Feder) had told me to report to his office upstairs at 11:00 a.m. today for my very first job review. And so's that is just exactly where I was, and to make a good impression, I'd even showed up maybe three or so minutes early.

Now Ralph Feder wasn't no hulkin' Brian Deacon or nothin'; he was just a short, chubby, baldin' dude with a pair of them little half-eye glasses perched on the end of a kinda puffy, reddish nose. And truth be told, the guy couldn't sit still for the life of him; he was always fidgetin'. If he wasn't wigglin' around in his chair, he was scratchin' his head or chewin' his nails like he was some-kinda nervous.

Peerin' through the cracked-open doorway of Feder's office, my fist all set to knock a coupla times, I caught me a glimpse of my boss rollin' his chair back a measure so as to unwedge the desk from his big round belly. Noticin' me, he glanced down at his black rubber wristwatch and said, "Oh... oh, Mr. Taylor, you're here. Very good. Yes, yes, very good. Please, uh, sit down." The man gestured across his cluttered office to a gray foldin' chair that was jammed between four stacks of what looked like business ledgers and a statue of a giant milk shake, maybe. Hard to say, but I thought it was most prob'ly strawberry.

"Yes, sir. I'm pretty sure ya told me to be here at eleven, yeah?"

"Well, yes... yes, I believe that is what I said." Feder reached over and shuffled the papers around on his messy desk until his pudgy pink fingers emerged from the crap pile, holdin' a clipboard. "Aaah, yes, let's see... where am I?"

Okay, *that* dude was a heart attack waitin' to happen, if I'd ever saw me one. Not that nobody'd asked my opinion on it, 'cause they sure hadn't. I was just sayin'. And besides, that there wasn't my concern, now, was it? My single concern was makin' a livin' so's I could take care of Cory. So's I sat up real straight in my chair and looked at Feder right in them spectacled eyes, just like Brian'd taught me to do, back at the Downtown Pub.

Feder shifted his narrow eyes back and forth from the paper-covered floor to me, until he found his train of thought. While chewin' on the cap of his pen, he mumbled, "Sho Mishter Taywa," then removed the pen cap from his mouth and started again. "Uh, rather, so Mr. Taylor, or, do you mind if I call you Brett?"

I nodded, shook my head, and then nodded again, but somehow Feder seemed to get that it was okay to call me by my first name. And I had to fuckin' struggle to keep the eye contact goin' strong.

"Brett... yes, Brett. I called you here to, uh... uh...." Head roll, nose rub, balls adjustment, possibly (hard to say just what the guy's hand was doin' under his desk); the man couldn't keep his ass still. Couldn't imagine that dude sittin' through a church service, or somethin'. "Yes, I've called you here to review your work so that we can... uh, progress toward... the, uh... future. In a p-positive manner, right?"

I nodded. "Yes, sir."

Where in hell is this here conversation goin'?

"And, uh... firstly, I'd like to inform you, uh, that I've had a great deal, oh, yes... a great deal of, uh, let's say, *difficulty*, keeping this position filled in... the, uh... past, yes." Leanin' butt scratch, nail bite, stifled yawn. Then that pen cap got stuck right inside the dude's left ear, and the truth was, it was more'n a little bit nasty, but I schooled my face away from lookin' revolted. (At least that was the plan; I hoped like hell I'd pulled it off.) "Let's... let's... uh, let's face it, uh, Brett; working at the B&G is like working at ... let's say, an enormous fraternity party. The past managers, uh, all students, you see, well, let's say that they... uh, *took advantage* of the relaxed environment. Yes, I... uh, think that would be, uh, accurate."

Sometimes keepin' yer lips sealed is just the right way to go. So's that's what I did, but I kept my ears wide open.

"Let's just say, well... uh, let's just say that, as the Food Services director here at Leighton University, the B&, uh, G has long been my, well, let's call it my *Achilles' heel*."

Yeah, okay. Whatever. I didn't have a clue what the dude was sputterin' on about or what the fuck was wrong with his foot, but I stayed shut up.

"Well, let's just say, well, uh... it looks like I found the right... uh, man for the uh, job."

Frankly, I thought that Feder looked rather relieved to've spilled that there piece of information, but it also looked like he might be expectin' me to say somethin' back to him. Short and sweet, that's just how I was gonna keep it. "Thank you, sir."

That worked, huh?

"Since I... since I... since I have to, uh, oversee all of the food services, uh, well... let's just say my plate is very full."

Judgin' by the size of his belly, I was pretty damn sure the dude's plate was full most of the time. And since it seemed that my evaluation was goin' pretty good without none of my verbal contribution, I decided I'd just nod again.

Finally, them spectacled eyes rose up offa the messy floor to look real hard at me. I shifted in my seat, knowin' full well that my value was bein' weighed up. "What can I say, uh, Brett? There are… let's just say there are no problems being reported from the, uh, B&G this year… well, not so far.

"Since, uh, since the day you took over the management… let's just say we decided to go with a completely, uh, a completely *different* type of person, that's not to say that you aren't, uh, intelligent… yes, but I didn't hire a college student this time." Feder actually chuckled a bit. "Nope, I went with a high school dropout and, hey… uh, what do you know? You are, uh, working out… well, great."

And one more time, "Thank you, sir."

In one slimy stroke, that there pen cap forged a path right on through what little was left of Feder's kinda greasy hair. "Yes, indeed, uh… Brett. Your employees seem to… to really, well, *respect* you. They arrive punctually, yes, and they actually get their, ah, their jobs done. Let's just say that… uh, that never happened in the past. No, never."

Well, I didn't know nothin' about how much my employees respected me; I kinda thought that they was all just scared shitless of me. I didn't never even hafta say too much to them workers in actual words. Didn't need to 'cause my power was all in my eyebrows. Yup, ya heard me right. If one of 'em was slouchin' on the job, alls I had to do was raise up one eyebrow (didn't really matter which one—the left and the right worked equally good) and send 'im a nasty glare, and what d'ya know? Problem solved! That there worker was scurryin' to get his ass back on the job!

Then Feder pushed up offa his rollin' chair and was on his feet, real quick-like for a chubby dude. "And no more late night bar fights… uh, not so far this school year, that is. Last year I had the campus police complaining in my office, let's just say every

Monday morning." He'd moved to stand right in front of me. And I mean, *right* in front of me; my nose nearly brushed the dude's protrudin' belly.

So's I looked up at the dude and sent him a super toned-down version of my evil eye, hopin' he might back off a coupla steps. Which he did. The dude stumbled back 'til he was mostly sittin' on his desk. (Uh-huh. As Cory'd said to me a bunch of times, "That scowl you send all your employees to keep them in line is quite an effective tool for discouraging undesirable behavior." You said it, kid.) Looked like it worked on bosses too.

"And the kitchen equipment... well, nothing breaks anymore...."

Just call me Mr. Fix-it.

By the random twitchin' of his right eyelid, I was pretty sure that Feder'd sat down smack-dab on his pointy pen cap.

"And I can't forget the accounts... well, uh, they are all balancing. No discrepancies, uh, at all."

"Well, I got me Barry to help out with all of the money countin' shi—stuff." I rubbed my chin. "And he's real good."

Reachin' out to shake my hand, Feder seemed to get more tongue-tied than he usually was, which really was sayin' somethin'. "Yes... well, I... ah, I...."

That there was my cue. I stood right up, grasped the man's clammy palm and said, "I'm real pleased that... that *you* are real pleased with my job performance. And thank you for your input, Mr. Feder."

Keep up the eye contact with them spasm-y eyes, Taylor. Even if it kills you.

"No, no, no... Brett, please call me Ralph... uh, okay?" At this point, he was pretty much beamin' at me with more'n a little love in his eyes.

Is the dude gonna hug me?

Frankly, I wasn't too comfortable with that there idea.

"Now, uh, Brett... do you have any, you know, any questions for me?"

Now to put it real short an' sweet, I thought I oughta get outta there while the gettin' was still good. Ya know, quit while yer ahead, right? "No, sir, or rather, Ralph. Anyhow, I figure I better just mosey on back to the B&G, keep things runnin' smooth and all, 'kay?"

"Yes… of course, Brett. I'd never want to keep you… uh, to keep you from doing your job. So, uh… so thank you for your hard work. It's, well, let's just say it is paying off nicely."

So's I kinda spun on my boot heel and got the hell outta that there stuffy little office, but I gotta say, my face was wearin' one fuck of a huge shit-eatin' grin. Soon as I got to the stairs, I let this big whoosh of air rush outta my lungs. And then I felt a burnin' need to call up my baby and tell him all the good news 'bout my job. Who better to share it with than the dude I was buildin' a future for?

October 5, 2007
Brett

SHIT, them waitresses can't get enough o' me!

Sure, that might sound like a slice o' heaven to most men, but for me it wasn't nothin' but a fuckin' pain in my ass. And I aimed to squelch the romantic hopes of each and every one of them fresh-faced college gals who was fixed on gettin' themselves a little taste of their wrong-side-of-the-tracks boss man. Yeah, might as well add "turnin' off horny chicks" to my already jam-packed job description.

Most of the time I got that there job done real easy-like, with a coupla sharp words and one of them "evil eye" dirty looks that I was so good at. But there was this one particular young lady—yup, there was always one bad apple in the bunch—who I just couldn't manage to shake off. No, sir. Fuckin' determined, that's what Megan Trasker was. That there cocktail waitress had them coffee-colored cat eyes o' hers superglued right onto my ass, which wasn't no public property. In plain words, I didn't have even a spark of interest in the girl, seein' as I wasn't no longer on the market—y'know, all married off to Cory. Not to mention that she wasn't interestin' to me, neither.

The rest of the male population who frequented the B&G didn't share my lack of interest in the so-called "sexy" Miss Trasker. Them Leighton University wanna-be studs couldn't barely keep their paws offa her pushed-up boobs and her sturdy, jeans-clad ass. So's this here situation led to what I'd started callin' "the damsel in distress game" that Megan liked to play. With me. Which sucked.

IT WENT like this: first, Megan Trasker'd flirt her curvy ass off with Tom, Dick, and/or Harry. And I mean, she'd tease 'im real good 'til the guy got himself a stiffy, and she got herself a response. Next, one of 'em drunken losers would make his move; he'd ask her out, grab her arm, or follow her to the bar. Got the picture? Then all of a sudden, hot-to-trot, "come and get me, boys" Megan morphed into Polly Purebred, all sugary-sweet and innocent as the day was long. And you got yourself one guess 'bout whose job it was to save that bitch's round ass.

Yes, one knight in shining armor, Brett Taylor, at your service!

And this fucked-up routine was surely gettin' old.

Looked like another round of "the damsel in distress game" was in progress tonight. Yes, sir. After once again failin' to score with yours truly in the walk-in fridge earlier in the evenin', which was apparently Megan's Plan A, she'd moved on to what I'm gonna refer to as Plan B. So's she proceeded to drape herself all over this tall, skinny (and super clueless) dude who sported a spiked-up jet-black Mohawk hairdo. Yeah, Mohawk-man pretty much thought he'd died and gone to friggin' beautiful-babe heaven when light-haired, dark-eyed Megan's big tits got stuffed right into his face as she'd served him a beer, droolin' all over him like he was the cat's pajamas.

In no time at all, he started firin' off his pickup lines, real noisy and disruptive. Prob'ly already mostly drunk, he was. "Hey, Miss Meggie, where you been all my life?"

Standin' over by the bar, I could already see where this shit was headin'. Downhill, and fast.

Then one of them pointy boobs got pretty much thrust into the dude's left ear when Megan leaned over to serve his buddy a brew. "Where do you think I've been? Right here, waiting for you, honey." She kept the volume of her voice on the down-low, 'cause it wasn't part o' her game for me to know that she'd been leadin' him on. But still I could hear her flirtin' words, since my ears was always perked up for trouble. That there was a part o' my job.

A soft giggle, a coy smile. Five, four, three, two—"Hey, shithead! Get your hands off my ass!"

I looked over. *Just* as expected. Guess I can predict the fuckin' future.

"Brett, Brett! This asshole is manhandling me!" Tears of outrage soon followed. *Also* expected.

Only because it was my fuckin' job, I was at Megan's side in a flash. She wasted no time before turnin' to me and smashin' that there hefty set o' boobs into my ribcage. And for the record, I gotta say that Mohawk-man looked real confused—nah, I'd hafta call that there expression he was wearin' shell-shocked.

"This animal can't keep his dirty hands to himself!" Now them crocodile tears was rushin' like the Colorado River in springtime. "Can I take a minute... to collect myself... in your office?"

I was real proud of myself 'cause I didn't roll my eyes at her none. See, this here type of scene happened with Megan at least three times each week. "Sure, go on ahead, Megan. I'll come talk to ya in a coupla minutes."

Meanwhile Mohawk-man was kinda stutterin', "B-but, sh-she wanted me. Really, she d-did." Snappin' out of his state of horny-shock and divin' headfirst into pissed-off-ness, he was. "She w-was asking for it!"

Well, that line wasn't gonna fly at this here bar. I'd seen my own Cory get harassed plenty enough at the Downtown Pub; I wasn't about to allow no attitude like that fly, not even if it was aimed at trampy Megan. "Sir, I'm gonna hafta ask ya to leave the bar. There ain't no touchin' the waitstaff allowed at this establishment, see?"

"But ask anybody—she was coming on to me!" The dude looked around at his buddies for support, but alls they did was shrug and kept suckin' on their brews.

"Let's not make this into no big problem 'tween us. It's simple, sir, ya grabbed ahold of a server, and that ain't allowed." Everybody in the bar'd got real silent, and they was gawkin' at us like we was a made-for-TV movie. Thankfully, Mohawk-man stood up, plucked his jacket offa his stool, and made for the door, all the while shakin' his head and cursin' a bit.

I felt it was my duty to shout out after him, "Don't wanna see yer face 'round here for a month o' Sundays! And when you do come back, if ya hafta, sit on yer fuckin' hands!"

Dealin' with Mohawk-man was the easy part.

Now comes the tricky shit.

After I made sure that all was settled down in the bar, I knew it was time to check on Megan, who was waitin' for me in my office. Openin' the door wide, and bein' damned sure to leave it that way, I could hear the sounds of snifflin' and whimperin'. Yup, Megan'd planted her cryin' ass right onto what I sorta thought of as "Cory's spot" on the couch.

Cory's spot. Just the thought of the sweet kid made me wanna smile. Surely did.

"'Scuse me, Megan…. Um, I just wanted to let you know that I kicked that there dude outta the bar, and he won't be comin' back here for a long while." Them sniffles still got louder. Okay, looked like I was gonna hafta try a measure harder here. "Um, one more thing—I'm real sorry that happened to ya." Duty done, 's far as I was concerned.

So's why ain't she gettin' up offa Cory's spot and makin' tracks to the door?

Nothin' usually goes like you plan it, huh? But on the bright side, the girl's tears'd pretty much stopped. On a dime, more'r less, which had to make ya wonder some.

"Thank you *sooooo* much for saving me, Brett. I was *sooooo* scared!" And in less than a millisecond that there girl'd launched herself right up offa the couch and into my stiff arms.

Workin' to untangle myself from them perfumey curls and clingin' arms, I said, "It's my job to look out for *all* of the servers— it's my *job.*" Uh-oh… I was pretty sure that them pointy-nailed fingers'd got locked solid 'round my neck. "Megan, you gotta let go o' me, huh?"

Loosenin' her hold just enough to lean back and look in my eyes, Megan continued with her evenin's agenda. Let's refer to it as Plan B, part 2. "You really came to my rescue in there…. How can I *thank* you?"

I did this kinda karate-spin-kick-thingy (minus the kick part) so as to unhitch the girl offa me the rest o' the way, and then, like in that kid's game, I took me one giant step backward. "Ain't no need to thank me. Was just doin' my job. Now, I figure that you're gonna want the rest of the night off, to calm yerself down, right?"

I got this kinda coy nod from Megan: head tiltin' down, eyes tiltin' up. Got the picture?

"And I'm gonna have one of them bouncers walk you back to yer dorm." Got myself grabbed again, I did, this time by my shoulders.

"I want *you* to walk me home." Them hands slid right down my arms to my hips. Uh-huh, I'd heard this here song and dance before a time or two… or two hundred.

"Well, I'm sorry, Megan, but I gotta get back to work. You'll be real safe with Billy Miller. He can take ya back, so's try to relax and enjoy yer evenin' off."

Shit on a shingle! Them spidery fingers was climbin' north, up my chest now.

"No, Brett… I want *you* to take me home. And when we get back to my place, I can show you my *appreciation* for how you saved me from that asshole. It'll be fun."

Not on your fuckin' life, Trasker; this here's a married man yer propositionin'!

Enough was sure as shit enough. I sorta batted her hands offa my chest, and none too gently, I must admit. "Sit down, Megan." So's the pair of us sat down on the couch; I was careful to plant my ass on the opposite end from the spot where she'd planted hers. "We gotta have us a talk."

Megan'd already started poutin' like a schoolgirl, so's she musta sensed the direction I was headin' in. "What do you wanna say?"

Knowin' that it usually scared folks off, I started out by sendin' a level eight (on a scale of one to ten) evil glare her way. Just to set the stage, so to speak. Well, I figured at least it couldn't hurt, right? "It's like this, Megan: I am engaged to get married. Got me a fella' who's wearin' my ring."

The girl fired back with a "so, what?" kinda look. Yup. Silent, but deadly.

"I ain't even slightly interested in messin' around with nobody else." That there was plain-speakin', huh?

"But your *boyfriend* doesn't even have to know that we got together." Before I could say nothin', the chick'd lunged across the sofa and had landed her ass pretty much in my lap. "Just come back to my place and we'll see what happens—it doesn't have to mean anything—"

I stood right on up, and Megan kinda half slid and half fell to the floor. "I ain't interested." And I shook my head hard, not givin' her so much as a "you okay?" glance.

"Don't you want to get a little *girl-on-boy* action?" Standin' up slowly, she reached behind herself to untie her apron, all casual-like, as if we was discussin' somethin' as dull as the weather. "Everybody knows that you're not even gay."

Them words hit me like a slap. Took me a second to find my voice, but when I did, I fuckin' yelled. "I *said* I ain't interested, and I ain't gonna explain myself to the likes of you! So's you'd better hear what I'm tellin' ya, Megan, or go find yerself another job, got it?" I hoped the bitch'd quit right there on the spot, but I didn't have me no such luck.

She sorta strutted all wiggly assed across the room to the door. "It won't hurt me any if you want to keep on fooling yourself into thinking that you're gay." Megan turned around and looked back at me with what I took for an expression of pity. "And I'm perfectly fine to work the rest of the night. I'm not about to miss out on a whole night of tips for nothing." And with a haughty flip of that shaggy rug of light-brown hair, the girl was gone.

Well, at least I thought she was gone, but I ain't never been a particularly lucky dude in most areas of my life ('cept for in gettin' Cory). So's a moment later, after I'd let my breath whoosh out and my shoulders slump down in relief, that there cat-eyed gaze was back in the doorway, starin' me down once again. "And one more thing, Brett Taylor, keep in mind that I'll be around when you come to your senses and realize that you're straight as a fucking arrow."

Now it was my turn to be shell-shocked. Alls I could do was stand there and gawk at the now empty doorway. But soon my mind went and got all cluttered up with thoughts of Cory, and how opposite he was from Megan. How sweet and pure he was, how classy he always acted, and how he was the smartest person I'd ever met. Mostly I was just glad that I had a person like him to go home to every night and call mine.

And I decided right there and then that Cory wouldn't never learn about all of the disgustin', slutty shit that went on with girls like Megan Trasker. What the kid didn't know wouldn't hurt him none. I'd make goddamned sure of that.

October 6, 2007
Cory

I ALWAYS got a seat of honor at the bar on Saturday nights when Brett had to work. The last stool on the right side of the long bar, directly in front of the cash register might as well have had my name stenciled on it. And it was the place I allowed myself to cut loose on an occasional evening, instead of burying my nose in books. Well, being underage, "cutting loose" didn't include drinking any alcohol, but I still had my share of fun. I ate greasy bar food, drank iced tea, and did no insignificant amount of people-watching.

Now, over the past few years of us working together at the Downtown Pub, Brett had become more and more what could be referred to as *dangerously possessive* of me. Or maybe you could call it *intensely protective*. Or, more accurately, probably, a combination of both. So normally, when anyone, male or female, young or old, tall or short (I could go on, but I think the sentiment is already quite clear), even so much as looked in my direction, they were putting themselves at risk of incurring the wrath of Brett. Which included, at minimum, receiving a rather menacing glare, and at most, well, I'd seen him bloody more than one out-of-line customer at the Downtown Pub. Which wasn't much fun for anyone.

Tonight was different. Don't get me wrong, the students were behaving no differently from usual; they were drinking, playing bar games, snacking on greasy, fried snacks, laughing together, and of course, attempting to hook up with one another. Anything it took to unwind from a week of hitting the books, I supposed. But Brett wasn't glaring at or lurking menacingly close to any customer who dared to come within a two-foot radius of me.

Maybe I should feel Brett's forehead; he could be coming down with something.

At that moment, from his spot behind the bar, Brett looked up from his paperwork, glanced over at me, and smiled easily. Yes, you heard me right—he actually smiled. And it wasn't one of those smirking grimaces that let me know he was barely holding himself back from slipping into "attack mode", or so he called it, when he felt it necessary to defend my honor. It was also not out of the realm of possibility that he may have also just winked at me.

My husband appeared relaxed... and happy. Come to think of it, I'd seen a lot of "relaxed and happy" on Brett lately. Ever since he'd slipped that thin, jeweled band on my ring finger. *Hmmm.*

"This seat taken?"

I quickly made my way from *The Brett Zone* back to planet Earth and turned to see the face of a young man wearing a rather expectant expression.

"I asked if this seat was taken, not what the population of Zimbabwe is."

"Oh. Oh, no. I mean, *no*, that seat is empty." It was almost always empty whenever I was at the bar, thanks to Brett's excellent bodyguard service. "You can sit there, no problem." I folded my hands neatly on the bar.

"What are you drinking?"

Not that I cared one way or the other, but this cloud of sweet-but-still-manly cologne engulfed me when the guy sat down. I looked at my hands. "Iced tea, uh, not the Long Island kind. I'm nineteen, so...."

"Say no more, I get it. No booze for the little dude." The guy signaled to Barry that he wanted a beer from the tap. Then he called out, "And, Barry, another iced tea for him."

I looked up. "Thanks." And then the guy smiled, which did a great deal to brighten his rather sullen-looking face. Taking in the overall dark and grim effect of his carefully planned black attire, I concluded that he considered himself Goth or New Age, or something on that line.

"Hell, I wish I could buy you a beer, seeing as you're old enough to go to war and take a bullet for your country. But you're not old enough to sip on a brew at a bar, which is just not right." The guy ran his fingers through his spiky black hair, hair as sinfully dark as my father's.

"Don't worry about it. I mean, I'm fine with iced tea." I lifted my glass and tilted it around a little so that that ice cubes splashed in the bottom. "Really."

Reaching over the bar, the guy snatched the beer out of Barry's outstretched hand. "You're always on the ball and ready with my beer, buddy. Thanks." He slapped some money down on the bar. After sucking the foam from off the top of his beer, he asked, "You a student here?"

Another quick glance at the guy told me that his eyes were lined generously in dark purple. It didn't bother me; I'd just noticed, that's all. "Yeah. I'm a freshman… School of Business."

"Oh. One of those yuppies-in-training?" Dark eyes flashed me a derogatory glance. "I see."

Now, as I said earlier, Brett had seemed more secure in our relationship since we'd made love, but that didn't mean he was going to lie down and roll over when someone tried to move in on his territory. I wondered just how and when Brett's "DTs" (or so I called the "discouragement techniques" that he used to dissuade both men and women who showed too much interest in me) would begin to unfold.

You see, on evenings that I visited the B&G, Brett selected certain opportune moments to swing by my bar stool to stake his claim (on me). Sometimes, if his nasty glare had proved ineffective in damponing the interest of an eager suitor, he'd step up behind my stool and drop a lingering kiss behind my left ear. (That certainly spoke louder than mere words *or* his evil eye, plus I really liked it.) And over the past week, he'd started reaching across the bar and none-too-subtly fiddling around with my ring, all the while staring meaningfully into the hopeful gentleman's eyes. In fact, Brett had developed a complete repertoire of nonverbal "DTs." Suggestive hair-ruffling, conveniently timed drink delivery, a manly shoulder rub accompanied by the flirtatious arm slug—well, he had mastered many strategies by which to deliver his less-than-understated message. His DT repertoire was actually rather impressive (and effective); it was as if I wore a label on my forehead that said "taken." And I really didn't mind at all.

In any case, the time for DTs was well overdue. Yes, its time had come and gone.

"I'm a junior, fine arts major. And old enough to buy beer, but just barely."

I smiled only a little, unsure if the guy was just being friendly or if he was interested. I never encouraged *that kind* of interest. So when there was a surge of movement toward the bar, I expected that I'd be cleverly extricated from my bar stool and safely ensconced in the arms of my fiancé before I was trampled in the stampede. But Brett was nowhere to be seen. Weird. *Really weird.*

However, my new friend at the bar stepped in front of me, and his voice rose over the rumble. "Hey, hey... guys, you almost flattened this dude sitting here at the bar! Mind your manners!" He then moved between my bar stool and what appeared to be a significant portion of the L.U. Football Team that had spilled forth from out of nowhere.

"Sorry, Ian, but you *told* us to meet you here, so... here we are." Now, Ian, the Goth dude, wasn't short, but he was dwarfed, at least in wideness, by the guy who had just stumbled forward to speak to him. "And who's this kid, anyways?" He took a long look at me. "Man, he looks kinda young. He's not jail bait or anything, is he?"

Ian just rolled his eyes and turned to look at me. "Sorry. These oafs usually restrict their tackling to the opposing team, but every once in a while they get carried away."

"Funny, E." The huge guy slapped Ian on the back with a grin. "Now order us some beers, we're thirsty... and introduce me to your boyfriend, here."

Following a second dramatic eye roll, Ian said, "This, unfortunately, is my roommate, Ben Reed, running back, and those hulks backing him up are Christian Gates, special teams, for now, at least, and Hunter Fleming, who wishes he was the first string QB.

And I'm Ian Webster, lucky suite-mate of these two and a few oversized others."

I nodded. "Names *and* positions... nice."

"Who's the boy?" This time it was the burly, red-haired Christian asking. "He your boyfriend, E?"

"It is *so* hard to be smooth with these animals around." Ian sat back down on his stool in utter defeat. "Guys, this is not my boyfriend, and probably never will be thanks to your unwanted help tonight. In fact, I just met... uh...."

"Cory." I supplied the guy with my first name.

"Yeah, this is Cory." He smiled at me and then looked out across the sea of athletes. "And right now Cory is wondering how many points you guys get for flattening a five-foot seven-inch business major."

"Way more points than we get for an old lady!" I couldn't tell exactly where that crack came from.

"I think it might be the beer they're after, not me. I should know better than to sit at the bar on a victorious game day." I had to laugh. "Go Hawks!"

"I like the little guy! Let's keep him!" Again, a voice from the crowd piped up.

Ben, the African-American running back, tapped me lightly on the shoulder. "So, Cory, are you gay?"

This time Ian rolled his eyes and groaned at the same time. "Charming, Ben." He turned his lined eyes toward me. "I am so sorry. Ben feels he has to be my own personal match.com service." Ian turned to his friend. "Ben, honestly, I don't need your help. I do *fine* all by myself."

But apparently the Leighton University Football Team did not agree with that sentiment. A chorus of deep, masculine grunts of disagreement could not be missed, and then the guy named Hunter shouted, "Ian, who do you think you're kidding? You don't get any action at all!"

"Picky, picky, picky—that's what you are!"

"Maybe E's luck is about to change. Right, Cory?" Ben was certainly persistent.

And just as suddenly as they'd swarmed up to the bar, the L.U. Football Team dispersed throughout the bar in search of cocktail waitresses, noisily reliving their "slaughter" of a team called the Panthers earlier that day.

As Ian settled back onto his bar stool and ordered another beer, I waited for Brett to initiate the first stages of his DTs, genuinely surprised that they hadn't already been launched.

Brett

LIKE a rock in my shoe, that there punker asshole is.

But then, you could look at a rock stuck insida yer boot in one of two ways, couldn't ya? You could see it as a small, but real painful problem, chippin' away at yer ability to keep yer head in the game. Or, you could view that there pebble as nothin' but a fuckin' minor irritation, sure as shit not somethin' that you liked or hoped for, but somethin' you could put up with if ya hadta.

So's in honor of me and Cory's honest commitment to each other and that there ring the kid wore on his finger that'd sealed the deal, I was gonna choose option two. 'Cause I knew that all of them dudes who wanted to get busy with my baby wasn't gonna get nowhere with him, was they?

Not to say that right about now it ain't well past time to shake that fuckin' annoyin' little rock right the hell outta my work boot, huh?

Enough was enough already. So's I eyeballed Barry, who was standin' pretty much smack-dab in front of Cory and that there Goth dude, with a "is that there sucker hittin' on my baby?" sort of look, and he didn't shoot back no SOS eyes, so's I figured I was safe to go out back to check on my nearly always shorthanded fry cooks.

When I got back, though, and I was only gone for a coupla minutes, mind you, Cory was hidden behind a wall of muscle-bound, thick-necked giants, all wearin' green and white L.U. Football T-shirts, sweatshirts, and jackets. Now, I didn't wanna seem like the kid's keeper or nothin', but on the other hand, I didn't let nobody fuck around with what was mine. And Cory was mine. Done deal. Yes, sir.

So's one more time I peered over at Barry, and his eyes didn't so much send me no SOS, but he did seem kinda miffed, and that there was enough to have me shovin' my way through all of them massive dudes to get to Cory's stool. *Better safe than sorry, huh?* And before all of them gawkin' monsters and their vampire-lookin' leader (who was surroundin' my baby like ants on honey) knew what was goin' on, I was passin' by, stickin' my fingers into Cory's silky hair, clear code for "this here boy is mine." And Cory grinned at me. Real cute, he was.

A big part o' me wanted to ask, "Any questions, losers?" but I held myself back outta respect for my husband.

Prob'ly shouldna held back, though, seein' as that was when all of them dudes' posin' and flexin' got started. Like them hulksters was peacocks an' my Cory was some sort of... little... little *peahen*, or somethin'.

"Look at us, pretty peahen! We's so big and strong and feathery!"

And that there vampire dude just sat there with his eyes superglued onto Cory's pretty face, all smug, like he was the peacock king.

What the fuck? Is them dudes for real?

Okay, so's my first attempt at what Cory called my DTs had failed more'r less miserably. Guess I didn't get my meanin' across to 'em like I'd hoped; maybe they was a little bit slow or somethin'. But Plan B'd work. The lingerin' neck kiss had always been a very effective tool in discouragin' other gay men from fuckin' with my boy. Uh-huh, it surely had. Yeah, it was time for Plan B.

Eyes on the target... ready, set... launchin' Plan B.

I straightened up my shoulders, so's I looked real cool, not even one bit stiff-like, and then I walked all slow and cocky right past Cory's bar stool, pausin' at the strategic moment just long enough to get my nose stuck right into Cory's sweet-smellin' hair and my mouth onto his neck, and then I dove lips-first into that there little hollow behind his left ear. And my boy, well, he shivered 'cause he knew who he belonged to. He sure did. Then I continued on my way by, sure as shit that my message'd been sent, clear as the Pemi River on a still day.

Behind the bar, Barry and me had a fuckin' huge drink order waitin' to be filled, so's I got myself busy, sparin' only a second to glance back and check out how well my DT'd worked. Fully expectin' that all them guys'd cleared their rugged asses right the fuck outta my boy's personal space, y'know?

No such luck. Them beefy athletes and their wiry-assed ringleader was all clustered around Cory, like my boy was the sun and they was all planets circlin' round him... even closer than they was before. It was like I'd performed some kinda ET (Encouragement Technique) by accident.

Time to pull out the big guns....

Yes, it was time to launch what Cory called "the ring trick," which I'd just developed over the past week (seein' as yours truly'd just stuck that there ring on his finger a little over eight days ago). It was made up of me stoppin' by and fiddlin' around, real super obvious, of course, with the band on Cory's left hand. And, for Christ's sake, if I had to yank that fuckin' ring offa the kid's finger, kneel down on that beer-soaked floor, propose marriage in a boomin' voice, and then slide that thing right back on Cory's hand where it sure as fuck belonged, I'd be happy to do it if it got my point across. Strike *happy*, I'd be *fuckin' thrilled* to do it.

Then I got me this brilliant idea. I'd do two DTs at the very exact same time; it'd be kinda like takin' out an insurance policy on the first one, huh? Yeah, I'd combine the ring trick with the nose tweak. 'Cause them dudes clearly needed a super straight-up message, seein' as they wasn't too clever.

Bye, bye, pebbles in my fuckin' shoe. Hope you all fall into a goddam pile on the floor and get swept right outta the door with the rest of the dirt.

So's instead of reachin' across the bar to get the job done, I decided to approach real sneaky-like from behind, and when I got there, I figured I was gonna reach around the kid's shoulders to tug at his ring with one hand, while my other hand found his cute little nose. Or that there was the plan, at least. But once I'd reached Cory, I didn't even have no chance to get my arms 'round him before I felt my six-foot three-inch, two-hundred-pound body gettin' jerked all awkward-ish up into the air by four or so sets of massive paws.

What the fuck is goin' on here?

Them jolly green giants'd actually lifted me up offa the ground and was just kinda holdin' me there, sorta suspended in midair.

"You know this joker?" that there little spiky-haired vampire asked my Cory. "Or do you want my friends to show him the door?"

Cory took one look at me hangin' there, and that there little shit burst into a fit of—of friggin' uncontrollable giggles. (Adorable, yeah, but *so* not the time for it.) "No, I don't want you to get rid of him… he… he's… he's my fiancé!" After laughin' some more, pretty much 'til he was mostly cryin' if I was gonna be honest, Cory added, "I was rather hoping to keep him."

This here situation ain't nothin' but shameful.

I was gettin' manhandled by a pack of wild gorillas, who was tryin' to protect my Cory from his very own lovin' husband! And I was gettin' giggled at on top of it all!

Them meatheads all exchanged these sorta frustrated glances, and then they dropped me to the floor like I wasn't nothin' but a sack o' flour. But, I had to say, I was pretty sure I seen them massive shoulders all slumpin' down in defeat.

That's what I like to see.

Reachin' for my hand, which was actually all clenched up tight into a fist right then, Cory cleared his throat real proper-like, and started makin' polite introductions as if we was at a garden party. "Brett, please meet my new friends Ian, Ben, Christian, and Hunter.

Guys, I'd like to introduce you to my fiancé, Brett Taylor, the manager of the Bar and Grill."

"Charmed."

"Nice to meet you, I guess."

"Whatever."

"Hhmph."

Them dudes wasn't too enthusiastic in their greetin's, I gotta say. And them super defeated, humble-soundin' voices made me feel fuckin' good, they did, so's I smirked at 'em all from over the back of Cory's head. "Pleasure's all mine." None of us stuck out our hands to shake, though. And since I was now pretty sure I'd staked my claim onto Cory, I added, all gracious-like, "You gentlemen have yerselves a nice evenin'." Then I swaggered back behind the bar and got busy with collectin' empties.

The thrill of victory!

No sooner had I got my mind back on business, though, than Barry was jabbin' me in the belly with his elbow. "Brett, I know that guy, Ian, from Lit class, and he's not a bad dude at all, but... I still think you ought to check this out."

What the fuck?

Now there was eight strappin' ballplayers along with that there Goth dude, Ian, huddled close around my baby, hangin' on his every word. Like they all knew my secret: that the whole fuckin' world revolved around Cory.

Well, just as long as they keep them overgrowed mitts to themselves....

However, I felt it was my husbandly duty to stroll on over one more time, all ready with a big glass of iced tea, extra lemons stuck in, just exactly the way Cory liked it (strategic drink delivery), and a super-lovin' shoulder rub (my final attempt at a DT) for my boy.

You can't never be too careful with precious things, y'know? Not when you had yerself a diamond like Cory for a lover.

October 10, 2007
Cory

I BELIEVED with beyond 100 percent certainty that Brett hadn't been particularly pleased—no, that would be putting it far too mildly—that Brett had been highly agitated when I had informed him that Ian Webster was in my biology class. Not to mention the fact that the professor had assigned us as lab partners—Butana & Webster, the first and last names on the class roster.

So, three times each week when I had Biology 101, Brett not only escorted me to the classroom, but he took me by the hand, led me right to my seat, pulled out my chair for me, and laid my backpack on the table. Sometimes he even unzipped it. And I really shouldn't neglect to mention the blush-inducing kiss and demonstrative hug that was delivered to me by my enthusiastic husband, for the sole benefit of a rather irritated audience of one— Ian Webster—who simply snarked, "Get a room."

And lucky Ian was also treated to an encore performance at the class's end. Sometimes before the professor had even finished speaking, Brett would be edging his way across the room from the door to our lab table, his big hands reaching for a handful of my hair to caress, and wearing an ominous expression directed squarely at my eye-rolling lab partner.

Today was no different, with the possible exception of the fact that not only was Brett wearing my backpack over one broad shoulder, but he also had insisted on carrying my cup of coffee, leaving my empty arms to swing uselessly by my sides. After our titillating good-bye kiss, which honestly left me sitting there with an uncomfortable bulge in my jeans, I tried to get my mind back on science, or at a minimum off of Brett's lips. So I reached into my backpack and pulled out my laptop, all the while forcing my brain onto nonerotic subjects such as elderly nuns, oyster crackers, and knitting lessons.

"So, what's it like to have a full-time bodyguard? You must feel like Paris Hilton."

I chose not to respond. For a full minute Ian and I sat shoulder-to-shoulder, our lips tightly sealed, waiting for class to begin. But for some reason I can't fully explain, I turned to look at the young man beside me, one sculpted cheekbone resting on his palm, his head tilted and spikey hair pointing skyward, his eyes agitated, but, as always, trying to appear bored. If you liked the tortured artist type, this guy would be a heartthrob. "Actually, I really don't mind it at all. Brett says that precious things need extra care."

"Things?" Shifting his dark eyes to catch hold of mine, Ian added, "You are so *owned*. Do you have to ask for permission to go to the boy's room?"

I shrugged, turned away, and then lifted my coffee to my lips to discourage further discussion.

But Ian wasn't finished driving home his point. "That dude is smothering you. And besides, he's not even gay."

All right, so that last remark caught my attention. Jerking my head around to stare at him, hot coffee splashed up on my lips. I might have hissed a bit, but I still refused to acknowledge that Ian's words were starting to get under my skin.

"Yeah, you heard me right. Your *boyfriend* doesn't play for *our team*, and I'm pretty sure that the thought has crossed your mind a time or two."

Despite this inner voice literally screaming at me to remain stoic and stare blankly at the white board, I heard my actual voice sputter, "W-what do you m-mean?"

"Let's discuss it over dinner."

At that moment the professor entered the classroom and switched on the white board projector, so, with a brief snorting sound, I shifted my attention to the front of the room.

Ian leaned in toward me. "Now, don't go getting your knickers twisted over having a simple dinner with me; we can break bread as friends, rather than the lovers that we will most certainly be in the very near future."

"Knickers twisted?" I snorted with more vigor. Someone in the row in front of us turned to me and said, "God bless you."

"And while we're breaking bread together, I'll tell you about how your American Eagle model-looking boyfriend is as straight as a ruler, and how I'd be the perfect Jacob to your Bella."

"I'm on Team Edward."

"So what about dinner?"

This time I leaned over toward Ian, and speaking softly so I wouldn't disturb the professor, I replied, "Thanks for the offer, but I'll be eating with my *Edward* at the B&G tonight. My fiancé... remember? Or do you have a short memory?"

"Princess, let me tell you, nothing about me is short." Before I had a chance to roll my eyes, straight white teeth flashed me a wicked smile. "Sorry, I kind of went off on a tangent there, didn't I? What I really want you to know, Cory, is that I'm going to do whatever I can to change your mind."

"What are you talking about?"

"Listen, I respect the bonds of holy matrimony as much as the next guy, but until you walk down the aisle with that breeder, I consider you fair game." He stopped talking and pulled his laptop out of his messenger bag with a certain air of finality.

By this time, the professor, oblivious to our discussion, was starting to get into the meaty part of the lecture. I, however, couldn't drag my stubborn brain off of what Ian had said about Brett being straight.

And just why am I obsessing over Ian's allegation?

Well, the answer was actually very simple: the notion that Brett wasn't quite as gay as me *had* crossed my mind. And it hadn't just simply skipped past my mind at a leisurely pace, pausing briefly to admire the spectacular view. Oh no, not at all. To be honest, the notion that Brett was straight had induced terror-based heart pounding—and more than a minor amount of sweating—on an occasion or two. Yes, when *that* thought crossed my mind, it left a trail of destruction in its wake. Complete and utter panic, I guess you could call it.

Maybe Brett really *had* confused protectiveness with love... or perhaps he had fallen into this relationship because he relished the familiarity and comfort it provided.

And then there was Brett's guilt—he had felt completely responsible when I'd been assaulted last summer.

What if Brett isn't gay?

Somehow, I managed to bury the bulk of my worries beneath the wonder of unicellular protists. However, I couldn't deny that Ian had managed to open a can of worms that until now had been just loose-lidded.

October 11, 2007
Cory

SHE always acknowledged the two of us with such a warm smile, so I headed for what had become my usual seat in the second row from the back of the lecture hall, next to the gorgeous black girl, in my Women in American History class.

"Hi there, boyfriend." She was just so friendly. "How are you and your man doing this fine fall afternoon?"

I slid into my aisle seat and pulled down the desktop. Brett immediately got busy shrugging off my backpack, and then he went so far as to unload it for me, which had me blushing. Computer, notebook, pen….

"Here, kid, I got you a bottle of water, and um, I got one for you too, uh…." He nodded to the girl beside me.

"Ally. Ally Jenkins." She reached for the bottle of water. "And thanks. That was very thoughtful of you."

Brett glanced at the floor and replied, "Not a problem." And then looking back up, he said, "Ah, I'm Brett Taylor, and this here is my… is Cory. Cory Dutana."

We all smiled at each other.

"You look so familiar, Brett. Haven't I seen you over at the B&G?"

"Yes, ma'am. I'm the manager over there." His pride was unmistakable.

"Oooh, that must be a fun job." Ally grinned as if she'd had a lot of fun there herself.

"It ain't never borin', that's fer sure."

"Well, you must be doing a good job. It's running a lot smoother than it did last year." Ally grimaced. "Last year, the police were there every weekend."

Well, Brett's chest had puffed out about a mile, and I have to admit I was rather proud too. "Yes, he does a great job there."

Ally Jenkins was a beautiful girl, in this runway model way. I estimated that she was almost six feet tall in her sneakers and was built like a willow tree, thin and wispy. And I just wanted to reach out and touch her flawless brown skin; it looked so smooth. As she reached up and slid her manicured palm over her tight cornrows, I noticed how exotically shaped her eyes were. Then I wondered if Brett had noticed as well.

"My boyfriend practically lives at the B&G with his teammates. I bet you've seen them there."

"Teammates?" If Ally's undeniable allure hadn't caught Brett's attention, then that comment certainly had. "What team does yer boyfriend play on?"

"Ben plays for the Hawks' football team. He's a running back—black, six one, built like a brick house... have you seen him?" Ally's pride in her boyfriend was every bit as obvious as Brett's pride in his job. Brett, however, had suddenly stopped being so chatty (not that you could ever really call him that).

"Yeah, I know who he is." Brett reached possessively for my shoulders before glancing toward the door. The football team and their "ringleader," Ian, was a touchy subject for Brett.

"It's such a small world up here, Ally. It seems like everyone knows everyone else, you know what I mean?" I decided to pick up where Brett had so abruptly left off in order to avoid the lapse in conversation that was surely about to set in. "As a matter of fact, we just met your boyfriend and his roommates last week at the bar." A pained look ghosted across Brett's perfect face, but it was gone almost as quickly as it had come.

And Brett was suddenly in a big rush to leave. "Well, I gotta head out now. Gonna hit the Quik-mart and get us some laundry detergent." Brett leaned down and placed a quick peck on my cheek. No need for the classroom make-out session when Ian wasn't watching, I guess.

"I'll see ya after class, babe." I couldn't miss that he didn't so much as glance at Ally on his way out.

"Was it something I said?" Ally stared at Brett as he headed for the door. "The man practically turned into an ice cube the second I mentioned Ben."

What do I say so as to give her a clue, but so as not to stick my foot too far into my mouth?

"Oh, it's nothing. One night last week, Brett and some football players just got caught up in a little bit of male rivalry at the B&G, that's all. You know, the usual sparring over, well… over—"

"Over *you*?" She started nodding like the truth had suddenly become crystal clear to her. "Oh, I know exactly who you are! You've got to be the guy that Ian Webster fell in love with at first sight last Saturday night! God, he won't shut up about you."

I felt the beginning of, as Brett referred to it, my "flamingo face" starting. In other words, a predictable blush had already begun its slow bloom up my neck. I fanned my face with my notebook. "I'm just a passing fixation for Ian. It'll blow over."

"Chill out, mister. You look like you're gonna have heatstroke." Ally pushed my water bottle into my hands and then sent me a harsh glance. "So, let me get this straight, Ian has no chance with you? 'Cause he's really a great guy."

I shook my head. "No chance."

That dark gaze softened as she studied my face with rekindled interest. "You're really crazy about your man, aren't you?"

"More than 'crazy about'. He's pretty much everything to me." No need to elaborate on that, was there?

"*Everything*… that's really sweet." She seemed to mean it. "This is not an average, everyday relationship with you guys, is it?"

Yes, I realized that even the least perceptive of people could recognize the intensity between Brett and I when we were together.

And Ally, being the insightful type, hadn't missed our powerful connection. But this was normally where I slammed the door on inquiring minds; what had happened between Brett and me just wasn't anyone else's business. But for some reason I couldn't explain, I gave her a closer rendition to the truth than usual.

"Brett and I have been through some very tough times together, Ally. Actually, I wouldn't even be here at the university if it weren't for him."

"Why not?" She looked concerned, rather than merely curious.

"I don't usually talk too much about this." Most of me hoped the history lecture would begin a few minutes early. But a little part of me wanted to share.

"Oh, you don't have to talk about it if you don't want to." Ally made a big show of rifling through her purse, finally pulling out a pack of minty gum and offering me a piece; she probably did it just to take the pressure off me.

I shook my head and then said, "No, I don't mind telling you, I guess. You see, something bad happened to me last summer. I… uh, somebody hurt me." My fingers flew straight to the scar beneath my eye, without my even realizing what I was doing. "And I don't like to be alone… too much… at all."

"Is that why Ben and Ian said that you have a bodyguard?"

I nodded, my embarrassment renewed. "Uh-huh. Brett… well, after it happened, I'd say he pretty much put my pieces back together, Ally. I don't like to be away from him very often."

"I get it: you have a lover and a bodyguard wrapped up together in one smokin' hot package, right?" She didn't appear to be disgusted by my neediness at all. In fact, she actually smiled.

"That *is* what Ian says, well, minus the smokin' hot part." Yes, flamingo pink was the color of the afternoon. My cheeks absolutely burned.

"Well, then you two must really think that you need the protection."

The professor cleared his throat and began to speak, but that didn't stop the shudder of trepidation that I felt at Ally's words—at the reminder that I, indeed, required a full security detail.

AFTER class, Brett was waiting for me in the lobby, hovering stealthily behind a wide, ivory-colored pillar, his green eyes fixed on the lecture hall's double doors. The very second he saw me, he bolted to my side.

"Hey, baby... missed ya, so much." And judging by the ravenous way he was looking at me, I believed him.

"Cory, want to go jogging with me? You told me that you like to run at the gym, but it's so nice out today." Ally came up on my other side. "What do you say?"

Brett and I exchanged glances.

"But we should really put a move on so we can run while it's still light out."

This time, my husband stepped up to the plate before an awkward silence could ensue. "Ally, that's a real nice offer and all, but ya see, I usually go with Cory... uh, when... when he's out and about the campus."

I could almost hear the door slamming on my budding friendship with Ally. But Brett was speaking a truth that I'd honestly come to embrace. "Yeah, I don't usually go anywhere without Brett."

However, it's a fact: nobody wants a friend who can't go anywhere with you.

I stood there and waited for the speech to begin. You know the one—the "you're all grown up and don't need Brett's permission to do what you want to do" speech. But instead, Ally stepped a bit closer to us and looked directly into Brett's eyes. "I understand that, Brett. But I'm six feet tall and a lot stronger than I look. Nobody will mess with the two of us. We'll look out for each other."

Still, I didn't turn on my pleading, "please let me go" eyes. Over the summer, I had entrusted Brett with the task of keeping me safe because I hadn't wanted to even *try* to bring Steven Percy to justice. I had simply wanted to forget that Steven was out there in the world. And in order for either Brett or me to have a moment's peace (knowing that the man wasn't in jail but out on the streets, free to return at any time), this is how it needed to be. No, I didn't even look up.

"I don't know...." After a long pause, though, Brett spoke again, but kept his eyes on the floor. "Where exactly was you plannin' on goin'?"

"Just a few loops around campus. And, if you want, we can stay away from Lower Mountain Road." Ally kept her cool, not acting too eager; she had quite an effective poker face.

"Yeah... yeah... Lower Mountain Road is way too fuckin' remote." I looked up to see Brett rubbing his forehead with both hands. "Don't go down there, 'kay? And how long do ya think you two'll be?"

I smiled because it looked like maybe I was going to be able to have a friendship with Ally.

"Well, we can walk back to your place now so Cory can change, and then we'll run for an hour or so."

"Can you two end yer run at the B&G?" He was looking squarely at Ally, his expression stricken as if he was literally in pain. "I'll be working and—"

"Of course. That's a great idea! Have some ice water ready for us, okay?" Ally stepped past me and pulled Brett aside. "You're okay with this, right?" She placed a hand on his shoulder.

It was quiet for a moment while Brett thought. "You won't leave him alone?"

Okay, I was turning red again, and I hadn't even started running. I apparently required a babysitter when I was away from my bodyguard.

"Not even for a minute." Then Ally looked over at me. "And you know, I hate to run alone. Cory, you'll be doing me a favor, really."

What a sweetheart she is!

Brett again nodded, and then grasped me by my shoulders. He looked at me with such a fierce expression that I didn't know what to think. "Have fun, Cory... I love ya."

I could feel his gaze on my back as we walked away.

October 17, 2007
Cory

WE'D finished our lab write-up and all of the other preliminaries on Monday, so we were all ready to perform today's osmosis diffusion lab. This particular lab involved a full hour of waiting around while the eggs and potato slices soaked in various solutions, which translated, at least in Ian's mind, to an abundance of time to spend trying to persuade me to date him. I privately referred to it as "the cat and mouse game," because I knew that's the sort of thing Brett would've called it if, in fact, he'd known about it. Which he didn't. No sense in upsetting him.

Oh, and in case you hadn't figured it out already, Ian was the cat.

"How's the best-looking dude on campus doing today?"

I rolled my eyes, a skill of which I had mastered the finer aspects in the past few weeks as Ian's lab partner. "I don't know, but when I see Brett, I'll be sure to tell him that you asked." Sometimes it sucked to always be the mouse.

"You are a funny guy, you know that?" Ian placed both elbows on the black-topped lab table and laid his head down between them, closing his eyes. "I guess I didn't get enough sleep last night, but such is the single life. So many dudes, so few hours in the day...."

"I wouldn't know."

"Maybe I'll take a nap right here while the eggs do their thing."

At that, I lifted my nose in the air. "I'm sure that would make a positive impression on the professor."

Ian continued as if I hadn't spoken. "But, you know, I'd sleep so much better if you'd cuddle up with me. Come here, baby." He lifted his head off of the desk and then started to drag my chair toward him.

Once again, I felt my eyes rolling back involuntarily as I firmly placed my feet on the floor to stop the sliding of my chair. "I'm getting married this summer; give it up, Ian."

"I'll give it *all* up to you, Cory."

Huffing loudly, I opened my laptop. "Whatever." *I so don't need to deal with this.* I began to type.

Apparently, Ian felt it was time to step up his game. "What are you doing now, Cory? Googling 'gay for you'? Because if your buddy Brett is gay, I'd bet my left nut that it's *only* for you." He spoke as if this was all a big joke, when it was my *life* he was talking about.

So I bounced right back with, "Only the left one? I thought you had more confidence in yourself than that." Nonetheless, my fingers had frozen on the keyboard. And I'll admit it: my curiosity won out over my common sense. I heard myself ask, "Why do you keep on saying that kind of thing, anyways?"

Sitting a bit straighter in his chair, Ian shrugged, and then replied with authority, "My gaydar is 100 percent accurate; it hasn't ever failed me. Your beloved Brett is not a true member of the Rainbow Brigade, so to speak."

"Your *gaydar?* You're basing this entire 'Brett's a het' theory on your *gaydar?*" I exhaled in quasi-relief. "I suppose, then, I'll worry about it once you have your gaydar scientifically tested for accuracy and I read the results in the *American Journal of Psychiatry.*"

"Believe me or not, but it has never been wrong."

"Everybody knows that gaydar isn't infallible."

"Then let's use simple logic instead, what do you say?" Ian reached out and pushed the top of my computer down. "So, you told me you've known Brett for about four years, or so? Tell me about when he came out."

Well, there wasn't a response I could give to that, because Brett had never officially "come out of the closet."

Had he ever been in the closet? Had he ever even realized that there was a closet to come out of?

"Okay, then, try this one on for size: how many guys did he date before you?"

"I never dated before Brett, either." My voice sounded rather whiny.

"Has he ever left a *Playgirl* magazine open on the coffee table? And I'll bet my *right* nut that he's never asked you to watch some steaming hot male porn with him."

"Those things don't mean anything—I don't get into porn, either." I lifted the top of my computer back up as if in challenge. "Besides, we have each other; we don't need porn."

"Fair enough, girlfriend." Leaning back, Ian pushed his knees up against the table. "I'm not big into stereotypes, but I do believe there is a *hint* of truth to them. So, do you ever find Brett listening to show tunes when you hop into his truck? Does the dude give a hoot about Fashion Week? Or decorating? Does he even like to go shopping at all?"

I gaped at the man beside me, trying to categorize the blur of thoughts that were rushing through my mind.

"I really don't need to point any of this stuff out to you; you're not stupid or blind. But your man doesn't meet a single requirement of queer-ness."

If it weren't for those submerged eggs and potatoes, I would have just gotten up and left. I certainly didn't need to listen to all of the ways Brett didn't fit into gay stereotypes. Next, Ian would be telling me that Brett couldn't be into me because he didn't worship at the altar of Barbra Streisand. And, although I hated to admit it, the worst part was that some of what Ian had said rang true to me.

If it doesn't look like a duck, walk like a duck, or quack like a duck, then maybe it's not a duck.

"So, my thought is that you ditch the het-dude. Find yourself a man who loves men, who has always loved men, and always will. Like, say, yours truly."

Glancing at my watch, I said softly, "Not a chance, Ian. I'm in this with Brett for as long as he wants me."

"Well, that's sad."

"Maybe so, but it's also true. So, I hope you're still up for being partners with me, but strictly in the *lab* sense." I got up and walked around the table so I could examine our experiments rather than further examining Brett's sexuality. "If you don't think you can still work with me, we should talk to the professor soon, though."

Frustrated, Ian just shrugged. "There's no need to be rash. But don't forget, when you get tired of swimming against the current with your so-called fiancé, let me know. I'll be waiting for you on the beach wearing a tiny black Speedo, with a little Rufus Wainwright playin' on my boom box."

October 19, 2007
Brett

A FUCKIN' pitiful excuse for a man, that there's exactly what I was. In fact, when I first seen her, I thought I was losin' my marbles.

This here ain't happenin'. Can't be.

Next, I decided that I musta been havin' one of them flashback-thingies, which was actually kinda the same as losin' my marbles, wasn't it? And that there was bad—real bad—seein' as I was at work, where I needed to be in control.

Find yer marbles, Taylor, and find 'em fast!

Shit, I hadn't had me one of them flashbacks for so fuckin' long.

Why now, huh?

Well, it didn't take too long at all 'til I became pretty dammed certain that I wasn't havin' me no flashback at all; the haggard-lookin' blonde sittin' at the bar was, in fact, my old lady. So's once I'd accepted that it really was my mama, her skinny ass jacked up on a stool, *at my very own B&G*, I hadta wonder what the fuck she was doin' here. It wasn't as if she'd missed me so fuckin' bad and wanted to have us no little drinky-poo and chit-chat together for old times' sake. No, sir. 'Cause them old times'd surely sucked.

And my next reaction was completely typical of me. Yeah, you guessed it—I was off to the can to lose my lunch. My belly just wasn't ready to accept what my brain was slowly graspin': Mama was here at my very own workplace, tossin' back a shot o' whiskey, glancin' all coy-like over her scrawny shoulders, kinda like she was expectin' somebody.

Duh! Get yerself a fuckin' clue, loser!

Mama was lookin' around for her sweet baby boy.

So's after I'd pretty much emptied out my belly in the men's room, I made myself get a mental hold on the fact that the lady sittin' at the bar, suckin' booze down like it was goin' outta style and tappin' a closed pack o' cigarettes onto her palm, wasn't none other than Sheila Taylor. Sheila fuckin' Taylor herself.

Uh-huh, this here is really happenin'.

Made me a decision right then, I did. I was gonna take care o' first things first. Which meant I hadta step down hard on my mental brakes so as to slow down my racin' brain. So's I sucked in a coupla deep breaths and blew 'em back out real slow. Then I did this counting backward from ten thingy that Cory'd taught me. It usually worked pretty good.

Okay, what do I gotta do next?

Peerin' out from the wall beside the men's room, like the ball-less coward that I was, I let my eyes loose to study the woman. She looked real old and tired, and super wore-out. But hard livin'd do that to a person, huh? Them years that'd passed us two by hadn't been no friend to my mama.

Sheila Taylor's bleached blonde hair hung down her bony back like hay against a flimsy barn door. And the rest of her body was real skinny and wiry too, 'cept for her belly that looked sorta bloated. Her once-pretty face was blotchy and dotted here 'n' there with some kinda sores, all o' the rest of her skin was dull gray, like a squirrel. But some shit hadn't changed none at all: them sharp, severe lips was drawn into that thin line I remembered far too good for comfort, and them hard eyes, well, there wasn't a measure of softness to be found there, neither.

Ain't never been no softness to my mama.

Next, my eyes somehow got pulled on over across the bar from Mama to my own personal good luck charm. Cory sat there at his usual place near the cash register, a sweet angel from heaven sittin' across the room from an evil devil from you know where. Them pretty pink lips was smilin' at somethin' Barry'd just said, and them gorgeous blue eyes was flashin' with soon-to-spout laughter. Then Cory took a little suck on his soda straw, just the way a little kid'd do.

Fuck, I adore the livin' daylights outta my boy.

It was really somethin' else—lookin' at my friggin' horrific past squarin' off against my super hopeful future—right there, in front of my eyes. Hadta blink a coupla times so as to be sure it was real. Which it was. And I was sorry to hafta admit that it didn't look like the evil half of the equation was gonna be goin' nowhere no time soon. Mama'd clearly settled herself on that there bar stool, seein' as she'd slung her purse over the bar stool and had sat on the strap, and she'd laid her smokes down on the bar.

Didn't wanna, but I knew I hadta. *Gotta find out what the fuck she wants outta me.*

Was an ant moseyin' on up to a can of Raid, I was right then. And the sorry truth was, once, or maybe twice, in my short walk from the bathroom to the bar, my feet kinda got froze onto the floor. Yup, I had me a coupla froze-up Eskimo's feet, and for some reason at the very same time I was sweatin' kinda like a marathon runner at mile twenty-five—in plainer words, I was pretty much a basket case. *Go figure.*

But somehow, I found the nerve to propel my body over to the bar where my mother'd planted her ass. Didn't even need to tap her on the shoulder or nothin'; she musta sensed that I was comin', even though she was the one who smelled like a cigarette-makin' factory. Coulda smelled her a mile away, yes, sir. Soon as I was right behind her, Mama spinned her stool around so's she could face me.

"Brett." Her voice was raspy, and her breath stunk to the high heavens. "Been a while, huh?"

Kept my face still like a statue, I did. I wasn't gonna give nothin' of my heart away to the likes of her. "Mama." Still, I ended up soundin' just like I did when I wasn't nothin' but a boy.

"Hey—ya recognize me! Sure thought that you'da forgot yer old mama even walked the earth no more." The woman grimaced, but on second thought I decided that she mighta actually been tryin' to smile.

Why don't you just cut to the chase, Mama?

"How'd ya find me?"

Her hazel eyes was dull and flat. "Wasn't too fuckin' hard, boy." She chuckled a bit, exposin' a coupla gaps where teeth used to be. "Didn't take no rocket scientist to put the word out at the Downtown Pub. Nice place, here."

I felt another spasm in my belly. "Sure hope ya ain't plannin' on makin' no habit of stoppin' by this here establishment. It's my... my workplace, y'know?"

Mama lifted a hand to push a stray strand of straw from offa her weathered face. No, sir, I didn't flinch none when she raised her arm up like that, the same way she'd done it when I wasn't nothin' but a boy and she was windin' up to slug me. (At least I wouldn't never admit it if I had.) "I'll do what I damned well please." Yup, she was annoyed but not pissed off yet. "An' that ain't no way for a boy to talk to his mama."

That's 'cause you wasn't never no mama to me. Sure wished I'd've dared to say them words out loud, but truth was, I'd only just thought 'em in my head. What my *real* voice'd said was, "This ain't no social call, so's, what d'ya want?"

I ain't fuckin' stupid, Mama. Just spill it.

Them used-to-be-pretty features sorta twisted themselves up some, and I found myself swallowin' hard in the face of her anger. So's in order to not completely lose it, I stole me a quick glimpse of my baby, sittin' over there at the other side of the bar. And Cory just so happened to be gawkin' at me too, them blue eyes all filled up with concern. Had that cute little worry-wrinkle in his forehead too, he did.

Just get to the point, Mama, so's we can get this here done with. "I asked ya what it is that ya want."

Mama stuck her bone-thin finger right into my face. "What do ya *think* I want, son? You got yerself one guess."

Nope, Brett Taylor wasn't born yesterday. "How much?"

"How much ya got on ya—in cash?" She kinda looked at the floor and her gray skin'd turned reddish. So's it seemed Mama wasn't too proud of her actions. Maybe she was a human bein' after all. (A fuckin' bad example o' one.)

"Got me about five hundred in my office."

"That'll do."

I hadta work real hard to keep my face on the stern side of blank. "Well, if I give it to ya, I don't wanna see yer face 'round here no more."

Liftin' her glass to her lips, Mama tilted it and sucked a coupla ice cubes into her mouth so's her next words came out all slurpy and lazy-soundin'. "Ain't gonna make no promises, but I'll do my best to steer clear of this joint."

I stared at her like I meant business, but truly, I was tremblin' more'n a little on the insides.

"Now run along and get me that cash, an' then I'll make myself scarce." Wonders never cease, 'cause I'd say Mama had herself the good grace to look a tad guilty.

I spun on my boot heel and headed for my office. As I passed him by, Cory slipped offa his stool and followed right along behind me, just like I knew he'd do.

Soon as us two was all safe in my office, I slammed the door behind me and then pulled Cory up against me real rough-like, buryin' my nose in that there silky sweet-smellin' hair. *I just need you so fuckin' bad right now, baby.*

Rubbin' the sides of my face so gentle, Cory asked, "What's going on?"

"My… uh, my… that there's my… uh…." Yup. I was freakin out.

"Sssh, now slow down, Brett. It's okay." Them soft fingers kept right on movin' in little circles, soothin' both o' my temples like he was tryin' to put me in a trance. "Talk to me."

"My… my p-past…." I really did wanna crack a smile so as to stop Cory's frettin', but I just couldn't make that there happen. "My past—it's come b-back… to haunt me tonight, it surely has."

"That's your mother out there, isn't it?"

Uh-huh, Cory's blue eyes reached right insida my soul, grabbed a hold on it, and held it safe; so's I knew it was okay to answer. I nodded.

"What does she want?"

Like some kind of angry tornado, memories started swirlin' around insida my brain. Years of beatin's, burns, neglect, and hatred.... I'm pretty sure all o' them things was why I was movin' my mouth, but no words came outta me just then.

Graspin' my shoulders tight with them little hands, Cory again said, "Talk to me, Brett... share it with me. It'll be better then, you'll see."

After a fuckin' huge courage-seekin' breath (and a helluva lotta faith in what my boy'd just said), I managed to answer. "First, I'll tell ya what she don't want, 'kay? Mama don't wanna find out how I been for the past six or so years, an' she sure as shit don't wanna dish out no big 'I'm sorry for what I done to you'. No, sir, them things ain't it."

"She wants money, doesn't she?" This severe look of pissed-off-ness crossed over my husband's delicate features. After all, Cory was the one who got to live with all of them nasty aftereffects of Mama's torture. No fuckin' wonder he was pissed. "What are you going to do?"

My face got all hot and red. "I'm gonna fuckin' give it to her." I yanked myself outta Cory's grasp and moved behind my desk, and then with a single firm tug, the bottom drawer where I always kept a pile o' cash (in case me 'n' Cory had us an emergency) rolled open. And I truly expected Cory to be all bent outta shape 'cause I was such a weaklin'-loser-coward that I was givin' in to that evil bitch, givin' her a big pile of our money. So's I grabbed the cash and made for the door without even glancin' over to see that there pity and disgust that was sure to be written real plain all over Cory's face. But as I passed him, one o' them little fingers of his snagged me by a belt loop of my jeans.

"I get it, baby. I understand."

Huh?

I just knew I was gonna start wailin' like a kid who'd dropped his ice cream cone on the street, outta the sheer fuckin' relief that Cory wasn't put out on account of my shameful behavior. "I'm sorry, Cory; I'm such a fuckin' loser."

"No, no... Brett, you aren't a loser. You're *normal.* Maybe somewhere deep inside, you just want your mother to love you." Them blue eyes was lookin' up at me, all sincere.

The truth wasn't quite so noble, was it? "It ain't that, honey. I just want my mother to get the hell outta here and to leave me the fuck alone." That admission, in itself, was downright disgraceful, but it didn't stop two of the world's most lovin' arms from wrappin' around my shakin' shoulders. Yeah, I was completely freaked out, but with my baby beside me the world was still mostly sane.

"Listen, buddy. I'm gonna go with you when you give her the money." The kid pressed his angel-like face against my chest. "I'll hold your hand if you want me to. You don't have to do this alone."

Hell no! I wasn't about to let Mama so much as lay her filthy eyes on my Cory. "I'm fine to do it by myself."

"Okay. Then I'll go sit in my usual place. Come see me when you're done."

He started to walk away, but I pulled him back. "Hey, have I told ya that I love ya yet today?"

Cory grinned, and he just looked so fuckin' cute. "Only a couple of times; I'm *sooo* deprived!" Pretended to be wipin' away tears, he was.

Taking my boy back into my arms and squeezin' real hard, hard enough so's he'd still feel it once I let go, all o' this crazy shit suddenly didn't matter so fuckin' much. "Well, for the record, I'm tellin' you again. I love you more than I can possibly show ya here. So's right after I'm done with Mama, you and me's outta here so's I can spend the rest of the night showin' you *exactly* how I feel."

"You've got yourself a deal!" Cory sounded kinda breathless.

Looks like things is gonna be okay, huh?

October 20, 2007
Brett

TONIGHT'S nightmares was the worst that I'd had since... well, since *ever*. Before I'd fell to sleep I'd tossed and turned, and when I'd finally got myself off to dreamland, it wouldn't last. Like a fuckin' clock, every hour they'd show up along with them bad dreams: shiverin' and sweatin' at the same time (go figure), pantin', and bellyaches. Finally, I jerked up outta bed; there wasn't no need for Cory to lose a full night's sleep on account o' my mental hang-ups.

But, as Cory always told me, in a kind and lovin' way, mind you, he couldn't sleep next to a man with big time stress problems and not realize when something was seriously fucked-up. (Them wasn't his exact words, but ya get my meanin'.) In fact, last week Cory told me he'd taken a detour from his studyin' at the library to read up on what he called "PTSD." Flashbacks, nightmares, and as the book'd said (and I'd pretty much memorized Cory's words—wrote 'em down and everythin'), "intense physical reactions to reminders of the traumatic event," which I guess would explain all o' the sweatin', shakin', and barfin'. Uh-huh, them things all fit my symptoms to a tee. There was also "psychological" (yup, another Cory book-word) aftereffects of PTSD too. Not bein' able to trust, feelin' real super alone in the world, taking unnecessary risks with yer life, and havin' sleepin' difficulties—looked like Cory'd won the jackpot when he'd got himself roped up with me.

But things'd been different with Cory as my partner. Not fuckin' perfect but so much better.

'Cept for right now, huh?

Already, Cory was holdin' me against his chest, and truth was, he had been for a while now. Squeezin' my clammy limbs, smellin' the sweat that spelled out my sufferin', prob'ly waitin' for the barfin' to start up. Nope, there wasn't no way in hell that I could hide all of this shit from my husband.

"We need to talk." Cory'd been awake for so long that his voice wasn't even sleep-crackly no more. I felt like a piece of shit for inflictin' this drama on him yet again.

And that there was the very moment that I knew I was gonna hurl. "Bathroom—now!" I made a run for it. A coupla minutes later, when I emerged from outta the bathroom wearin' only a towel and a real sheepish expression, I stood at the foot of our bed, my head hangin' low. "I'm real sorry it happened again, Cory."

"Come here." Like always, Cory opened up them perfect arms for me. And I pretty much poured myself, like a glass of warm milk into a waitin' mug, right into his embrace. I snuggled against his bare chest as he rubbed little circles with his fingers onto my damp shoulders. "We have to talk about how upset you got tonight. Are you up to it?"

I nodded against his chest.

"Do you remember last summer when you took me to Maynard Beach, after… after I got hurt?"

I hated like hell to think about that there time, but again I nodded.

"Well, I'd been having bad dreams about what Steven did to me."

I felt my whole body stiffen, and not in a good way. "Yeah, I remember."

"And remember how I told you all about what had happened to me on the night he hurt me? I told you how painful it was and how I was so scared." Cory stopped talking, so's I nodded again. "Well, after I told you about it, my nightmares went away."

I pulled outta Cory's arms and flopped down flat on the bed. "So's yer sayin' if I tell you about all of the shit Mama done to me when I was a boy, maybe I'll feel better?" Before Cory even had a chance to answer, I added, "What if it stirs up more shit in my head?"

"Then we'll talk about that too."

I thought on it a moment, real unsure.

"Sharing your pain with me might make it less threatening to you. It can't be healthy to keep it all locked inside." Cory pulled himself up so's he could lean against the headboard. He even crossed his legs like he was gettin' ready to listen to some kinda long sob story. "You know I've been reading up on Post Traumatic Stress Disorder—"

"Disorder? That there word makes it sound like I'm a nutjob!"

"Not at all, Brett. Post Traumatic Stress Disorder can happen to anyone, from going through any really frightening event. And I think your entire childhood qualifies as frightening, don't you?"

Couldn't argue with the kid on that one. "But still, I ain't nuts, and I ain't gonna go to no head shrink... 'cause Cory, I-I just can't do that! Ya see?" I was losin' my cool. See, I'd do about anythin' for my boy, I just hoped to hell he wouldn't ask that of me.

Cory tried to pull me into his arms again, but I shoved him away.

"Listen, Brett, you aren't crazy at all... if anyone is crazy, it's your mother. And you don't have to talk to a professional about this if you really don't want to, but just, please, talk to *me*."

I sat up and dropped my legs over the edge of the bed. "Honestly, Cory, ain't you sick of wading through this pile o' shit with me, over and over again?" I knew that I'd sorta rudely presented the kid with my back, but I just couldn't look at him right then. "If I ain't sweatin' and shiverin', I'm pantin' and barfin, and usually in the middle of the friggin' night, when you're tryin' to sleep."

I felt Cory moving to kneel behind me on the bed, and soon his arms was curlin' down around my shoulders. Felt like heaven, when he done that. "Your feelings are not a burden to me. So don't think you can get rid of me that easily, bud."

I fuckin' love him so much.

"But you gotta know, nothin' I'm gonna tell ya'll be too pretty—it sure ain't no picture-perfect fairy tale. Besides, I never really wanted you to know all o' this shit. It's fuckin' humiliatin'."

"I need to hear the truth; I don't care if it's pretty or not. And I'm listening, so whenever you're ready...."

I didn't never talk about what Mama done to me so's it was hard to know just where to start. But here I was, all wrapped up in the lovin' arms of the man who'd promised me his whole entire future, so's I guess it didn't matter one way or the other where my story began, huh? I turned around and moved us so's me and Cory was sittin' and facin' each other. And then I started talkin'.

"First memory that ever got stuck in my head when I was a kid is of what Mama'd call my 'playpen'. See, when she needed to get somethin' done without no kid in tow, she'd stick me in the trunk of her car. Had herself this big old sedan, and I fit in there, well, let's say fer way too many years." That first little tell-all already had me sweatin' bullets, but I kept on spillin'. "And then there was our broom closet. It was real dark and dusty—I couldn't hardly breathe in there."

"She put you in a closet too?" Cory didn't appear to be too happy with that news.

"All the friggin' time." I swallowed hard, surprised that the nausea hadn't yet come back to torture me. "But I got why she did them things... you know, she needed to stick me somewhere so's she could go somewhere else and didn't have to pay nobody to take care o' me. Them two places was like my babysitters." I peeked at Cory, and I gotta say, it looked like my bellyache'd found him, seein' as he'd pretty much turned green.

But he nodded, like he wanted me to go on with my story, so's I did.

"There was plenty of beatin's, and Mama used all kinds of shit to beat on me with, whatever she could get her hands on fast, but when she... when she burned me, well, that was what freaked me out the most."

Still green as a pond frog, Cory took himself a deep breath and asked, "Was it because the pain of being burnt was so much worse than the pain of the beatings?"

I shook my head. "Nah, that there's true, but it ain't the reason." I couldn't fuckin' believe we was talkin' 'bout this shit—all honest-like and out in the open. "See, when she put me in the trunk or the closet, I could understand why she done it. And when she beat on me, it was 'cause I'd been a little shit, y'know? Like I'd got into somethin' I shouldna. But when she burned me, there wasn't no reason that I could figure. I'd've been sleepin', Cory, that's all I done."

Cory took a hold on my arm and them fingers traced over my burn scars, one by one.

"I couldn't never understand why she went and burnt me like that. And finally, it sunk into my thick skull—she did it outta pure fuckin' hate."

It was quiet for a minute before Cory asked, "When did she do it? You know, when did she burn your arms?"

This was gonna be tough to say out loud, 'cause sayin' shit out loud made it so fuckin' real. So's I took me a coupla steadyin' breaths. "I don't really wanna... don't wanna talk about this part. But... but I want you to know what I been through, so's, so's I can get fixed... and...."

Looked like Cory needed a coupla steadyin' breaths himself right then, it did. And after he took 'em, he said simply, "Brett, just tell me."

"Okay... so's, uh, so's I didn't have me no bedroom, seein' as my bed was the livin' room couch. And when Mama'd come home real late after partyin' it up, or whatever it was she'd been doin', she'd come in the front door and see me sleepin' there, and I s'pose it'd remind her of how she really didn't want no kid to care for."

"What would happen then?"

"Alls I can say is when I got woke up, I was screamin' out in pain, and she was sittin' beside the couch on a stiff chair from the kitchen, lightin' up a smoke."

Cory wasn't lookin' too good; my little song an' dance was gettin' the kid all worked up. Don't know just why, though, but I couldn't stop yappin'. "I was always scared as shit to go to sleep at night."

"Maybe that is why you can't sleep very well when you're upset."

Or maybe it's because I'm a fucked-up looney tune.

Yeah, my lips was motorin', and it seemed that I just couldn't hit the brakes. "I ain't never gonna forget the way she looked at me when she was doin' it. You know, burnin' me with them smokes o' hers. When I woke up, Mama was always fuckin' smilin' like it was some kinda sick game… like it was fun for her. And she always burned me in these rows of three. She usually had to light up a coupla times to get the job all the way done, which is pretty fucked-up all by itself."

"Why three?" The kid's eyes was puffy and pink, all on account of my loose-lipped ramblin'. "Why rows of three?"

Oh, yeah. Brett Taylor wasn't nothin' but a spillin' machine. "See, number one was 'cause I'd done somethin' to piss her off, at least that's what she told me when I woke up screamin'. And number two was 'cause I fought her off when she stuck me the first time. And she didn't give me no reason for number three, so's I figured it was just 'cause she fuckin' hated me."

That there arm of mine Cory was holdin' onto got pulled up to them pretty lips, and he rained down tiny kisses all over it like *I* was somethin' precious. Or more likely he was tryin' to take away all of them fucked-up memories with them sweet kisses. Which I gotta say, kinda worked.

"There was too many beatin's to count, but they didn't scar me none, at least not scars you can see on the outsida my body." I could see that this here chat was really takin' its toll on Cory, but, of course, Cory already knew the truth: there was plenty more scars on my heart and soul than I had on both o' my arms put together. "It ain't too hard to figure, really, Cory. I wasn't never s'posed to be born, but I got born anyhow, and I fucked up her whole life. So's she made me pay fer it."

At first, Cory didn't say nothin' to my pathetic little "Once upon a time there was a boy named Brett...." story. After all, what the fuck could he say? But I loved him and trusted him, so's I knew he'd make it okay for us. Finally, after a real deep breath, my boy said, "No one deserves that kind of treatment, especially not an innocent child." What Cory said next really shocked me, 'cause Cory didn't never say no swear words. *Never.* "You didn't 'fuck up' anything, baby, because it was your mother who was already 'fucked-up' long before you were even conceived. She just blamed her misery on you."

"Well, sure looks like I gone and spilled enough shit for now, huh? I got my sweet boy cursin' like a sailor...."

"No, Brett, I want to know everything—I mean *everything!*"

The kid really seemed to mean it, which was super considerate and all, but my belly was startin' to nag at me to make a return trip to the can. And since I wasn't up for spendin' the next forty-five minutes hurlin', I decided we was all done with discussin'. At least, for now.

Sometimes enough is just plain old enough, huh?

"She can't hurt you anymore. Now that you've started to share it, you and I will just grow closer and stronger than ever." My face got pulled real close to Cory's by them determined little hands. "And right now I want to be as close to you as I can possibly be."

Oh.

Time for a bit of good news, ain't it?

That there sweet, husky voice of my husband wasn't cryin', no, sir; it was *wantin'.* So's I placed my lips real soft onto Cory's, and I swore to God that I tasted the flavor of carin', with plenty of passion mixed in too. And yeah, we'd already done the deed twice on the couch before we hit the hay, but I wanted more. Guess I kinda needed more. "Wanna make love to you again, baby."

As soon as I spoke, that there wriggly little body started humpin' and grindin' on my leg, and I knew that he was up for it too. The time for talkin' was done. I drove right on into his sweet mouth with my hungry tongue, and my hands started touchin' and squeezin', and, Christ, suddenly I realized that Cory'd been right. I felt a whole hell of a lot better after sharin' my fucked-up story with him. You know, lighter, like a Mack Truck'd got lifted up offa my shoulders. And even more fucked-up than that (but at the same time amazin') was that Cory seemed to feel better too, now that I'd spilled out some of the shit that'd been stuck insida my head for so damned long. At least, that's how I was readin' the crazy passion he was showin' me right about then.

Before Cory got himself too overexcited down there beneath his belly, I pushed him offa me, not unkindly, and said real soft into his ear, "Now, you gotta slow down a measure, boy. I got me some plans." He breathed real deep a whole buncha times, and I could tell he was tryin' to drive his desire in reverse.

Ya see, Cory knew that sometimes I liked to take him from zero to sixty-five, sexually speakin', that is, without no help from them humpin' hips of his. I liked to start things up when his male part was soft as a pillow, and then I'd kinda tease him and coax him along, all slow and thorough-like, 'til he'd give up his right arm if I'd just let him fire one off. And once I got him to that point, I liked to keep 'im that way for a good long while, just so's it'd build up real nice. Then when he was turned into nothin' but a rollin'-around, moanin', horny mess of a man, he'd know that sure as shit, *I* was the one who'd made him into that. All of Cory's burnin' need was there by *my* doin'.

Yup. Brett Taylor done that to you, baby.

And Brett Taylor's the one who's gonna ease that there burn, as well.

I can't explain to ya how them types of thoughts made me feel—but sayin' somethin' like "real hot for my boy" might be a good way to start.

And tonight was one of them "zero to sixty-five" types o' nights for me, it was. Needed to know that I still had me some power, I s'pose. So's when the kid'd cooled down a measure, I made my move. This time I used both of my hands, one at the front door and one at the back, to get him, um, let's call it "all hot and bothered," and once I'd got the kid just exactly how I wanted him, I somehow managed to put words onto all o' them questions that was swirlin' in my brain. "What'd I ever do to deserve the likes o' you?"

Cory was breathin' real heavy so's I knew I was gettin' him good in just the right spot, his release just a moment away, so's he didn't answer me. And I ain't fuckin' with ya when I say that no brilliant explanation shot into my own mind neither, 'cause them little hands of his was slippin' underneath that there towel I wore, and they was surely distractin' me.

Sometimes talkin' is the right way to go, but other times there ain't no need for more words, huh?

October 21, 2007
Brett

YUP, it was happenin' again. The truck radio'd gone and sang me and Cory's story once more:

> *You are the strength that keeps me walking.*
> *You are the hope that keeps me trusting.*

It seemed like every time I turned on the radio, the song playin' on it was tellin' the story of my love for Cory. In that there Lifehouse tune called "Everything," the love seemed religious, just exactly like the worshippin' feelin' I had for my boy.

And then take last night when I'd been washin' the supper dishes. I'd just got the sink filled up with hot sudsy water, when Cory'd called out to me, "A little music might make my studying less monotonous…. Um, *big* hint!"

So's I'd dried off my hands and gone straight over to our boom box, and then I'd switched it on, so's it was playin' real loud.

> *This life, this love that you and I've been dreaming of for so long*
> *Would all be as good as gone without you.*

Yeah, that there's a fact. Gotta love the way Keith Urban sings a ballad, huh? And come to think of it, the other mornin' when the alarm clock'd started spewin' out its wake-up tunes, I'd found myself grinnin' then too.

The dawn is breaking, a light shining through
You're barely waking and I'm tangled up in you. Yeah.

Didn't know who the hell Howie Day was, but his song'd sure made me take a second to appreciate the way me and Cory was tangled up in our big purple nest together: four arms twisted together, four legs pretty much in a knot. Yup, us two was pretty much nothin' but one big human pretzel. And right then, I'd had to admit that them Gods of Music had again gifted me with the perfect song. But I didn't tell Cory nothin' about the Gods of Music, see, 'cause maybe it was just too goofy to share.

I hopped outta my truck when I got to Ally's apartment where my boy'd been studyin' all afternoon. Climbin' the stairs, I could hear music blarin' in the stairwell. It was apparently comin' from outta the apartment on the top floor, Ally's place.

And guess what? When I pushed open the door, all ready to nag at them two for partyin' it up 'stead of studyin', I found Cory and Ally jumpin' up and down on the sofa singin' along real loud with Kelly Clarkson. And they was beltin' out the refrain, "My life would suck without you!"

Made me smile, that there did.

October 25, 2007
Cory

"NO WAY, that's crazy thinking, Cory. Brett is *so* into you."

I bent down to retie my sneaker lace.

"Come on, let's go! It's getting cold out here…."

We didn't waste any time in getting back to our jog; both of us were well aware that we had only fifteen minutes left before Brett expected us at the B&G, and because we'd taken an extra-long detour from our regular route, we were farther away than usual. But our faster pace didn't prevent us from chatting a little while we ran.

"I mean, is there anything at all about Brett's behavior that suggests he's not completely nuts over you? Because there's absolutely nothing I can see, boyfriend." Ally sucked in several short breaths in rapid succession and then went on to say, "The guy watches you like a hawk, he escorts you everywhere, he makes sure you eat and sleep enough… and I'll bet he's very careful to make sure you're *never* sexually frustrated."

Actually, Ally wasn't even slightly off base about any of those things, but she'd completely missed my point. "I didn't say that Brett doesn't care about me… and feel responsible for me. We're pretty much each other's only real family, so of course he's very attached to me." I turned down the gravel path that cut through the quad. "All I'm saying is, it's possible that, well… that Brett's not gay."

"He sleeps with you every night, doesn't he? And it's not all about sleep when you two are snuggled up underneath that shiny purple comforter, is it?" Ally was breathing more heavily now, as we were making very good time. "So, yeah, I think that pretty much makes him gay."

Shaking my head, I dared to disagree. "No, Ally, that doesn't make him gay. It just makes him devoted and loyal." After a few more steps I slowed down so I could read the expression on Ally's face. "You know, he never dated men before me."

"From what you've told me, Cory, he never dated *anyone* before you."

Finally, we reached the grassy courtyard in front of the B&G. Both of us crumpled in half to catch our breath. "I think we went five miles today. That's our farthest distance yet. But Brett'll be lonely for you soon; we're a little bit late."

She was refusing to hear what I was trying to say at all, and it was frustrating. "No, he'll have plenty of company, believe me. Haven't you noticed the way the girls in there stare at him?" I nodded toward the B&G. "They certainly don't sense any gayness in Brett."

Ally stepped closer and then sort of tumbled me down onto the grass so that we could stretch. "You, my friend, are creating a problem where there isn't one. Mark my words, the split second your man catches a glimpse of you in that bar, this adorable, dreamy expression will invade his pretty face, and next thing you know, he'll be drooling all over you like you're nothing but a grape Popsicle."

I had to laugh at that image. "Well, I may not *be* a grape Popsicle, but I have one in my pocket...."

Ally leaned over and swatted me with her empty water bottle, and then she fell back on the ground, a mass of giggles. "You're too much, you know that? And that's a visual image that no one but Brett really needs... but baby, you've got to let this whole bit of lunacy go—Brett Taylor loves you to death!"

In a very small voice, I again inserted my own two cents, still unwilling to drop the subject. "I just want him to have the freedom to be certain that a male lover is what's right for him, that's all."

I never knew eyes could roll so far back into someone's head. Ally was becoming exasperated with me. "Whatever, Cory."

So I decided reluctantly to let the topic drop for now, and I stood up. Then reaching down, I grabbed Ally's arm and pulled her to her feet. As I did so, a new thought entered my mind. "Hey, have you sent me any prank-ish e-mails lately, you know, trying to be funny?"

"What do you mean, baby?"

"Well, I've been getting these kind of strange messages from e-mail addresses I don't recognize."

"You shouldn't open them; they could give your computer a virus."

"Yeah, you're probably right. But it's too late; I already opened them. Anyways, I thought maybe you were messing with my head a little, because you're such a *funny* gal."

Instead of seeing laughter there, confusion mixed with concern in Ally's dark eyes. "I don't know if I like the sound of that. Are these e-mails threatening?"

"Oh, no. It's nothing like that." I lunged forward to begin a final stretch of my calves, but Ally still stared at me, looking worried.

"Don't worry about it, Ally. Forget I said anything, okay?"

Now it was Ally's turn to refuse to let the subject drop. "At least tell me what the messages said."

I was fairly confident that my face was already blushing as red as a radish based on the amount of heat that was radiating from my forehead (enough to roast marshmallows over). "This is so stupid. Someone just confused my e-mail address."

"Tell me." She meant business. Now I knew how she kept Ben in line; her voice could be very stern when she wanted it to be, almost scary.

"Okay, okay. The first said, 'There you are, found you' or something like that, and the second one said 'Still so pretty.'"

"Sounds like you have yourself a secret admirer. Were there any more e-mails?"

"Just one more that said 'We have some unfinished business.'"

Ally shook her head and mumbled something about some people not having better things to do with their time. Then, very bluntly, she pronounced, "That's just plain weird."

"I know. So you don't have *unfinished business* with me? Because I know you think I'm *still so pretty*." I was teasing Ally so that she'd lighten up about the subject, but she didn't take the bait.

"Those e-mails aren't from me, baby. You should let Brett know, don't you think?"

This time I ignored her suggestion—the last thing I needed was a paranoid husband—and I grabbed her hand. "Come on. Let's go get a drink before you head out."

Just as Ally had predicted, Brett's piercing eyes widened the moment he saw me, and despite the fact that a faraway, rather wistful, expression took possession of his even features, there was absolutely no Popsicle-craving drool involved whatsoever.

Well, there wasn't very much.

October 29, 2007
Brett

THE bar was packed, 'specially for a Monday night. There was just somethin' about college kids and Halloween season; they fuckin' loved it! Just what them kids needed—another excuse to drink!

"He's so freaking possessive, like, did you guys see him here at lunchtime yesterday? He lurked around Cory like a stalker the whole time I was talking to him."

No, sir. Ian Webster didn't even make no attempt at keepin' the volume of his voice on the down low. Not that I'd be able to escape Ian's verbal bullcrap even if I'd wanted to, seein' as he was sittin' up at the bar and I was right behind it, slingin' drinks. Plus he'd pretty much bellowed it out like a foghorn, all the while starin' me right in the eyes; the dude was challengin' me.

Another dude, one of them jock boys, chimed in with, "Why doesn't he let Cory decide who he wants to hang out with? If you ask me, Taylor thinks he owns the kid." Seemed like none o' them jock boys had a brain of their own; they all just went along with the crap that Ian preached.

"Well, since you brought it up, nobody actually asked you, Hunter." That there reply came from Ally's boyfriend, Ben. Up until right then, Ben'd pretty much stayed outta this particular conversation, probably 'cause Ally was sittin' beside him moniterin' their every word, and not lookin' particularly happy about the way things was goin'. And Ally, well, she was kinda a tiger; I, personally, wouldn't want to cross her. I was betting that her boyfriend felt the same way.

"Maybe he doesn't trust Cory, or he thinks Cory is into us. So he guards him." That brilliant conclusion was drawn by the carrot-head, Christian, clearly not no future brain surgeon.

"In Bio, I filled Cory in on the fact that his 'fiancé' Brett, wasn't nothing but his bodyguard." The beer had evidently loosened up Ian's lips, not that they had ever been particularly tight, huh? "Cory said he didn't mind having Brett as his conjoined twin, but I know that the kid's getting suffocated."

Looked like these dudes was gettin' themselves all riled up.

And I might be gettin' a touched riled up, myself. Just sayin'.

"You know what?" Ian sprang to his feet from offa the bar stool he'd parked his sorry ass on. "I'm gonna go tell that asshole just what I think of him and how he tries to control Cory's life!"

And he's callin' me the asshole?

I grabbed a coupla dirty glasses offa the bar and clanked 'em together real noisy-like.

Here I am, come an' get me!

But shit for brains, over there, wasn't done spewin' his venom yet. "That dude thinks he's such a badass, well, he doesn't scare me one bit! Yeah, I'm gonna tell him how it's gonna be with Cory from here on out—he's gonna have to loosen up on the leash!"

Before the runt could hop over the bar and give me a piece of his most likely puny mind, Ben stood up and pretty much shoved Ian back down onto his stool with a single thick mitt. "Hey, man," he said, his mountain of a body towering over Ian, "Ally told me that Cory's perfectly fine with how Brett treats him."

Ian looked none too happy. "It's probably because Cory's scared shitless of the guy—"

"No, that's not it." Ben's deep voice rumbled as he shook his head. He glanced over toward his girlfriend who was looking back at him with a stern warnin' in her eyes. Ben's voice dropped down real low. "I guess something really bad happened to Cory last summer, so Brett looks out for him, that's all." That there comment made the hair on the back of my neck stand up; yeah, somethin' real fuckin' "bad" had happened to Cory on account o' me bein' an idiot.

But Ian wasn't in no mood to see reason. "So that's what Taylor calls it? 'Looking out for him'?"

"Stop acting like a giant asshole, E. Cory's not the new kid in town that you guys have to fight over so he'll be your BFF."

"Well, I'm sick of that dude, Brett Taylor. He acts like Cory's his property." Now Ian was starin' into his beer, all poutin' and grumbly (I couldn't help but notice).

So's now that I got me the complete picture of what Ian and his gang of jolly giants was thinkin', I didn't need to stick around and watch Ben try to drag Ian's head outta his ass. In fact, Ben could leave it up there the rest o' the night, for alls I cared. I moseyed on over to the cash register where I rung in my latest sale, and, not that I gave a flyin' shit, I glanced over at them asswipes just to see… well, I don't know just why I done it, but I looked on over at 'em. And it didn't come as no fuckin' surprise that Ian and all of them super-jocks was glarin' back at me like I'd drowned their pet kitten. That is, 'cept for Ben, who was lookin' at the ceilin' all casual-like, and Ally, who was starin' over at me and shruggin' like she was real sorry 'bout them boys' bad behavior.

I didn't have no more time to waste on them assholes, so's I got my ass back to work. But before I'd mixed up the next drink I broke into this sneaky sorta grin, 'cause I knew that Cory was sittin' on his spot on the couch in my office, his cute little nose stuck in a textbook. Right where he fuckin' belonged.

November 1, 2007
Cory

"TIME for yer chocolate fix, kids." After seating me and removing two bottles of water from my backpack, and then actually opening them for us, Brett slipped a small brown bag from out of his denim jacket's pocket.

"You sure know the way to my heart." Ally looked up at him and batted her long dark lashes a few times before reaching into the bag. "Yummm—I *love* malted milk balls!"

"Chocolate knows the path directly to my heart too." I held my hand out for a few.

Brett elbowed me lightly in the shoulder. "That there's pretty much what I'm countin' on." Those words were followed by a sexy wink, and I felt my heart melt—no malted milk balls required to get the job done. "You two runnin' today after class?"

"It's Thursday, so, yeah." Ally answered, crunching down hard on a candy and then nodding to acknowledge Brett's meaningful "take care of Cory" look. Brett ruffled my hair a bit and headed for the door.

I watched as Brett sort of swaggered away, clad in denim and a black T-shirt and rugged biker boots. To a casual observer he'd appear aloof, even dangerous. Yes, Brett certainly had mastered the bad-boy persona. But I knew that wasn't the real Brett at all.

"That man is smitten. I don't care if you think he's not gay." Ally glanced at me cautiously. "But Ben said that his friends all think he dominates you."

I shook my head. "I'm not even slightly dominated, Ally. Protected is a better word… and I agreed to this arrangement before we ever moved here. In fact, I asked for it."

"*I* know he's one of the good guys, Cory. You don't have to convince me."

"Does *Ben* know it?"

Ally shrugged, clearly unsure. "You know, boyfriend, I think it's time we *showed* him how great Brett is, don't you?" She allowed a crooked smile.

"What are you up to, Al?" The professor and his assistant entered the room, so I opened my computer and switched the power on. "I can always tell when you're being devious."

She followed suit with her own laptop, and then she flashed her eyes at me and said, "I'm developing a brilliant plan…." When the power came on she typed a few words quickly and then asked me, "What do you think of this?"

At first, the homepage of Leighton University flashed on her screen, soon to be replaced by the Undergraduate French Club's page. "The L.U. Annual French Club Fashion Show?" I didn't see how this had anything at all to do with Brett and Ben.

"Yeah, it's Saturday night, a fund-raiser for the French Club's annual Paris trip. I went last year; it was a blast. Can Brett get the night off work? Because I think we should dress up the boys, have them treat us to a nice dinner at the Tavern on the Green, and then hit the fashion show!"

"Um, Ally, do you want them to have fun, or do you want to *torture* them?" Dropping another malted milk ball into my mouth, I suggested, "Because if you want them to have fun, you should think more in terms of *sporting events*. Too bad the World Series is over already. They definitely would have had fun watching the Red Sox wallop the Rockies."

Ally was enjoying my confusion. "No sporting events—this is one of Ben's only Saturdays off from football this fall. I'm not about to find myself sitting in another sweaty stadium, and besides, this is going to work like a charm." There was a twinkle in her eyes.

"How so? Sorry, but I just can't see it."

"You need to be more devious, Cory, really you do." After one quick spurt of laughter, she said brightly, "Ben and Brett will be forced to bond over their mutual misery!"

November 3, 2007
Brett

THE Tavern on the Green wasn't no casual, down-home waterin' hole. No, sir. And it sure wasn't aimin' to please the less-than-discriminatin' tastes of no Mr. Fix-It-Barkeep like Brett Taylor. None-the-fuck-less, that was exactly where I found my ass planted tonight. At the moment, me and Ben Reed was starin' at each other real awkward-like across this fancy-set table, both of us fiddlin' with our cloth napkins that was folded up sorta like crowns... in the warm glow of candlelight. Which woulda been romantic if our dates weren't off in the bathroom.

Ben broke the silence. "So, are you up for a fashion show tonight?"

"Will I *ever* be up for a fashion show? That there's a better question." I glanced down at my one-and-only fancy-ass "uniform": the very same white oxford shirt, khaki pants, and navy blazer that I'd wore to Cory's junior year Casino Night, his National Honor Society Induction, and his high school graduation. But tonight Cory didn't make me wear my banker's tie.

"Yeah, I hear you, man. I hate it that I have to wear my dress-to-impress outfit." Ben glanced down at his own clothes. "Ally actually pulled it out of my closet and placed it all out on the bed in the shape of a person for me so I wouldn't screw up getting dressed. How'd you get out of wearing a tie?"

Yeah, me and him was in the same fuckin' boat in the dressin' up department. S'pose the both of us was also pretty much whipped on our lovers. Didn't matter none to me; I'd go any damned place Cory wanted me to go, whenever he wanted me to go there. And I'd wear a pretty smile on my face to match with my fancy-assed clothes, whether I fuckin' liked it or not. Case closed.

Callin' to mind the fact that Cory wanted me to make a good impression on this dude, I tried my hand at makin' small talk. Which I sucked at. "So's Cory's gone joggin' with Ally just about every Tuesday and Thursday since they met in history class." That there was friendly conversation, huh?

Ben nodded and grunted his agreement. "Ally's kinda nuts over Cory."

"Yup. Same for Cory… about Ally, that is."

"What happened to Cory last summer? Ally told me he got hurt, but didn't get into the details."

My heart sped up, and I couldn't think of no words to answer him with.

Here we go….

"So, what happened to him?"

Well, that was real fuckin' direct. "Uh, it's just that… one of them customers at the bar where we used to work… he *liked* Cory, uh… and that there feeling wasn't mutual. And the asshole wouldn't take no for an answer. Get what I'm sayin'?"

A light seemed to suddenly turn on insida Ben's head. "Did he get… like, um, how do I say it? Did Cory get *raped*?"

"Nope. Not that… but he got beat on real bad." I couldn't fuckin' believe I was actually havin' this particular discussion with this here dude who was still pretty much a stranger to me.

"Is the asshole in jail?"

Ouch. A major sore spot, that there was.

"He oughta be, but he ain't. Cory begged me to leave it alone, so's I did. It's a long story." I studied the flowers painted on them pretty plates real intent-like, as if I actually could appreciate shit like that. See, I just couldn't look up right then on account of my eyes was waterin'.

"So that's why you watch out for Cory all the time, isn't it?"

I could feel his eyes studyin' me, takin' in the details. So's I nodded real quick.

"That's cool. I'd do the very same thing if it'd happened to Ally, man. I'd never leave her side again."

At that point Cory and Ally came back from the bathroom. Had to admit it, both of 'em looked kinda relieved to see me and Ben sittin' there, chattin' like a coupla school girls. Prob'ly thought they'd come back to find us wrestlin' on the floor, or worse. Almost told 'em all exactly what I was thinkin', but the waitress came just then with our salads. Prob'ly that was a good thing, huh?

Ben hadn't swallowed his second bite of Caesar salad, when he got this really funky look on his face. "Uh, excuse me… I need to use the men's room."

That there dude ran with impressive speed, almost like he was chasin' down a pass, directly to the can.

"He didn't look too good, Ally," Cory said, all super concerned.

Ally frowned and started to get up. "I'm going to go and see if he's okay."

Real fast, I jumped up onto my feet. "Sit down, Ally… and Cory, you keep her company, 'kay? I'll go and check on him."

IN THE men's room, from outta one of them stalls, I heard the sorts o' sounds that come with major-league sickness, if ya catch my drift.

"Ben, you okay, man?"

Silence. A big-time burp. And finally, "Not really."

"Your belly's achin', ain't it?" I got my answer from the sound of the dude losin' what was left of his lunch. I leaned against the sink and waited.

After a coupla minutes, the door to the stall opened to a much more haggard-lookin' version of Ben than I'd seen just a coupla minutes before. And his dress-to-impress outfit was mighty rumpled. "Brett, I think I might be sick."

"*Ya think?*" (Okay, I admit I sounded sarcastic right there, but the dude needed to get real.) I reached out to loosen up Ben's tie. "We gotta get yer ass home."

"What about the fashion show? Ally's gonna be so disappointed.... I can go. I'll be okay... just give me a second...." Then he made a return trip to the toilet.

After this round of barfin' stopped, I told him, "You ain't in no shape to go nowhere but to bed. I'm gonna go talk to Cory and Ally, and then I'm bringin' you home."

"But... but...." Time for more barfin', round three, or was it four?

"Just rest easy, man, and I'll be back." Alls I got for an answer was a nauseated groan.

"OKAY, here's the deal: Ben ain't feelin' 100 percent peachy tonight, so's I thought I'd give him a lift back to his place. Now, that there won't take me too long, and then I'll come back and the three of us'll get our fine-lookin' asses over to the fashion show, huh?"

Ally got outta her seat, fiddled a bit with the tie on her silky blouse, and said, "No, no, Brett... I'll go back with you guys, and then I'll stay with him."

Placin' a hand on Ally's shoulder, I kinda nudged her back down into her seat. "Look here, Ally, Ben don't want no company tonight, believe me. And besides that, he made me promise that I'd take you two to that there show. Ya think he's tryin' to punish me?" That there last part was an attempt at a joke. "Death by fashion torture...."

Ally smiled weakly. "All right, if that's what he wants, and what you want too."

"What about your dinner, Brett? You'll be starving!" Cory was always tryin' to feed me.

"Don't worry none about that; I had me a big lunch at the B&G." I leaned over and gave my boy a kiss right on them super sweet lips. "Now you two go on ahead and have a real nice dinner, and I'll be back in less than an hour."

I HADTA pull my truck offa the side of the road three times on the short drive back to Ben's apartment so's he could throw up in the woods. Poor dude was in a real bad way. And when we pulled up in front of his place, I insisted on helpin' to drag him up the stairs, and then he pulled off his clothes, droppin' 'em into a pile on the floor, and I got him into his bed.

"I stuck this trash can next to the bed when you was in the can, in case, y'know…." I cracked a half smile. "Hope you don't need it." Then I stepped over to the bed.

It seemed to take Ben a helluva lot of effort to lift up his head offa the pillow to look at me. "Thanks, Brett, but you'd better stay away from me—I don't want you to catch what I've got; this isn't any fun at all."

"Don't worry, man, I ain't gonna kiss you or nothin'. I just wanna give you somethin' to drink." I handed him a bottle of water that I'd swiped offa his desk.

Leaning back, Ben mumbled, "I owe you, man."

"Now, go to sleep, if ya can, and I'll get back to them two at the restaurant."

Ben already seemed to be dozin' off. "Thanks for *that* too "

"Not a problem, Reed. But I got me one question before I leave."

Ben's dark eyes cracked open.

"You sure you ain't fakin' sickness to get yer sorry ass outta this fashion show tonight?" I had me a quick chuckle on account o' the look on his face. "'Cause if you are, dude, payback's gonna be a real bitch!"

In response, Ben lifted up the wastebasket and pretty much stuck his head right in.

SO'S tonight I had myself two gorgeous dates to the French Club's Fashion Show. Sure, my belly rumbled a bit, complainin' all noisy-like that it wasn't too pleased with missin' out on supper. But Cory'd put my dinner in a to-go box, and I scarfed down what I could on the ride across campus to the theater. Still, it was worth it, 'cause I thought I mighta scored a coupla extra points in Cory's book for doin' what I done. (I didn't really care a hell of a lot 'bout nobody else's scorecard.)

November 12, 2007
Ian

ONE night at the B&G, after giving my efforts at courting Cory yet another try and failing miserably (which was pretty much par for the course), I decided that it was time I did my homework. I mean, time I *really* did my homework. No, I wasn't talking about an American Lit or Bio assignment; tonight I was going to wrap my brain around the real Brett Taylor. You know, study the guy. Okay, okay, so I was going to stalk the man as he performed his duties at the B&G, in order to learn the facts I needed.

No, I'm not too proud to admit it; in any case, the ends would justify the means.

I took a minute to wonder why Cory was so unwaveringly devoted to this guy. The two of them clearly didn't have a single thing in common: Cory was sweet and sensitive; Brett was gruff and surly. Cory was smart and clever; Brett was one step above caveman. Cory was interested in fashion and art and music; Brett was, well, one step above caveman. It was a wonder that the man had managed to evolve beyond the fur loincloth into those faded Levi's that he seemed to live in.

So, anyways, tonight I was going to discover, firsthand, the reasons for Cory's devotion, even if it killed me. Which it might. I could easily choke on my beer; I was so damned frustrated with this whole situation. *Somebody* in this equation was blind, and I meant to find out who it was. Either I was blind to Brett's gayness (as well as his greatness), Cory was blind to Brett's straightness (and his total thuggish-ness), or Brett was blind to his own straightness, or.... Well, whatever the case may be, there we sat, me and Ben, slumped over a pitcher of beer at a back corner table.

And I wasn't leaving until I had my answers.

"What the hell does Cory see in a guy like Brett Taylor? Oh, other than the fact that he's king of the pretty boys—but I have to say that he's a king in dire need of a proper hair style." I lifted the pitcher to refill my own beer and then Ben's. "Maybe all it takes to get a guy like Cory is to be a potential contender for Mr. January in the 2013 Hunk of the Month Wall Calendar."

"Cory's not that shallow, and you know it." Ben took a long sip of his beer. His devious expression told me that he was going to stick it to me now. As in get me, and get me good... and enjoy it fully. "Yeah, Brett's definitely 'a sweet piece of eye candy'—isn't that what you always say about the players when we watch ball games on TV?" He made air quotes with his fingers when he said my words for a hot athlete. "Remember that time when us guys all tried to pick out the perfect Red Sox player for you? That was a fucking awesome night! Yeah, good times.... But anyways, you really shouldn't hold Brett's good looks against him—it's not nice."

"Well, it's common knowledge that God doesn't overbless, so Taylor's probably seriously lacking between his ears... or, I've got it—I bet it's *between his legs* where he comes up short!" I made the universal sign for a tiny penis with my fingers.

Ben's last sip of beer seemed to have found its way down the wrong pipe. Looked like I was the one who got him good in the end. "Holy crap, Ian! That's cold. Taylor's not such a bad guy." He coughed forcefully, a few drops of golden lager trickling from his nose.

"You've got eyes, Ben. Take a look around at all the women... and I mean *all* of them. You must admit that they clearly don't see 'homo' when they look at him," I continued, barely acknowledging that Ben was a participant in this conversation. "They literally lick their lips when they look at him; he might as well be an enormous bowl of triple chocolate brownie ice cream smothered in hot fudge."

"You *know* how much college girls like ice cream, Ian." Ben leaned back in his chair and added, "And chocolate too. Apparently, Brett Taylor's got both areas covered."

Okay, so what if I completely ignored Ben's half of this discussion? What he was saying didn't amount to very much, anyways. At least I could be thankful that I had a warm body sitting across the table from me so nobody would realize that I was actually talking aloud to myself. "I haven't done too badly with guys here at school, have I?"

Ben looked at me cross-eyed. "You haven't done anything *at all* with guys here at school; that's more the size of it."

Well, who asked you, anyways? Oh, yeah… I did.

Moving right along….

"In fact, there's even been a time or two that I had to fight 'em off, wouldn't you say?" Maybe I was stretching the truth ever so slightly.

"Like last Halloween? When you managed to ward off that cute little dude dressed up like a Catholic schoolboy as well as that other guy decked out in drag like a Catholic schoolgirl? *That* was classic! Wish like hell I had video of you trying to fight the two of them off, all dressed up as a piece of corn on the cob! Can you say YouTube?"

"Corn on the cob, my friend, was a stellar costume…." I glanced at Ben, whose eyes were streaming giddy tears, as he mumbled something about a food fight in a parochial school cafeteria. "You're laughing *at* me not *with* me, aren't you?"

Ben was rapidly becoming far too enthusiastic about this topic. I didn't like it one damn bit. "And after winning football games, E, women really want us bad, you know—us guys on the team. It's more like they actually have to have us! Not that I'm interested, 'cause of Ally and all. But it feels good to be in demand, you know?"

"But neither of us have ever been in demand like this guy, and I don't even think he graduated from high school—he's one small step up from a hoodlum. And just look at all of the chicks staring at him… *just look*… you see, Ben? Some of them are actually obnoxious, the way they're trying to get his attention. Look at that one…." I attempted to point nonchalantly with my elbow.

"The one with the big—"

"Hair—yeah, the one with the big *hair*.... See that? She just dropped her purse right in front of him."

"I'd say it's more like she pitched it at his feet. Geez, that fastball must've hurt like hell when it hit his ankle. The babe is hot, *and* she has one hell of a windup." We watched as Brett bent over and retrieved the girl's purse, and then spoke politely as he handed it to her. "Her strategy worked."

At this point I was starting to feel like a sports commentator doing a play-by-play. "Look, her lashes are fluttering at him like her eyeballs are trying to take flight. The dude must be fucking blind—he hasn't even noticed her flirting her ass off with him!"

"From where I'm sitting, it looks like that gal's ass is completely intact. Uh-huh."

I slugged Ben's arm hard for Ally's sake and watched as the girl shimmied her way over to Brett's side and then pressed one abundant breast boldly against his bicep. "He's gonna make a move on her now, just watch. No het dude can resist a boob in that kind of close proximity."

Ben nodded in agreement. "Yeah, Taylor took a direct hit with that girl's hooter, that's for sure. Tough to pass up... and I'm speaking from heterosexual male personal experience."

Now, Brett could've easily taken a handful of that willingly offered breast, but the only thing Brett took was a single step backward, retreating from the fluttering lashes and the large boob that was clearly crowding his personal space, his eyes leveled at the floor.

How utterly disappointing.

"Sorry, dude, but Brett Taylor hasn't even realized she's *female*. Or, maybe, it is just possible he doesn't *care* that she's female." Ben didn't seem particularly astonished by this revelation.

Well, you had to hand it to her; this young lady certainly was no quitter. She persisted in putting on quite a titillating show for Brett's exclusive benefit. At the moment, she was arching her back seductively, reaching to adjust the buckle on the side of her boot, the other arm slung carelessly across a thrusting hip, and her eyes raised in a coquettish expression. All at the same time. Now, that took coordination.

But still no reaction from Brett, and I'm talking about zero.

It's almost as if he isn't interested in her. Hmmmm.

"I'm *gay,* and I'm getting kind of hot from watching her… um, her little display. What's up with this guy?"

Ben picked up a menu off of our sticky table and proceeded to fan himself. He was clearly not unaffected by the little lady's shenanigans either. Then finally, after one last desperate slide of her pink tongue over her sparkly teeth, the poor girl's shoulders drooped in defeat as she gave up on the man and trudged away, not even a trace of spring left in her step, or wiggle in her walk, or whatever. Ben dropped the menu on the table and filled his glass yet again, sucking the entire beer down in a single gulp as if to cool himself off.

I wasn't finished with my case study yet, not by a longshot. My specimen had merely passed test number one, but no straight man in his right mind could resist a double whammy, and it looked like Seduction of the Bartender, Phase Two, was strutting Brett's way. I'd heard that Megan Trasker, one of the B&G's waitresses, and the recently crowned Miss Leighton University (which proved that she had her attractiveness act together, didn't it?), refused to take no for an answer when it came to getting the guy she set her sights on. Rumor had it—rumor being defined as Darlene Wilcox, my Renaissance Art class study partner and, coincidentally, Megan Trasker's big-mouthed roommate—that Megan and Brett had a history together. Granted it was a one-sided history. Megan had been chasing Taylor's ass around the B&G since school had started. (In fact, I'd made it my business to tell Cory *all* about Queen Meg's designs on his "fiancé"—in vivid detail, of course. What kind of a friend would I be if I left out the specifics?) I watched with bated breath as Megan marched right up to Brett and started performing her well-rehearsed male-tantalization repertoire, but it was immediately clear that her attempts were going to be as miserably unsuccessful as her predecessor's.

No dice for pretty Miss L.U. either. And she didn't look particularly pleased.

Maybe Brett Taylor has no sex drive. None whatsoever. He's a redneck, right? Maybe he lost his libido in a hunting accident.

I scanned the crowd of mainly women, most of whom were gazing hungrily in Brett's direction. "Look at the man, Ben; he hasn't even realized that any of those babes are alive, let alone that they are more than ready and willing to jump his bones!"

"Well, you've got to admit, Ian, Taylor's a good-looking dude. I mean, you don't call him 'The Ken Doll' for nothing, right? And he may not be a varsity athlete like me, man, but check out the dude's pecs. That guy's put in his share of hours at the gym."

I'm gay, not visually impaired.

Yes, I had already taken ample time to inspect Brett's arms and shoulders and face and butt and… and, well, let's just say that the whole package had been closely scrutinized. And I'd reluctantly admitted that the "whole package" had passed the rather stringent list of requirements to qualify as a hottie in my book. With flying colors. But that was neither here nor there. "And what is it with the whole 'tortured soul' thing he's got going on?"

"I don't know, but the chicks seem to dig it." Ben got up with a grunt and headed off to the men's room leaving me alone to wallow in my bewilderment. I wasn't yet finished stalking my unknowing prey. I continued to observe the subject through narrowed eyes. Twenty-five or so eager, horny, and slightly tipsy women surrounded him (easy pickings for the straight man, or so I hear), all clamoring for his attention, but it was nothing but business as usual for Brett Taylor.

Oh, but when Brett approached his beloved Cory, still perched at the bar on the very same stool where he'd shot down my most recent, and quite creative, I must say, come-ons, all I could do was watch helplessly. The two of them pretty much melted into a couple of piles of mushy goo the very second their eyes met. No doubt about it, there was a raging love fest in that glance. *Yeah, get a room.*

And I was forced to admit that Brett Taylor had *handsome, chivalrous, devoted, tortured,* and *faithful* all wrapped up and stuffed deep in his back pocket where I couldn't get at it. Time to face the music. (Quite possibly it was well past time for that, but who was watching the clock?)

I have no chance with Cory.

That sad fact was becoming increasingly clear. Brett Taylor couldn't see anyone but Cory. And vice versa.

Let me reiterate it so there's no room for confusion: I am the snowball in hell. That pretty much sums it up.

Just then Ben wobbled back to our table grasping another full pitcher, beer sloshing onto his wrists with every step.

"I've been thinking," I informed him gravely, "I might just back off from Cory a little. You know, give him a chance to come to me."

Ben winked at me, a knowing look in his eyes.

"Maybe, and don't get too excited, Ben, because this is only a *maybe,* Cory's destined to be like a little brother kind of buddy to me." I felt my heart sink right down to the tips of my combat boots. I guess I wasn't yet feeling too enthusiastic about a completely platonic state of affairs between Cory and me.

Ben put his hand up to slap me a high five, looking enormously relieved at my sudden change of heart. "You've already got four brothers at home, and all of us guys who live in the suite are like your brothers too—another bro is just what you need for your collection!" Ben was laughing, but he sobered quickly when he saw my expression. "Seriously, E, Brett isn't such a bad dude. And he really does love Cory a lot."

Despite the fact that I was planning to let up a bit on my hot pursuit of Cory, I wasn't planning on crowning Brett Taylor as some sort of saint. Therefore, I successfully managed to completely ignore Ben's most recent defense of the man. "I guess having Cory as a kid brother is better than having nothing with him at all." I lifted my glass to my lips knowing that tonight I'd studied hard and learned the cold and bitter facts firsthand: Brett Taylor plus Cory Butana equals True Love Always.

Brett

STANDING at the bar beside my trusty bartender, Barry, I struggled with Cory's "friendship" with the entire L.U. Hawks varsity football team and that there artsy-Goth dude who might as well've been their fuckin' quarterback; them dumb jocks hung on his ev'ry word. And it wasn't no secret that Ian Webster was basically knocking himself out to get into my husband's skinny jeans. "That guy is so into my fiancé. Check out the way he's gawkin' at Cory," I complained to Barry, noddin' toward Webster and his bulgin' eyeballs.

Barry glanced over at me, and grinned. "I recognize the smitten expression, Boss—it's written all over *your* face too!"

"Believe me, I know it is; I gotta see this here lovesick mug in the mirror every mornin' when I shave." Lookin' over at where Ian sat with Ben, his dark eyes gapin' all the way across the bar at my baby, I gotta say, I felt a tiny bit sorry for him. Just a tiny bit, though. 'Cause who could blame the dude for bein' hooked on Cory? Nobody could, that's who. My adorable little husband had it all—brains, beauty, sweetness... *fuckin' everythin'*. And I could deal with all of the kid's football buddies and head-over-heels Ian Webster 'cause I knew for a fact that I could trust my boy with my life, and more important, with my heart.

But still, I didn't enjoy watchin' a crowd of high testosterone levels in the human form flock around my pretty partner.

November 15, 2007
Cory

My CELL phone vibrated in my pocket at exactly the right moment. The Women in American History paper I was toiling over was not coming together as easily as I'd hoped; in fact, it was going nowhere fast. I looked at my phone as I pulled it out of my pocket. It was Ally. "Hello, honey."

"Cory, are you at the library?"

"Yeah." I whispered so as not to disturb the other students around me. "What's up?"

It took merely a few seconds for Ally's worries to gush forth. "Ben and Christian and most of all Hunter are completely lost in their calculus class. They can't even begin to do their homework, and if their grades sink too low, baby, they'll be put on academic suspension, and they won't be able to play…. And Lord, Cory, I'm a history major. I can't even begin to help them—"

"Okay, okay… calm down, Ally." I got up and walked toward the stairwell where I could talk. "Now, listen, I'm pretty decent at math. Want me to take a look at their assignment?"

"God, yes!"

"Well, where are you guys?"

"We're at their place, and Ian's with us too. But we'll come over and get you, you know, so Brett doesn't freak out that you went somewhere alone."

Um, that's embarrassing.

"No, how about you guys meet me in the lobby of the library in fifteen minutes. That way we can go study at my apartment, and

Brett can come straight home after work instead of, you know, having to get me at their place."

"Saint Cory of Calculus! We all praise you!" I heard Christian's relieved shouts coming from somewhere near Ally.

"Tell Christian that he's a laugh a minute, and I'll see you guys in a few."

Ally spoke again, this time more hesitant. "We aren't interrupting any major studying, are we?"

I had to smile. "No, as a matter of fact you're probably saving me from jamming a pencil in my eye."

"Good. See ya!"

After leaving Brett a hurried voice mail attempting to explain the situation, I packed up my things and headed downstairs.

FOR the next several hours I got to play the part of "calculus teacher," one with extremely oversized students. I sat cross-legged on the recliner holding a notebook that was now covered in largely printed practice equations, facing my three rather bulky students, who lounged comfortably on the big bed's shiny purple comforter. Somehow, though, the bed didn't look so big anymore, as Ally also had taken residence there, sort of spooning Ben as he worked.

"It's a miracle! I get it. For the first time this year, I can honestly say I understand calculus!" Christian held up a hand for a high five, which I rather proudly returned.

"Yeah, and it's not like I'm gonna become a math major or anything, but I think I see the light! You sure saved my ugly butt, Cory." Ben was equally jubilant.

A sleepy feminine voice from behind Ben chimed in, "I think you have a cute butt, baby."

"Me too...." Ian popped up from where he was lying on the couch. "But no matter how I beg, Benji, you just won't let me near it."

Ben sort of dove off the end of the bed onto the couch, and that's how the wrestling match got started. The two of them rolled to the floor with a thump in heated mock-battle, so I looked at Ally and suggested, "I think it's time we called it a night."

"Ally! If you ever get sick and tired of Benji here, send him and his adorable ass my way, okay?" Ian's comment was met by the sound of a sharp slap on denim. "Do it again! I love it when you spank me!"

"Shut up, asshole!"

"Yeah, you guys're disturbing my sleep." Hunter now lay on the bed with his calculus textbook tucked beneath his head. "You see, if all of Cory's tutoring doesn't help, my backup plan is osmosis."

Ally glanced over at me apologetically. "They're getting completely out of hand, Cory. I think we missed their feeding time."

But I wasn't paying her my full attention; I was still beaming over my accomplishments as a calculus teacher. "Think of it, Ally, I may be single-handedly responsible for saving Saturday's game—no academic suspensions for my star pupils!"

Ally rolled her eyes. "We *need* to feed them."

By now Christian had gotten in on the act by launching himself off the edge of the bed onto the pair. "Double body slam!"

"I'll order pizza." Ally smiled her approval as I started to dial. "They earned it, hmm?"

"Hey, Cory, does Brett have any beer?" Ian extricated himself from the human pile and strode past me to the refrigerator. "Nope, guys—there's no brews, but there's some of those old-fashioned black cherry sodas...."

"Toss me one!" Christian was the next one to rise up off of the floor. Catching a bottle, he said, "Yeah, these are the all-natural kind—sweet!"

"The good stuff—the champagne of sodas!" Ben swiped Christian's soda and yet another wrestling match commenced.

"Help yourself, really," I teased. "I can make iced tea too."

"I'll take a bottle of black cherry," Hunter and Ally said in unison, and we all had to laugh.

"We conquered calculus with our secret weapon!" I was hoisted into the air by my two largest guests.

Yes, it was far past time that the zoo animals were tossed their slabs of meat.

Brett

I GOT home at about midnight to a pizza party ragin' full force in my apartment. And don't get me wrong, I ain't got nothin' against pizza… or parties, for that matter. But this here wasn't the sorta pizza party you went to in grade school. Nope, Cory's little get-together consisted of a pile of hulkin' football players fillin' their faces on *my* bed like they owned it, and the dude who'd been tryin' with everythin' he had in him to get into *my* husband's pants chowin' down on a slice of pepperoni on *my* couch; all of 'em suckin' down *my* black cherry sodas. And then there was Ally sittin' at the kitchen table, but she wasn't no problem.

The biggest fuckin' problem I had me right then was Cory. So busy servin' up drinks and pizza, he might as well've been back at the Downtown Pub on the job. My little host with the most, there, well, he was so goddamned busy playing waiter that he didn't barely even have time to fuckin' look up and smile at his husband when he'd got home from a hard night at work.

That there fact, all by its lonely self, had pretty much brought my blood to a full boil.

My place, *my* bed, *my* soda, *my* husband… and alls I got for a "welcome home" was a half a wave from Ally, a stuffed-full-mouth grunt from Ben, and a half-assed attempt at a smile from Cory. The rest of 'em didn't seem to've noticed that the other man of this house'd got home.

This here situation is fucked-up.

I was pissed off at somebody, which wasn't no abnormal feelin' for me 'cause I spent a lot o' time bein' pissed off. What *was* fucked-up about it was that the person I was pissed off at was Cory.

Cory

"YOU weren't particularly talkative when you got home tonight, Brett." I very rarely became annoyed by Brett's indifferent behavior toward my friends, but tonight was an exception. I tied my sweats low on my waist as I came out of the bathroom. "You know, maybe those guys would like you a little bit more if you made an effort to be friendlier to them."

Brett was already in bed, his bare back presented to me. I knew that he was not in a good mood at all, and it was easier for him to deal with his emotions when he wasn't actually looking at me. So I flopped down beside him, causing the mattress to jostle him around enough to satisfy my frustration. "Talk about this with me, Brett, God, you're acting like you're jealous or something."

Brett shot up off of the bed as if he'd had one of his bad dreams, and I'd have bet my life that he hadn't even been asleep yet. "Ya think?" He stared at me, visibly shocked. No, on second thought, he was angry. Very angry. "Yer goddamned right I'm jealous—I'm fuckin' green with it! And I'm ready to fuckin' lose it!"

That outburst was unexpected! But I guess my own shock was equally evident. I could feel my eyes bulging.

"You want yer freedom, Cory? That's what yer after, ain't it?" Now Brett wasn't yelling. His voice was quiet, carefully restrained, and needle sharp. No, he didn't need to shout in order to get his point across. With the same controlled voice, he queried, "Is it Webster you wanna date? Or one of them jock boys, huh?"

Like his voice, his glare would also have been perfectly capable of cutting glass. And I couldn't have been more surprised by his reaction if Brett had sprouted wings and flown right out the window. "You think *I* want *my* freedom?"

"Christ, Cory, it'd pretty much fuckin' kill me to let you walk, but yeah, I'll let ya go if it's what ya want." His eyes had puffed up like he'd inhaled something acrid. "It's okay, don't think nothin' of it, kid... I'll deal." The rims of his green eyes had reddened; the effect of the two contrasting colors was almost Christmas-y.

While I tried to digest what the heck was happening, there was a period of silence between us, and not at all our usual comfortable silence. This quiet was soon broken by the sound of Brett raving.

"Just say the fuckin' word, Cory, and I'm gone—I won't be nothin' but a fuckin' bad memory!" He stood in front of where I sat on the bed, slightly crouched down with his fists tightly clenched.

"*What?*" My own panic and confusion also hung thickly in the air between us. "I never said that... that *I* wanted freedom. But maybe... maybe that's what *you* want."

Brett didn't even stop and think; he just reacted. "Have you lost yer fuckin' marbles?" Completely agitated now, he began pacing back and forth in the narrow space between the bed and the window. "I ain't got no fuckin' clue what the fuckin' hell yer goin' on about!"

I reached out from the bed and snagged Brett's arm as he passed by, and then I pulled him onto the bed beside me. He was sweating and panting and—and I really thought he was having some sort of panic attack. "Look at me, Brett." Those wild eyes shifted from the floor to the ceiling to the kitchen table, but never toward me. "I need to see your eyes, honey, right now."

The man reluctantly dragged his tortured eyes over to meet mine. Yes, he was deeply upset but was still paying attention.

"Listen, Brett, there's something I've been wanting to talk to you about, and I haven't known exactly how to bring it up, but—"

"Holy fuckin' shit...."

I had to ignore his panicked murmur if I was going to get these next words out. "But I guess now is the right time, so... uh...."

"Just fuckin' say it, Cory." He turned directly toward me, those beautiful jade green eyes sparkling with emotion, barely kept in check. He was expecting to hear something earth-shattering. "Say what you gotta say, dammit." It was nothing short of a command.

I took a deep breath. *Here goes nothing.* "What I've wanted to ask you, for a while now, I guess, is… well, let's put it this way—"

"Jesus Christ, Cory, sp-spit it the fuck out, w-would ya?" His teeth appeared to be chattering. Then he hopped up and started back across the room.

"Okay. All right…. So, so you could go have any girl you want at the B&G or at the gym or—or pretty much anywhere you go. The girls around here, and probably everywhere else too, well, they stare at you, and they flirt with you… and I know about Megan Trasker's little obsession with you 'cause Ian told me all about it… and I want…." This was much harder than I thought it would be to say aloud. "I want you to know that it's okay with me if you want to… if you want to experiment with *women* some. So you can be sure, you know? And we can still be really good friends…."

Something was very wrong here; that fact was immediately obvious to me. Brett wasn't reacting as I'd expected. I mean, not even slightly. No guilty glance to the side, no blush to match the likes of my "flamingo face," no awkward, stuttering denial of his secret interest in women. Brett simply appeared flabbergasted. (It wasn't often that I had the opportunity to use the word *flabbergasted*, but I call them like I see them.)

He stopped, midpace, and blurted, "*Sure?* Fuckin' *sure* about what?" Momentarily, his mouth hung open. And not in an appealing way, either. I mean it was wide open, tongue falling off to the side — all-in-all, it painted a rather disturbing picture.

"What I'm trying to say, Brett, is that maybe you should date a few women—"

Brett had stopped pacing and had moved directly in front of me. "Why in fuckin' tarnation would I wanna do somethin' like that?"

He clearly wasn't catching on to the fact that I was setting him free. In all truth, he didn't look even slightly giddy with his newly found emancipation; no, the man looked much more as if he was going to be sick.

"Huh? I asked ya somethin'?"

So, I decided I'd help him out a little bit. I took both of his stone cold hands into mine, and then I let all my concerns just spill out. "You're asking me *why*? So you can be sure you're gay, that's why. Think about it for a minute—you've never dated before me, not men or women, and you've never *come out*, have you? And...." I was starting to come apart at the seams. "And Ian says that you aren't even gay, and his gaydar is like 99 percent accurate and...." And then I just unraveled. Thankfully, my freak-out (consisting mainly of frenzied breathing and an intense battle against tears) had closed my throat enough so that I was forced to stop babbling, that is, if I wanted to inhale.

Brett squeezed my hands, and then gripped me by my forearms and shook me a little, as if to be certain I was actually sitting next to him, spouting this crazy nonsense. "You... you think I don't *love you*? And that I don't want you, like, uh... like *in the sack*?"

I nodded, blinked once, and then I hiccupped. Not at all smooth.

Way to let him off the hook easily, Cory.

And before I had a chance to even think about supplying him with a more comprehensive verbal answer, Brett had crumpled into a pile on the bed. "I fucked it up with you an' me! I gone and fucked it up again!" His first few sobs prevented more words for a mere moment. "I tried... so fuckin' hard to show ya... how much... how much I love ya! Every fuckin' d-day... I tried...." Sobs interspersed with distressed words. Then he burrowed right down into the blankets and pulled a pillow over his mass of blond tangles, muffling his desperate groans. In no time at all, muted, but still desperate, apologies surged forth from beneath the pillow. "Cory, baby, I'm so fuckin' sorry.... I didn't show you enough of my love, and I kept too much insida me, 'cause I didn't wanna scare you off.... Sorry, so fuckin' sorry."

Brett was inconsolable; it was my turn to be flabbergasted.

"I fuckin' screwed *us* up!"

Still somewhat in shock, I reached down and lifted the pillow from off of Brett's head; oxygen deprivation was certainly not going to help this situation. "Brett, ssh… it's okay… it'll be okay…." He pressed his face into the mattress.

It was certainly muffled, but I could still make out his words. "It ain't gonna be okay if you don't believe I love the hell outta ya!" Still more guttural groans emitted from out of the back of Brett's throat. "Shoulda told ya 'bout them songs… shoulda told ya how them songs said all o' the shit that I never could put into words right…. I shoulda done better by ya!"

I then had my very own "what the fuck?" moment, at least that's what Brett would have called it. And though I was more than a little bit puzzled by his response to my suggestion that he take the opportunity to be sure of his sexual identity, I just had to touch him. He was in pain and it was my job to help him, no matter if we were lovers or mere friends. My fingers found his golden curls, and I tousled them a bit before I dug in and scratched his scalp just the way he liked it and whispered, "Tell me, sweetheart, tell me about the songs… I wanna know, so tell me now."

Brett rolled over, looked up at me, and sniffed. Then he rubbed his flattened palms painfully hard up and down over his face. After blinking once more to hold back any further tears, he replied, "You see, there's all o' these songs, y'know, all o' them love songs that I hear playin' on the radio…. Well, them songs all make me think o' you." He wasn't sobbing now, but a few stray tears straggled down over his cheekbones, causing my heart to break for him—for us. "They say all o' the shit in my heart so much fuckin' better than I can…. Shoulda told ya."

Slowly at first, the meaning of his words started to sink into my brain. And it didn't take long at all for the truth to hit me like a hard blow to the side of my head.

Brett is in love with me.

His feelings are real.

No experimenting with women was necessary, thank God. But since the topic was now out in the open, I knew it was time for me to put my doubts to rest. I placed my hands on each side of Brett's dripping face, and I asked, "So, here's the million-dollar question: I want to know if you are truly sexually attracted to me?" My stomach flip-flopped steadily—at least five times—as I waited for the answer.

Brett stared at me in disbelief. "Don't I seem it?" Pulling away, he shook his head back and forth a few times. "Don't I seem like I'm super into yer body, like... like pretty much every single friggin' night? And some nights twice?"

I nodded, my cheeks burning. "But you never *came out*, and Ian said that all gay guys come out... and that you're straight as an arrow—a *very straight* arrow."

Brett still appeared rather dumbfounded. "How the fuck does Ian know if I'm gay or straight? He ain't never hit the hay with me."

I had to smile a little at that. "You do seem to be *into it* when we're intimate."

That statement coaxed a hint of laughter from deep in Brett's chest. "Lemme tell ya, Cory, it ain't no act. I'm very, very *into it.*"

I was starting to feel better about things, but there was still a question that needed answering. Again, I took Brett's face into my hands so that he couldn't look away, and I asked him point-blank, "But Brett, are you even gay at all? I worry so much that you are very protective of me... and very loyal, and you have confused those things with being in love and...."

"Why do you gotta call it somethin'?" With a single finger, Brett stilled my rambling lips. And though his tears had dried up for the most part, his breaths still came in soft heaves. "To be honest, Cory, I can't say if you'd call me gay or straight or somewhere in between 'em... 'cause I really don't know what the *word* is for how I feel. But I can tell you what I *do* know: I got me no sexual feelin's for nobody but you."

He gazed into my eyes with an intensity that almost made me squirm. "Brett...."

"No, you gotta listen to me now... you just gotta, honey. See, I ain't never had no sexual feelin's for nobody before I met you... not a single one. Never wanted 'em."

We were both quiet, but I knew Brett had more to say. So I waited. Sometimes I had to be patient when it came to Brett and words.

"It's like this here: I'm a guy, and I only wanna make love to you, and you're a guy too, so... so's if ya really gotta name it, I s'pose that makes me pretty much *gay*, huh?" Brett shrugged as if his words made some kind of wacky sense. "Get what I'm sayin'?"

I felt as if a knot inside my heart had loosened and come untied. All of the tension that I'd held for so long dissipated the very moment I realized that although Brett may not be an all-around gay man, it didn't matter at all when it came to the two of us. Brett was mine. His heart, his mind, his body. How to label what we had? Well, I just didn't know. But whatever you called it, it was real. And it worked. So I simply answered, "Yes."

"Listen here, baby." Brett pulled me down beside him and dragged the covers right over both of our heads so it felt like we were in our own little corner of the world. "Yer my best friend, I ain't gonna lie about it. But that there fact don't take nothin' away from how I feel 'bout you as my lover, and as my husband. I promised you forever, and I meant it. Did *you* mean it?"

As I nodded, a deep shiver racked my entire body, leaving it tingling. Brett immediately sensed my shudder and moved to warm me. His palms found my arms, and he began to rub, creating friction beneath the blankets.

"I love yer body, baby, head to toe; well, it's a fact that I can't get me enough of it. Love yer pretty eyes and yer sweet lips and yer smooth chest and yer lovin' hands, the way they touch me and... love yer privates too... so fuckin' much, I do." Brett's breathing had evened out, and he spoke as if he was mesmerized by his own private thoughts of my body. "All of them things is perfect to me, Cory. You're alls I dream of, alls I need. And alls I want. I hope I didn't fuck things up 'tween us too bad."

God, I was a complete loser. Brett actually thought that he'd brought out all of these insecurities in me. I didn't know what to say.

"I gotta have me that there body of yers now, if you'll let me. I wanna teach ya, wanna show ya how much I love ya. It'll be so good, you'll see."

Brett

I MIGHTA screwed up with all of my not-said-enough words of love, but I damned well wasn't gonna screw up with my body! I aimed to show Cory ev'ry single motherfuckin' feelin' of love that was burstin' outta the seams of my heart by usin' touches.

Gotta teach him the truth... gotta make him know I'm sure.

"It's you who I wanna share my bed with, baby, and my whole entire life with... just you." And maybe it was kinda harsh, but I grabbed onto them slim shoulders, and I shook 'em some. Not to be a bully, mind you, but to show the kid that I meant business. "You're my husband, my partner, and just like them Hallmark cards say, you're my better half. And, baby, I ain't never gonna let you go, y'hear?" I hadta suck back all of my brain's over-thinkin' so's I could make way for the important shit—my feelin's. This here thing I had goin' with Cory was too fuckin' precious to take for granted, it surely was. "Mine, honey. You's all mine."

Them blue eyes that was gazin' back at me was all glazed over with love, and I'd say a hell of a lot o' lust'd got itself mixed in too. "Then use me."

Come again?

Looked like it was time for another one of them gawkin' contests 'tween us. I friggin' stared at Cory like he'd grown an extra eyeball, and he eyed me right back. "Say what?"

"Sex is always *all about me...* it is always you doing everything to make me feel good. But I want it to be *all about you* this time." Yup, the kid was totally serious. "Show me your passion, Brett. I want you to take what you want from me—just take it!"

I was fuckin' baffled right then. Guess it showed.

"Don't you get it, Brett? I want you to make love to me and be selfish about it. I need to feel the heat of your desire. Please, please, can you just do this for me?"

Them kisses that rained down on me then, wasn't even a tiny bit gentle. They wasn't soft, and they sure wasn't sweet. No, sir. Them kisses was hot and lusty, and they was designed to get me goin'. Which they did. Felt like I'd caught on fire, I did.

"Gotta get this here situation straight, honey. You want me to just take sex from yer body without givin' nothin' back to ya?"

"Believe me," Cory breathed right into my ear between them fierce kisses, "if you take what you want, you'll be giving me what I need."

And who the hell was I to say no? If Cory wanted that there enough to ask for it, then that's exactly what the little dude'd be gettin'. So's I flung him down onto the bed real forceful and once he was underneath me, I grasped them thin wrists and pinned 'em right down onto the bed, like I'd always wanted to do. As a matter of fact, I went right on ahead and did whatever the fuck else I wanted, too, I did. My mouth skipped over them pouty lips, and dove right onto them tiny nipples. And I sucked on 'em, one after another, and I did it hard, like a real hungry baby would on its mama's tits. And doin' that to my boy got me even hotter, 'specially 'cause of the way he wiggled around beneath me like he almost couldn't take it no more, so's I decided that I wanted to get me a better taste of him. I ripped them sweatpants right offa Cory's legs, and I wasn't even a measure polite about it. No, sir.

"Don't ya move yer arms, Cory, hear me? Keep 'em up there over yer head… want ya to grab onto the headboard or somethin'…." My voice came out all rough and gravelly. "Don't ya move a friggin' muscle, now."

Cory's breathin' was heavier than I'd ever heard it before. He nodded and wrapped his fingers 'round the bedpost, them wide eyes stuck onto mine. So's I bent down and pressed my lips real firm into that crease between his crotch and his leg, and I kissed and I sucked and I even bit that there spot a little. Which got me so fuckin' heated up, the next thing I knew, I'd plunged right on down so's his whole manhood filled up my mouth and my throat, and I slurped it up without no tenderness at all. Like a starvin' man, I helped myself, and seein' as my boy was hard as a friggin' granite boulder, I think he kinda liked it too.

After a coupla minutes of doin' that, and Cory hangin' onto the headboard like it was a life raft, I made me another demand. "Turn yerself right on over, baby. Onto your belly now, hear me?"

My boy looked up at me with an expression that I ain't never seen on him before—a sorta blend of shock, scared-ness, and a fierce wantin'. But again, he nodded and obeyed real quick, which I gotta admit, gave me a bit of a rush down there 'tween my legs.

That there beautiful roundish butt was starin' straight up at me, and it looked like maybe Cory's legs was squirmin' some and them little hands was surely shakin'. "I'm gonna take ya now, but I ain't gonna hurt ya none." I leaned over and pulled the lube outta the bedside drawer. "I'm gonna get ya ready, kid." And then I prepped his backside real good for what was surely gonna be the roughest ride I'd ever took him on. When I was done, and let me tell you I did a damned thorough job of fixin' him to be ready for me ('cause that there was exactly what I wanted to do), I lubed up my rock-hard part, which had me groanin' as much as the kid was.

"You ready?" Kneeling over him, I reached down and pulled Cory up by the waist 'til his ass was tucked all snug against my privates, and then I covered the rest of his body with my own, makin' sure to grab onto them hands so as to keep 'em pinned down to the bed real firm. But I hadta let go of one hand just long enough to grab a holda my male part and press it against his ass, and I said, "See how hard ya make me? Do ya feel it?" Then I pushed my way fully insida Cory's body in one fast and forceful stroke, and it felt damn good. The kid shuddered, but he didn't beg me to pull out none, in fact, he tried to push back onto me a measure more. And knowin' he was all filled up, prob'ly strugglin' some to take all o' me in, I kinda muttered out, "This here is how much I want ya...."

And so's I had my way with him.

That there lovin' I dished out wasn't soft and sweet at all; nope, it was mostly what you might call rough-and-ready, but that there was the way I wanted it. And that there was exactly what Cory'd asked me for: to take everything I wanted from his body without no regard for his needs, it sure as shit was.

"Feels like heaven, baby... yer insides're just grabbin' onto me...." I wasn't gonna last long. No, sir. And then, just 'cause I wanted to, I reached up with one hand and took a hold of Cory's stiff male part, and I rubbed it up and down and up and down until he was callin' out my name, pleadin' for more.

"Brett, oh, Brett… please… please…."

Them beggin' sounds actually had me grinnin' real wide. "What do ya want, Cory? Tell me right now, y'hear?"

"I wanna let it go…. Can I, please?"

"You can let it go… once ya… once ya feel me firin' off insida ya… but not … not 'til then, 'kay?" I couldn't barely even think right then, but somehow I formed them words. Maybe he nodded, maybe not; I just kept on poundin'. I didn't give the kid no mercy from my lovin'. No, sir.

The very split second after I started goin' off, I felt Cory losin' it right into my hungry hand. And it was so fuckin' good, so fuckin' amazin'. It was surely ev'ry thing a man could ask for in the sack and so, so fuckin' much more. We was both left pantin', in fact, I'd pretty much collapsed right on top of Cory's sweaty back. And then I heard him say it.

"Thank you… thank you, Brett."

Looked like I'd gave the boy just what he'd needed too.

November 16, 2007
Brett

THAT mornin', if the sun was to peak into the window besida our bed, it'd see two men curled up together without even no skinny sheet separatin' their warm flesh. See, last night I'd tried to fall asleep with as much of my skin plastered onto Cory's skin as was humanly possible, so's we'd wake up all warm and snug. It looked like I'd gone and done a damned good job of it too, 'cause we was pretty much stuck together as if we was one single dude.

"What we talked about last night, Brett, none of that was your fault." Cory's husky early-mornin' voice kinda rumbled outta deep insida him. He lifted his mop of brown silky hair up offa where it lay on my heart, and he looked at me. "You really don't have anything to be sorry about."

"What do ya mean?" There had to be a better way to describe the color of them beautiful eyes than just plain blue. Right then I wished I knew more words.

The kid cleared his throat, almost like he was nervous. "You've been great—you've showed me how much you love me every day… in so many ways. What I mean is, it isn't your fault I doubted your feelings for me."

"So's tell me why, and maybe we can stop it from happenin' next time." That there'd seemed a lot like somethin' Cory'd say to me; s'pose you could say I was learnin' from him how to be a good man. Come to think of it, the kid'd sounded a little bit freaked out, like maybe he figured I was gonna be pissed off at him for what he was tellin' me right then, but I wasn't. I was just so glad to still be his husband.

Cory turned kinda pink and looked away, saying shyly, "I got insecure, I guess. And Ian seemed pretty sure that you weren't gay. I guess I bought into what he was trying to sell me. I'm the one who's sorry."

"He told you that shit 'cause he wants you all for himself." Not that I could blame him none. My husband was a gem, huh?

"Well, he's going to have to settle for us just being friends, if that's still all right with you."

He looked at me for my answer, but I wasn't no ogre. I wasn't gonna tell Cory who he could and couldn't be friends with. "Yeah, baby. You go on ahead and be Ian's friend and his lab partner too. After last night, I know for 100 percent sure that your heart belongs only to me. Ain't worried no more."

Then my boy snuggled back down against my chest, dropping a kiss or two on my skin as he settled himself. When he got his little feet all stacked up in between mine, just the way he liked 'em, I heard a happy sigh.

"And one more thing, Cory; you ain't got no reason to be insecure." I drew some hearts on his shoulder with my finger 'cause I loved him so damned much. "You's super hot to look at, real smart, and always smilin' and friendly. Hate to say it, but you's way too good for the likes o' me."

I could feel his head shakin' back and forth against my chest. "Well, I can't agree with you there, Brett. I've loved you since I was fifteen years old because you have the very best heart I've ever known."

"Alls I got me is the best heart this side o' the Mississippi River?" Now I was teasin' him 'cause it was fun. "So yer sayin' I ain't good-lookin'?"

"I'm not about to build up your ego any further." Cory'd raised up his nose and looked away, but I could tell he was smilin' by the way his voice sounded. "And Brett, maybe it's good all that happened last night… because I had some questions, you know, and now I have my answers." He was quiet for a minute, before he added in a low voice, "And the sex was unbelievable…."

Cory sure couldn't get a glimpse of it, seein' as his head was now planted on my chest, but I felt my face heat up prob'ly to bright pink. "*Was*? You think I'm done with lovin' you so soon this mornin'?"

My baby giggled a little, and it was just so fuckin' adorable.

"I'm never gonna upset you like that again, though, Brett. I'm gonna make you as happy as you deserve to...." The rest of Cory's words kinda got cut off on account of our mornin' love makin'.

November 20, 2007
Cory

As ON most weeknights, Brett had deposited me "all nice 'n' safe" (his words) in my usual spot on the library's third floor. In the rear, near the stairs. And he'd be back to retrieve me at eleven o'clock on the dot. You could set your watch by my husband.

And I'd be lucky if I even got through half of my Basic Accounting homework by then; I was having serious difficulty concentrating. I'd become rather obsessed with last night's little "misunderstanding" between Brett and me. My mind kept flipping back and forth between guilt because I knew that I was completely to blame for it, and relief because I now knew that Brett was completely mine, gay, straight, or somewhere in between.

The vibration of my Blackberry on the wooden table alerted me to a new e-mail. Without thinking, I opened it and started to read.

"I ALWAYS GET WHAT I WANT."

I stared at the little screen, dumbfounded.

It can't be him.

However, any scrap of doubt I had been allowing myself the luxury of enjoying slowly dried up and then blew away when those words fully sank in: the exact same words that had been spoken into my ear right before I'd been sexually assaulted last summer. I could never forget those words. I knew that because I'd tried.

And only one person had ever used those words in my presence in a way that sticks out in my mind.

No, this message doesn't need to be signed. I know exactly who it's from: the person who hasn't yet gotten what he wants from me. Steven Percy.

With a sweaty palm I clutched my phone and deleted the message, my fingers trembling, and then I did the same on my laptop. Just as I'd deleted the other strange messages I'd received recently. As if that could truly make their impending meanings go away.

How does the man who attacked me last summer know my e-mail address?

I didn't even have a computer at the time I'd been attacked. Had he been back to the pub and asked someone who worked there for information about me? Had he found my e-mail address through the university? But at any rate, you didn't really need to be Sherlock Holmes to figure out someone's e-mail address.

More questions rushed into my head.

Does he remember where I told him I was going to college?

Does he know where I live?

Has he been watching me?

In no time at all I was sucking in shallow breaths, and my forehead was perspiring.

This is not happening. It can't be happening.

But I don't have to worry; Brett will protect me. He promised me he'd never let anything bad happen to me again.

And who's to say this e-mail is even from Steven Percy, anyways?

I closed my textbook on the Basic Accounting work that was going nowhere fast. Biology would be a better distraction.

I am safe.

Maybe if I kept on telling myself this, it'd be true.

I am safe.

This was kind of like self-hypnosis.

I am safe.

This newest e-mail was nothing to worry about.

I am safe.

And even if it was from Steven Percy, he was probably just trying to scare me.

I am safe.

It had worked.... I was scared.

His band Dirty Laundry was still on tour, wasn't it? And the man had far better things to do with his valuable time than to harass *me*, right? And he'd never make the long trek back to a random college town in northern New Hampshire just to teach some stupid kid a lesson, would he? And if it was sex he was after, he surely had more willing potential partners than he could count within a few feet of where he was right now, and they'd certainly be much more fun to be with than me. *Yeah. Sure.*

Nothing will come of this.

Whatever you say, Cory.

Hands on my shoulders, grasping and squeezing, nearly had me falling out of my chair. I spun around. "Jesus Christ, Brett, don't sneak up on me like that!" My voice was shrill, accusatory.

"Hey... hey, baby... I'm sorry. I ain't tryin' to scare ya...." Shamed, he hung his head. Then he bent down behind my chair and wrapped his arms around my shoulders. "You okay, kid?"

I need to pull myself together.

But I had absolutely no plans to inform Brett of my suspicions about Steven Percy. Hadn't I promised him and myself just last night that I wasn't going to cause him any more distress?

Brett was really happy here at L.U. He loved his job; he loved his home; he loved me. There wasn't any way in heck that I would even consider robbing Brett of the joy that he was finally able to experience in his life by blabbing on and on about all of my groundless worries.

Without looking up to meet his eyes, I started to pack my things. "I'm fine.... I guess I'm just a bit tired, that's all."

Lifting my heavy backpack from off of the table and slinging it easily over a shoulder, Brett asked, "Did you hear from yer dad 'bout Thanksgivin'? Get an e-mail from him or anythin'?"

I couldn't help it; I turned toward him, and with a clipped voice replied, "I didn't check my e-mails." And I headed for the stairs.

Brett

"NO!" CORY cried out loud enough to wake up the both of us. And prob'ly them two dudes across the hall, as well.

I didn't waste no time. I reached out and pulled my baby up against my chest. That there slight body felt all trembly and heated-up. I sure as fuck recognized them nasty-ass symptoms. "Bad dream?"

Pushin' himself offa me so's he could sit upright, he mumbled somethin' that coulda maybe passed for "Uh-huh."

"You ain't had no bad dreams since last summer when... well, you know when." I reached up to rub Cory's shoulders. "You dreamin' 'bout that asshole? Percy?"

Too quickly, Cory stuttered, "I, uh... I don't... I don't remember my dream, *okay*?" The "okay" part sounded kinda pissed off.

Nope. I wasn't buyin' what Cory was tryin' to sell me right there. "Weren't it you who said we gotta talk about the shit that's eatin' at us? Huh, baby?"

Droppin' back on the bed on his side like he was collapsin', Cory said, "I just want to go back to sleep."

Sure as shit, somethin' ain't right with my boy tonight.

Then that tiny raspy voice I only heard when Cory was scared or hurtin' sliced right into my troublin' thoughts. "Hold me, Brett, please... will you hold me tight?"

"You know I will." From behind him, I snuggled up real close and wrapped both of my arms around his narrow waist. And then I squeezed him good so as to comfort him. "I'm always gonna look after you. Got it, baby?"

I'd swear on a stack o' Bibles that the little body in my arms shuddered in fear.

Then I heard a loud sigh. "I know you'll try."

November 22, 2007
Brett

So's there I was in Roderick's little kitchen, bastin' our Thanksgivin' turkey. Even had a "Kiss the Cook" apron on, I did. The apartment smelled kinda salty and sweet at the same time on account of the bakin' that Cory and Roderick'd done earlier today when I was downstairs at the pub hangin' with Jon and Brian. Guess it was the smell of just-baked pumpkin pie mixed with what was risin' up from offa the turkey that was right under my nose. And somethin' about that there smell warmed up my insides in a way I couldn't explain.

Yup, I'd shared Thanksgivin' turkey with Cory and Roderick a time or two before. Actually, I think maybe it'd been three times, but this time was different. See, today I was part of this here little family. Me and my husband was gonna share our first married Thanksgivin' together and I, personally, had me a helluva lot to be thankful for. Yes, sir.

We'd arrived back in Belton real late last night. I'd closed up the B&G for the long weekend by seven and had headed right off to the bank to deposit all o' the cash. Then I'd went and picked up the items that Cory'd written down on a real important shoppin' list: a coupla cans o' pumpkin, a five pound bag o' sugar, some o' them fancy spices that come in tiny tins, and one of them roll-out crusts. But the kid hadn't wanted to tag along with me to work and the store, which was kinda fucked-up. He'd begged off so's he could stay home and study. Only thing was, Cory had himself a four-day weekend, plenty of time to get his schoolwork done.

So's why didn't my boy wanna come hang out with me at the B&G last night?

But that was okay, huh? Nothin' at all to worry about. We had us a whole weekend, just me and Cory in Belton with *our* family, to get my boy's head outta his backside, where it'd been stuck way too fuckin' much since Tuesday night. S'pose he'd just been hittin' the books too hard, that's all. The kid's brain needed a break from all o' his studies. *Yeah, that's it.*

So's speakin' of the whole "our family" thing I'd gone and blurted out a coupla seconds ago: I was as good as Roderick's son-in-law, even though he didn't know nothin' about it yet. And much as it surprised the hell outta me, I had to admit that the man'd been puttin' in a big-league effort to be a *real* dad to Cory. Hadn't thought that Roderick had it in 'im, but wonders never cease, or so folks like to say.

Since we'd split for L.U., there'd been plenty of phone calls to Cory from back home in Belton askin' the kid how his studyin' was goin', a coupla phone calls to me to see if we needed nothin', and once even a sloppily put-together care package filled with rock-hard peanut butter cookies with candy kisses stuck on top that Roderick must've baked himself. (Sure thought Cory was gonna break a tooth on them things.) But the biggest change in Roderick was that he hadn't got himself wasted on booze or no illegal substances, from what I could see, since Cory'd been away at school. The dude was straight. And truth was, when he wasn't fucked-up on booze or pills, I kinda liked Roderick. Yeah, maybe he was a wee bit clingy, hadn't taken his fuckin' hands offa Cory all day today, but my boy didn't seem to mind none, so's I was okay with it.

Well, all o' the veggies we'd cooked up that mornin' was already set in bowls on the table, so's guess it was turkey time, huh? I carried the turkey platter out to the livin' room 'cause we was gonna eat at the coffee table. I set the bird down on the rickety kitchen table that we'd stuck by the lamp, and then I got right to carvin'.

"Smells good, Brett." Cory was sittin' on the floor in front of the coffee table at Roderick's feet. The older man had his hand glued to Cory's shoulder, and Cory looked like the cat who'd swallowed the fuckin' canary. In plainer words, the kid looked *real pleased,* so's it was all good.

"Hope yer hungry."

"We have all weekend to finish off all of the leftovers, right? You two are staying 'til Sunday, aren't you?" The new, clingy Roderick's face got kinda twisted, all nervous-like, but Cory reached up and squeezed his dad's hand.

"Just try to get rid of us before this food is gone. You won't have any luck!"

Roderick relaxed a measure. "Oh, okay… good."

I sat down on the opposite end of the couch from Roderick, and we all filled up our plates. Cory hadn't been eatin' too good for the past coupla days, but it sure looked like he was gonna chow down today, seein' as his plate was full as an Irish pub on St. Patty's Day.

After passin' around the gravy, Roderick spoke up. "I noticed that Cory has a new piece of jewelry… on his finger."

S'pose he'd noticed that there sparkly ring. I looked at Cory to see if he wanted me to explain, and he answered me with this little nod. "Since you mentioned it, Roderick, guess me and Cory's got some news, some real good news, that we wanna share with ya."

That there man's eyes got wide, and Cory turned about six shades o' red.

"Seein' as how we been livin' together up in Leighton, and how us two spent the better part o' the last four years pretty much in each other's back pockets, I figure that you gotta know how we feel 'bout each other."

Cory leaned across the table and touched my sorta shaky hand. Which was sweet. Just like him.

"And seein' as I don't never wanna spend another Thanksgivin' or Christmas… or even any regular day without yer son, on account of how deep I love him, I went and asked him to marry me. I done it last month, Roderick."

"And I said yes," Cory chimed in, a shy but real happy smile painted on them lips. Super cute.

Roderick nodded. "You two are very young. Are you sure that you're ready for a step like this?"

The man didn't have much of a leg to stand on if he was plannin' on arguin' this here point, nonetheless, I answered, patient as I could be, "I'm sure... *we're* sure. I loved Cory pretty much since I met him, and...." What else was there for me to say? I hoped real hard that Cory'd start yappin' right then, which he did.

"Dad, I've never wanted to be with any man other than Brett. He's my best friend and my... well, I love him in *every* way. And he looks out for me—"

"He takes care of you like I never did."

S'pose that there is callin' a spade a spade.

Looked like Roderick was havin' a starin' contest with his peas.

"Dad...." Didn't think it was possible, but Cory's cheeks'd grew a coupla shades redder than they was before.

Roderick stood up and crossed the room so's he could gaze outta the window. Tiny dots of snow'd just started fallin' outta the cold gray sky. "Brett, I need to thank you for doing all of the things for Cory that I never did, you know, during his high school years." He turned to gawk at me, all serious-faced. "You picked up a lot of my slack, and I, well, *we* both are very thankful."

"Was my pleasure to do everything I done, and I ain't shittin' ya 'bout that." I glanced over at Cory, but he was still starin' up at his father, waitin' on what the man'd say next. "Just sayin'."

"And as long as it is real love, not appreciation, or need, that keeps you two together... well, then I'm very happy for you both." Roderick glanced back and forth between us, waitin' on his assurance. Again, it was Cory who took the wheel.

The kid got up, and 'stead of walkin' over to his dad to convince him of our true love, he came around the couch and plopped his little ass right down on my lap. Then them lovin' arms wrapped me up, surely tellin' Roderick all kinds o' shit that words just couldn't say as good. But he spoke up, as well. "Dad, it is a good point that you brought up, and we've talked that over. Yes, we appreciate each other, and yes, we need each other, but what we have is deeper than those things... deeper than friendship. There's magic between us." Gotta say, hearin' my boy say them words made hundreds o' goose pimples rise on my scarred-up forearms, they did. And then my baby bent down and kissed me, long and sweet, right there under his father's nose. So's I kissed him right on back.

Thanksgivin' Day… so, so thankful. Sure am.

Roderick smiled. "That's all I needed to hear." He sat back down and picked up his fork. "I want to throw you guys a wedding—the wedding of the century!"

Me and Cory looked at each other, and then the both of us gawked at Roderick. Truth was, we already felt like we was married in our hearts, so's we hadn't thought too much on the actual wedding itself. Least I hadn't.

"When are you planning on having the ceremony?"

"Uh… well, this summer, I s'pose. Huh, Cory?"

Cory nodded, them robin's egg eyes round. (Thought I'd change up my word for blue.)

"Then I would be honored if you let me put it together for you two. Just give me a list of who you want there, and I'll go to town." Roderick was still gazin' at them peas, or maybe it was the stuffin' his eyes was stuck on now, prob'ly afraid we'd shoot down his generous offer.

"Really, Dad?" Cory was apparently having some trouble digestin' his dad's enthusiasm.

"Let me do this, Cory. Let me be your father and give you away and… and send you off right." The man looked up at his son. Them jet-black eyes o' Roderick's had filled up like a kiddie pool in June, but them soon-to-be tears didn't really bug me none. 'Cause this here was an important moment for all three of us, so's I waited for Cory to answer, nice 'n' patient. Whatever Cory wanted'd suit me just fine.

Cory slid offa my lap and moved to sit beside his father. Roderick was lookin' at him real cautious, like Cory's answer'd make him or break him. "Will you let me? Will you let me plan your wedding? And give you away?"

With a tiny nod, Cory launched himself into his dad's arms, and I s'pose it was settled, huh?

For some reason the three of us was real starvin' all of a sudden, and we dove right on into our Thanksgivin' supper.

Yeah... so thankful.

Thanksgiving Day
Cory

IN A million years, I could never tire of looking at him.

I watched, almost studiously, the rise and fall of my husband's sculpted chest as he slept the late afternoon away, his stomach full of turkey and everything that had accompanied it, his heart filled with love of his newly gained family. He slept peacefully in the knowledge that he was loved, that he belonged. Wherever he and I were together, that very place was Brett's home.

Today had been picture-perfect, aside from the dark cloud with Steven Percy's name on it that seemed to follow me everywhere lately. My father, thrilled that I had come home for the holiday, had bonded with me over the baking of potatoes, the steaming of vegetables, the creation of a pumpkin pie. My husband, in charge of the turkey, had escaped downstairs to the pub to visit with his former bosses while the oven did its part. Then we'd eaten together and had spoken with my dad of our love, of our wedding, of our future. There had been time for football, for a few games of cards, for talking about how things had been, how things were going to be. Like a real family would do.

I ran my hand lightly over the muscular ridges and the striking V-shape of his abdomen; Brett certainly was stunningly made. I tangled my little finger into a fuzzy tuft of the blond hair that spattered his powerful chest, and then I raised my eyes to his face. Those perfect features were loose and relaxed in slumber; golden waves draped across my pillow. This fine-looking and deep-feeling man, right now a portrait of tranquility and satisfaction, was mine to keep forever.

As the afternoon progressed, I'd started to feel a sense of inner peace that I had thought lost to me. I'd felt better about my, well, I guess you could call it my *predicament*. The food, the family, the football… they all blended together to induce within me a feeling of safety. Of normalcy. And so I'd made a decision: there would be no more secrets between Brett and me. I'd tell him about the e-mails, and we'd solve this problem together.

But how exactly do I bring up the topic without rocking the boat hard enough to capsize it?

I'd struggled for so long with my dilemma that when I glanced over at Brett, I saw that he had dozed off on my bed. So I checked my assignments online, and then I made the stupid mistake of checking some more of my newly received, now less-than-mysterious e-mails. I mean, I couldn't ignore them. Could you? Each e-mail was a threat to my life, to my safety, to my future. And it had become an addiction of sorts: my need to know what tactic Steven Percy would use next in this game of mental torture that he'd designed exclusively for me. But when I read today's e-mail, all hell broke loose in my mind.

"IF YOU LIKE YOUR PRETTY BUSBOY KEEP HIM OUT OF THIS. I'D HATE TO HAVE TO HURT HIM TOO. ENJOY YOUR TURKEY."

And that's how my picture-perfect day came to its speedy conclusion.

This latest message put an end to any consideration I'd given to sharing my fears with Brett. If I talked, Brett would suffer. And Brett was not going to suffer any more because of me. I wouldn't let that happen.

Steven Percy was coming back to finish what he'd started with me last summer.

With me.

Not with Brett…

With me.

Me.

I snuggled down against my husband's side where I knew I was safe.

For the moment.

November 27, 2007
Brett

WAY too fuckin' early I got woke up to the sound of frenzied poundin' on our apartment door. Well, truth be, it was almost 8:00 a.m., but seein' as Cory'd had another night chock full o' fucked-up dreams, us two hadn't caught much in the way of shut-eye, so's I'd turned off the alarm clock and let us sleep in. Now, I slid offa the edge o' the bed, real careful-like so as not to wake up my boy, pulled on yesterday's jeans, and headed for the door.

"Jesus—hold your horses!" I muttered as I pulled open the door. "Yer fuckin' racket could wake up the dead."

Gotta say, I was more'n a little surprised (and less than stoked) to see Ian Webster standin' on the landin', leanin' on the doorframe. But instead o' wearin' his usual smug "I know somethin' you don't know" sorta expression, the dude looked all flustered like a little kid who'd got lost at the shoppin' mall.

"Hey, is Cory up?"

I pulled my bedhead-hair into the frayed elastic band I'd wore on my wrist to bed, then turned and glanced back at the bed. "Nope. Still sleepin'."

Ian looked over at the purple satin-covered lump in the middle of our bed, a coupla locks o' pretty brown hair stickin' outta one of the folds. "I need to talk to Cory… he'll know what I should do."

So's outta the goodness o' my heart, I stepped back from the door a measure, and I beckoned. "Why don't ya come on in, Webster?"

Now, just to get things straight, there wasn't no small amount of pissed-off-ness floatin' around in the air 'tween me and Ian right about now. No, sir. Let's just say you could almost taste the bitter tension in the air when you opened up yer mouth to take a breath. See, I knew full well that Ian'd been feedin' Cory stories about how "un-gay" I was, which'd made my baby worry himself sick. Which'd caused us a shitload o' trouble, which us two'd worked out... and in fact, we'd worked it out real nice. So's I guess it was all good, huh?

And knowin' Cory, he'd want me to step up to the plate and help Ian out, if I could do it. "Can *I* help ya with somethin'? See, I kinda wanna let Cory sleep in; he didn't catch too many Zs last night."

Ian hesitated 'cause the last thing he musta wanted was to take charity from me, his rival.

Yeah, we sure is rivals, seein' as the both of us is in love with the very same dude.

But clearly, the guy was desperate. "I left all the notes that I basically killed myself to get—from ten different sources—and that I need to write my history paper back in Rhode Island when I went home over Thanksgiving. And I really need them. The paper's already late, and the professor said I could have until class time tomorrow to pass it in, or he's gonna go to my advisor. If he does that, my advisor will suspend me from the yearbook staff, and I'm doing these awesome illustrations for it and...." He stopped rambling and scratched his head. "And Cory would know what to do."

I held my tongue while I laid out this here situation in my brain.

So here's how I saw it: Right in front of me stood Ian Webster, jet-black hair all messed up in a "please touch me" kinda way, eyeliner smudged some, but still doin' its job of makin' him look sorta sexy-pathetic, tight black shirt, tight black pants, black combat boots, black scarf, and these black... well, you get the picture. And this here superhot tortured-artist-dude'd snatch Cory right out from under my nose if he had himself a half a chance. And we both knew it.

"I think I can help ya." *This here is an example of me holdin' out an olive branch.*

"How?" It seemed that Ian didn't quite trust me.

"You can borrow my truck. Then you can run down to Rhode Island, grab yer notes, drive back up here, and finish yer paper-thingy."

"That won't work." When I looked at him again, the dude's whole face had this Snow White sorta thing goin' on; you know, his white-as-the-driven-snow skin'd turned all ruby red on his cheeks, all framed by that jet-black hair. "I don't have my license—too much time in high school spent painting, sculpting, you know, perfecting my whole starving artist identity. No time for practical stuff."

Shit! Looks like I'm gonna hafta take one for the team, huh? Team Cory, that is.

"So's I'll drive ya down there, then. But I gotta work for a coupla hours at the B&G 'fore we go. I'll work through lunch and then get shit ready for the dinner rush, so's we can leave at like... like at one thirty."

This here is much more'n an olive branch; seems I'm offerin' him the whole fuckin' olive tree!

"Well, yeah, that'd work. I could pull an all-nighter and get it done by class time tomorrow." Ian got this look on his face, both relieved and shell-shocked at the same time. "You'd do that for me?"

"Hell, no! But I'd do it for Cory. And Cory thinks a lot of you, as a *friend,* that is." Major emphasis on the word friend. Couldn't help it.

"Point taken." Ian glanced at the floor, maybe a touch frustrated. He didn't like what I'd just said, but he didn't argue it neither.

So's now I had me a favor to ask in return. "Cory has an afternoon class. I need you to ask Christian or Ben or Hunter to pick him up at the library at quarter of two and walk him over to the Statler Auditorium."

"Uh, Brett, Cory's a big boy. Don't you think he can walk there by himself?"

Every single goddamned muscle in my body got tightened up. "Listen, Webster, I'm willing to help you out, but I need you to get this here done for me. It's called a fuckin' two-way street, ever heard o' that?" I wasn't in no mood for no debate. "Set it up, or we ain't goin' nowhere."

Ian's dark squinty eyes turned round. "Okay, okay… relax."

"And then after class, Cory goes runnin' with Ally so's he don't need nobody to walk him back here."

Real wisely, Ian managed to restrain himself from makin' another "Cory's all growed up" kinda comment. But he sure didn't look too happy about it.

"And then I want yer football buddies to park their asses here tonight and have pizza with Cory and camp out 'til you and me get back, ya hear?"

This time Ian couldn't choke back his wiseass reply. "You mean to tell me that you want your pretty boyfriend spending the whole night in a room filled with horny football players, who just so happen to like Cory so much they'd consider switching teams if it meant they could have him?"

I sat my ass down on the futon, quickly glanced over at my baby who was still dead-to-the-world under them covers, and answered. "Yup. That there's exactly what I'm sayin'." Then I looked straight into Ian's eyes and added, "Not to say I'm thrilled with the whole situation, but I trust Cory and… um, and sometimes my *fiancé* don't like to be all alone." Emphasis on the word fiancé, seein' as Cory wasn't no "boyfriend" to me.

Ian nodded, so's I knew he'd caught my drift.

"So's you make sure yer buddies behave themselves tonight, and I'll make sure you get them notes you need, 'kay?"

"I'd say we understand each other."

"Good. Now you'd better get yer ass on the phone to make yer part o' the bargain happen, huh?"

"Consider it done, and, uh, no worries, man. They'll do it for me."

I got up and stepped straight to the door, and then I held it open and met them dark eyes straight on, suggestin' that it was time for Ian to leave. "B&G, one thirty sharp."

The dude nodded once more, but before he left, he took one last longin' look at where my baby lay sleepin' on the bed… way the fuck outta his reach.

WHEN Cory woke up, I was stretched out on the recliner lookin' over some menu revisions for the B&G.

"Mornin', baby."

The kid popped right up. "What time is it? It feels late."

"Nearly nine. I let ya sleep in a bit." Lookin' over, I tried to catch Cory's eye. "You didn't sleep too good last night."

Cory didn't say nothin', but we both knew I'd put it mild. The kid had slept like shit.

"Somethin's wrong; I can tell." I got up offa the recliner and went over to sit beside Cory on the bed. "You gotta talk to me."

This big, bright smile suddenly got pasted onto Cory's lips. "Everything's fine… except if I don't get going, I'm gonna be late for class." He leaned over and kissed me quick, then got outta bed.

Okay, then.

As Cory made up the bed, I explained the arrangements I'd made with Ian to go pick up his forgotten notes in Rhode Island today. "And so's, It looks like I'm gonna be gone pretty much all afternoon and night. Prob'ly me and Ian'll be back around eleven or so."

To say Cory seemed pleased that I was helpin' Ian out wouldn't be no lie, but still there was somethin' fucked-up about his reaction to my news. Them blue eyes darted around, lookin' everywhere 'cept for at me. Seemed like maybe he was scared or somethin'. "So… uh, so… so I'll be walking to class alone?"

"Not by a long shot. A coupla yer buddies are gonna meet you at the library and walk you over to the lecture hall; it's all arranged. You know I don't like you walkin' around campus alone." I noticed the way Cory's cheeks got all red, but I didn't miss the flash of relief that crossed his face. "And I hope you don't mind, but I told Ian it was okay if they stopped by here tonight for pizza. Thought you wouldn't mind it too much."

Noddin', Cory appeared a little bit more relaxed now, but still he didn't meet my eyes. "I can help them with calculus, right?"

God, he's fuckin' sweet. Them ball players'll be wantin' to party it up, and Cory's gonna make 'em crack open their books.

"Then it's all set, huh?"

"Yeah... yeah, it's all set." Cory went back to makin' up the bed.

Nope. Nothin' was all set, seein' as I was pretty sure that somethin' was fucked-up insida Cory's head. Didn't know just what it was, but I knew my husband well enough to know that things wasn't nearly as peachy keen as that bright and happy (and fake) smile on his face led me to believe.

So's there I was, pretty much hip-to-hip with the enemy. I hadn't never before noticed how fuckin' tiny the cab of my truck was.

Ain't this just super cozy?

I focused my eyes real firm on the road, and pretty soon the late-fall scenery was whizzin' on past.

Nope, not too many leaves're still hangin' onto them trees— winter's surely on its way.

Now, just 'cause I'd zipped my lips shut and was dwellin' on the weather didn't mean I didn't have nothin' to say to the dude dressed like the grim reaper, who was kinda slumped down all moody-like, in the seat beside me. And sure as moss grows on the north side of a tree, the dude in my passenger's seat surely had more'n a coupla choice words he wouldna minded sendin' my way.

But the fact was, neither of us planned on bein' the first one to spill our guts, so's for quite a long while it was just me, Ian, and WBLM (a down-home rock station outta Maine that *I'd* chose) insida that there truck.

Once Ian started yappin' again, I kinda wished our conversation'd stayed on mute.

"Uh, I'm... I'm, uh, I'm in love with Cory too, you know."

That there was one way to break the silence with a BAM! But I didn't even turn my head to gawk at the dude, who I gotta admit sure had a big pair of balls (steel ones) to say them words to me like that, plain as day. Eyes still fixed on the highway, I replied, "Yeah. I know."

And it appeared that the dude wasn't quite done with his tell-all. "I've tried every trick in the book to make him fall for me—but I just can't seem to make it happen."

I nodded so's Ian'd know I'd heard him, but I didn't have nothin' to say to that.

"So you win, okay? Cory's all yours...."

I knew for a fact that Cory'd always been all mine, but I didn't point that out.

Frustrated by my tight lips, Ian started to rant. "What is it between you two, anyways, man?" By now, that milky white skin on Ian's whole face'd turned an angry red. (It'd be fair to say that now he wasn't so much Snow White as he was Mr. Krabs.) Yup, flamin' crimson, he was. "It's like Cory's wearing one invisible handcuff, and you've attached yourself to him with the other one, and he doesn't even want the key! Or maybe the key is lost and—"

"Ain't nobody lookin' for the key, Webster... well, 'cept for you, that is."

"Whatever, man.... But I just don't get it!"

Ian was gawkin' at me, all scandalized-lookin', like I'd just flashed my ass outta the truck window at a bus full of nuns. "What don't you get?"

Reaching over to turn off the radio, Ian'd seemed to've decided that he was gonna lay it all out there on the line. He said softly, "I don't get why you're with Cory; I know for a fact that you aren't even gay."

Yup. I'd suspected it, but 'til now I hadn't been 100 percent sure. "You know that for a fact, ya say? How's that, huh?" Didn't even give the dude a chance to say his piece. "Gay, straight—or whatever you wanna call me, it really don't fuckin' matter, Webster." The last part got spoke real loud and clear.

"How can you say it doesn't matter? You *sleep* with the dude, for Christ's sake."

I didn't even pull outta the passin' lane to deliver my next verbal punch in the gut. "Maybe I ain't gay for you, or maybe not for no other man, but I'm gay as a picnic basket for Cory, ya got it?"

At them snarled-out words, Ian kinda bowed down his head, spiky black hair fallin' in his eyes. And he shut his trap.

Taylor: one; Webster: zero.

But bein' the sucker that I am, it didn't take too long before I was feelin' bad for the dude. Uh-huh, crazy as it may seem that there's true. After all, who could blame him for fallin' in love with Cory? So's I figured I'd spell the situation out for him, and then maybe he'd get it. "Listen, it ain't all that simple 'tween Cory and me. See, we been through a world o' hurt together, and I ain't shittin' you on that."

Don't know just how long I'd been lost in my thoughts about Steven the Motherfucker Percy when I noticed Ian was grumblin'. "That's *exactly* what Cory always tells me when I ask him how you two ever managed to get together. He says, 'We've got a very long, complicated history' or something along those lines." Ian pounded his black denim-clad thigh hard with his fist, super frustrated. "There's got to be a story behind all of this 'we've been through so much together' bullcrap—and I want to hear it!"

"Ain't my story to tell." I was shaking my head. "Cory's a real private guy."

"Well, I think you guys are being too private." He said it like it was an accusation. "Talk to me, man, and I promise you I'll back off of Cory. I really want to know." And right then I decided that maybe Ian *needed* to know so's he could move on.

The truck cab was silent as I gave this whole mess some thought. Sure as shit, this guy and me had somethin' fuckin' huge in common: we both loved Cory. He deserved at least the shortened-up version, huh? "Met him when he was just a kid, I did. He lived above the bar I worked at, and we got to be buddies. I looked out for him all during high school, and I s'pose you could say that our friendship gave me a reason to get up every mornin'."

Ian looked skeptical. "There's more to you and Cory's relationship than friendship."

"Well, yeah." I stole a peek at my sullen passenger. "I fell for him hard, even though I tried like hell not to. Couldn't help it, Cory was just so… he was just so—"

"I know *why* you fell; it's probably the same damned reasons I fell." Ian's dull expression suddenly got brighter. "Are you sure it isn't just some high school crush on steroids that Cory has for you? Or an attachment he outgrew but can't let go of?"

I glanced at him sorta sideways. "Hate to disappoint you, bud, but this here's the real deal. You know, it's love. For the both of us."

"Love," Ian repeated the word, his voice suddenly sarcastic. "So is *love* the reason you watch him like a guard dog?"

Felt like I got injected with a long needle right directly into my heart, it did. 'Cause I knew the *real* reasons I watched so close over my precious boy. "Nope. That ain't why."

"Well?"

If I was gonna talk about this particular subject, even if I was only gonna brush its prickly surface, I needed to focus. 'Cause this here topic ripped me apart every time I so much as thought on it. So's I pulled my truck over real abrupt onto the sandy shoulder of the highway and I turned to Ian. "Cory wouldn't want what I'm gonna tell ya to be public knowledge, so's keep yer trap shut 'bout it, okay?"

With them dark eyes gettin' wider and wider every second, Ian nodded.

"Webster, last summer Cory got beat up, or more like, uh, attacked. It was real bad."

Grabbing the sleeve of my sweatshirt, Ian demanded to know more. "What do you mean? Someone assaulted Cory?"

"Hell, yeah" was what I was thinkin', but I just said, "Uh-huh."

"Well, what happened? You can't clam up on me now!" I looked away super fast, but I knew that Ian'd already seen my eyes fill up with wetness. "Oh my God! Are you saying Cory got *raped*?"

Real quick, I blurted, "Nope, not raped. Cory didn't get raped." I hadta fight to hold them stupid tears in. "Listen, if Cory wants to share all o' this shit with you, that's fine. But I ain't gonna say no more; it ain't my story to tell. Just understand that me and him got real close afterwards."

Ian definitely did not want to leave it at that. "What the hell happened to him? And who'd want to hurt Cory? He's so sweet and—"

"Alls ya need to know, Webster, is this: I don't guard Cory just for shits and grins. See, I gotta live with what that son-of-a-bitch done to Cory every single fuckin' day—he friggin' tortured my boy—and I ain't gonna let nothin' hurt that kid again!"

And I could tell right then that Ian got the big picture. Yup, the fog lifted right up offa the harbor, and he could see out over the ocean for miles. The look in his eyes when he glanced over at me spoke louder than even a million words coulda. That there look was all filled up with sorrow, pity, anger, hurt... but mostly understandin'. The dude didn't say nothin' for a long while, so's I pulled my truck back onto the highway headin' south.

We didn't talk at all 'til we was well past Boston. Then Ian again grabbed my sleeve, this time more gentle, and said, "I think I get it now. I get how it is between Cory and you."

I smiled a measure, but I quit my stupid grinnin' when Ian said his next words.

"You must have killed that guy who fucked with Cory, huh?"

All of my calm just blew outta the car window. I felt them little muscles in my jaw start twitchin', and my belly clenched up so's it wasn't nothin' but a hard tight ball in my gut.

"So? What did you do to the guy?"

Swallowin' back the bile in my throat, I choked out a coupla words. "Cory begged me to leave him the hell alone. So's that's what I did."

"Well, did you get Cory into some decent counseling? Or at least teach him some moves to protect himself in the future?"

Them particular comments made me stop and think a measure, they damn sure did. 'Cause I hadn't never thought to do neither one of them things. Mostly what I'd focused on was watchin' over my boy like a hawk so's he'd never get hurt that way again. This time I didn't answer Ian, and I think he knew right then that the subject was closed. I reached out for the radio buttons, found me another rock station, and raised the volume up to brain-numbin'. That way, we surely couldn't talk no more, even if we wanted to.

Ian

"HEY, baby, did yer day go good?" Somehow Brett had calculated the very second that Cory'd be back in their apartment after his jog with Ally; he'd placed the call only after looking at his watch no less than fifteen times. "You sound funny—are you sure everything's fine on your end?"

I sat beside him, my eyes now shut, but he knew I was listenin'.

"Now, we's gonna be kinda late, Cory. No need for you to wait up, but tell all them dudes that they can crash at our place 'til me and Ian get back." Ever since he'd started talking to Cory, Brett's voice had softened to the point that I could actually say he sounded almost sweet. "Yeah, baby. Ain't used to not bein' with you, neither.... Uh-huh, love ya too."

Brett placed his phone in the center console, a syrupy expression of love on his perfect face.

"You sure have your caretaking job down to a science, man." I wasn't giving him shit about it. I was just thinking out loud. "I wouldn't mind having Cory for myself, but if he can't be mine, he deserves someone like you. You treat him like gold."

Brett looked over at me and shook his head. "You got it all wrong there, Webster. See, I'm just tryin' to deserve the likes o' Cory. Every day that's all I wanna do."

Brett

IT WAS dark now, and we was still on the road, but at least we was back in New Hampshire; it'd been a hell of a long day stuck in a truck. I thought Ian was asleep, but suddenly his head popped up offa the back of the seat, and he asked me, "If you level with me about something, I swear I'll *totally* lay off trying to snatch Cory away from you."

Glancin' at the dude, I asked with a skeptical smile, "What is it that you wanna know so friggin' bad?"

"Okay, so here it is: you pretty much admitted to me that you aren't completely gay, right? So aren't you tempted by all of the hot college girls who are constantly throwing themselves at you at the B&G?" Ian didn't look at all like he was merely curious; he looked much more like a desperate man bettin' every dime on his last chance at the roulette wheel. "Don't you just want a little taste of the ladies, if you know what I mean?"

"You gonna give it up with Cory if I come clean on this?" I kept on grinnin'. "Not that I'm worried about you or nothin'."

"I *said* I would, didn't I?"

Clearin' my throat so's there'd be no mistakin' my words, I gave the dude his answer. "Well, my man, I think my answer's gonna disappoint. 'Cause God strike me dead if this here ain't the truth: there ain't no temptation for me out there, not in the shape of a girl or a guy." I felt the smile fall offa my face when I considered the reality of the situation. "There ain't never been nobody else, Webster. And there ain't never gonna be. It's just Cory… just him."

"I hear you, Brett." Ian lay his head back down on the seat and really went to sleep this time.

IT WAS nearly midnight when we got back to the studio. And I gotta say, we was met by a kinda comical sight. Well, it was mostly funny but maybe just a little bit disturbin' 'cause, yeah, I still had me a coupla jealous bones in my body.

There was my Cory on the middle of the bed, all neatly tucked under our shiny purple comforter. And surroundin' him on the bed, the sofa, and the recliner was six enormous snorin' football players, who'd clearly missed curfew. Ben's head, which was jammed up against the headboard, rested stiffly on our single purple satiny throw pillow.

"Quiet, don't wake 'em up yet. This is too cute; I've got to get a picture of Ben to post on Facebook." Ian had his phone outta his pocket in a split second, and then he was shootin'. "He looks like a princess, doesn't he?"

Fuckin' adorable. Whatever. It was well past time to get these oafs outta my bed.

"Looks like they had a party." Pizza boxes, soda cans, bowls with a coupla oily popcorn kernels stuck onto the bottom, was kinda strewn all around on pretty much every flat surface in our place.

At the sound of Ian's voice, Cory'd jolted upright, his eyes all wild. "Who's here?"

I crossed the room real quick and had my boy clasped in my arms before he could even blink. "It's me, kid. I'm home now." I pushed that silky hair back offa his face and then lightly pressed on his shoulders. "Lie back down, now. I'll be beside ya in no time at all."

The sound of rustling blankets and the closing up of the recliner sorta brought me back to reality.

Oh, yeah. Six hulks makin' their midnight exit.

"We all turn into pumpkins at midnight, Taylor. You might have to roll us home."

"Shut up and get your backpack, Chris." Ian was doing his best to round 'em all up. "Sleeping Beauty—yeah, that'd be you, Benji. Rise and shine!" Then there was some more sleepy groans.

And when he'd finally got 'em all out the door, Ian stood in front of me and offered his hand. "Thanks, Taylor. You saved my ass!"

"Glad to do it, Webster."

And I knew that a truce'd got formed between the two of us men who loved Cory.

November 30, 2007
Cory

ALTHOUGH it was Friday night, I just couldn't drag myself to the B&G to hang out with Brett. When something was weighing this heavily on my mind, I just couldn't summon up the energy to do much of anything at all, except to dwell on it. So here I was, home alone, which wasn't really working out very well for me either. The door was bolted. The windows were closed tightly and locked, despite the fact that no one without the powers of a superhero could get into the windows of our second-floor apartment, and I was folded up on the recliner, arms wrapped around my knees, just trying to disappear. Which also wasn't working out as I'd hoped.

Something's gonna happen… and it's gonna be bad.

I had received two more disturbing e-mails this week. Numbers five and six, respectively. "YOU MADE ME WAIT FOR IT. NOBODY MAKES ME WAIT FOR IT" arrived when I was getting ready to leave history class with Ally yesterday. I'd tried to cover up my inner freak-out, but I don't think she bought my "changing seasons bring on my allergies" story when my eyes suddenly filled up and my face turned bright red. Severe fall-to-winter allergies? Not a very convincing lie at all.

The most recent threat had arrived a mere five minutes ago.

"NOBODY CAN STOP THIS."

No, not particularly comforting. Mainly because I knew it was true. And I was more than slightly scared about it, but I was much more afraid to let Brett know what was going on. He didn't know how sick Steven was and what a danger we'd both be in if he didn't get what he wanted.

But I knew. How very well I knew.

My brain scrambled in search of a handhold to grip, a ledge for my feet. Anything to prevent me from tumbling head first into the abyss of doom that was so likely my fate.

There has to be something I can do to stop my impending doom. But what?

Brett

IT WAS more than super-mega-fucked-up that Cory hadn't wanted to come to work with me again tonight. Come to think on it, Cory hadn't wanted to come out to the B&G even one night since before Turkey Day. No, sir, tonight wasn't the first or the second or even the third time my boy'd bowed out on a night at the bar, which he usually fuckin' loved, since my Cory was a people person. Or rather, used to be a people person.

But I had me a theory, I did. I believed right on down to my bare bones that Cory was scared sick about somethin'. Maybe that somethin' was real, or maybe that somethin' was all made up insida his head, but that there wasn't no matter. Whatever the hell it was had my boy shakin' like a leaf in the wind. And for some reason his lips stayed zipped tight about it.

Once again tonight I hadta thank my lucky stars for my good buddy, Barry. Not only was he the best assistant manager that a guy could ask for, but tonight he'd solved my problem with Cory. Not that he knew he'd just supplied me with the perfect answer, seein' as neither of us even knew that I'd asked him a question. But when he said it, well, it just hit me, y'know?

See, it was Barry's responsibility to report to me if one of the restaurant employees needed to miss an upcomin' shift at work so's I could make the necessary paperwork changes. Tonight he'd informed me that none of the female servers would be available to work next Wednesday night 'cause this women's club at Leighton University was sponsorin' a crash course in self-defense over at the Sports Complex, free for any student who was interested in attendin'. Now, Barry was squirmin' around in this big fuckin' tizzy 'bout who we was gonna get to wait tables on Wednesday night, so's he was pretty much astonished when I hauled him into my arms and hugged him real fierce. Nearly kissed 'im too; I was so friggin' stoked.

'Cause right at that very second I knew exactly what Cory needed, scein' as how he'd seemed to've been feelin' so scared lately. He needed to get his ass to that there self-defense course. See, if I was gonna call a spade a spade, I'd admit that the kid'd been afraid to be alone ever since that asshole'd attacked him last summer. For a while he'd controlled his fear by soakin' up my strength, y'know, by stickin' close to me and lettin' me guard him like a friggin' Rottweiler. But for some reason, *my* strength wasn't no longer enough to keep his fears at bay. Cory needed to get in touch with his *own* power; he needed to trust in himself again. He couldn't hide behind me no longer, and not 'cause I didn't want him to. I'd break my ass to protect that boy 'til kingdom comes and back again, and I wouldn't consider it to be no pain in my ass whatsoever. But I'd just now realized that Cory needed to step up and feel strong for himself.

Cory needs to know he's his own man, huh?

Tryin' to be real quiet, I let myself into the apartment, closed the door, and hung my coat on the doorknob. As soon as I stepped inside I got smacked in the face with a wave of scorchin' air; it was hotter than hell in there. Cory'd closed up all the windows that we usually kept cracked on account of the old radiator cranked out way too much heat at night. So's I moved to them windows without a sound, unlocked 'em, and lifted 'em open just slightly.

Cory'd left the light on in the can, and in the dimness I could see that he wasn't in bed, but instead he was all curled up like a puppy on the reclinin' chair, wearin' only a pair o' L.U. boxers. No wonder the kid was hangin' out nearly naked; there'd been a fuckin' heat wave in our apartment. Not that I had no complaints in that there department—naked was the way I liked Cory best, just sayin'.

So's for a coupla seconds, I stood there and let my hungry eyes feast on my boy's body. Yeah, he was a smallish man, but he was just so fuckin' perfect. I checked out his slender, but still-muscled arms, all wrapped up around his legs that was just the same. And them little hips—well, they was prob'ly one of my favorite parts o' him. Real narrow, with smooth skin that still had a little tan left over from the summer, made me think o' how it felt to hang on to them things when I was takin' my boy for a ride. And that slim chest, and that flat belly... uh-huh, my fingers was tinglin' with the need to touch.

I missed the hell outta you tonight, baby.

Truer words ain't never been thought, huh?

But I wanna remember what you was like before you was always frightened like a deer caught up in headlights, baby.

Yup. Somethin' sure wasn't okay with the insides o' Cory's head lately, but I had me a solution, which I was gonna share with my boy as soon as the time was right.

Looks like I got me a bit more work to do before I see that old Cory again, huh?

That ain't no trouble, though; Cory was worth any amount of work I had to do. I was just so goddamned sick an' tired of hearin' "I'm fine, I'm fine, don't worry, I'm fine" droppin' outta them pretty lips. 'Cause I knew *fine*, and that there dude curled up tight on the chair was not doin' fine. No, sir. But now I felt a little better about the whole fucked-up situation 'cause I knew how to help Cory to feel safe and happy again: self-defense was my answer.

And I ain't gonna let it fuck with my head that Cory ain't choosin' to share his fears with me. No, sir.

It was almost as if Cory could hear how loud and outta control my thoughts was ragin'. He started to wiggle and squirm on that there chair on account of he was wakin' up. And soon as he realized he wasn't alone in the room no more, he pretty much jolted up to his feet like he'd got struck by a bolt o' lightenin'. The kid was fuckin' petrified.

"Baby, it's just me." I reached out my arms to touch Cory's side, which was all sticky from the swelterin' air in the room. Them strong little hands reached around my neck and locked together, then they clung to the collar of my shirt super tight, like it was goin' outta style.

"I'm so glad you're back, Brett!" Lemme tell you, he meant them words.

"Yeah, yeah, me too." I lifted the boy into my arms real easy-like and then turned and slowly lowered him onto our bed. "Now, climb under them blankets; I cracked the windows, so it's gonna cool off in here real quick."

But when I tried to release Cory, he didn't let go. Just clung tighter, he did.

"Not yet… don't let go yet." He yanked me down so's I pretty much fell on top o' him, and then he said, "Just hold me for a minute, 'kay?"

Every man wants to feel needed by the person he loves, but I knew that this desperate neediness in Cory wasn't really him. It wasn't right. I pushed him back a little so's I could find them light blue eyes in the darkness. "Tell me, Cory… what's goin' on in yer head? I gotta know."

Cory answered real quick, like he was all ready for that there question. "Nothing is going on. I'm fine." He pulled me back down on top of him. "I just missed you."

Before I knew it, super soft lips'd raised up in the darkness to press against mine. And what was that there? Oh, man, it was my boy's sweet little tongue pryin' its way insida my mouth. It felt too good to quit, so's I put my worryin' on a shelf for later and focused on kissin'.

Truth be told, it was a fuckin' challenge to let go o' Cory long enough to rinse off my now super-wantin' body in a speedy shower (which I really couldn't skip, seein' as I stunk like a bar room.) Once I was done, I wrapped my towel real snug 'round my waist, and stood near the foot of the bed, searchin' for Cory's pretty eyes.

And then I found 'em.

Solemn eyes stared up at me in that there dim light. They studied my face first, and then dipped down a measure to take in the light hair scattered across my chest, and soon them eyes was examinin' my shoulders and my arms. Them eyes touched briefly on my waist and legs, before slidin' back up to rest once more on my face. Cory was surely checkin' me out, but not in the "you're so hot" way that I was used to at the B&G. And somehow, I felt that I'd just got measured up, like Cory was evaluatin' the strength of me, his protector. And after he got done with his little test, the kid still looked scared shitless, so's I guess I'd failed, huh? But I didn't let myself have no pity party about that 'cause I knew that there came a time when a man had to stand up on his own two feet, and Cory's time had just now got here.

"Wanna make love, Brett." Strangely, his voice had this unusual sound o' sureness in it; almost demandin', it was.

I moved to the bed and knelt down beside him. If Cory needed to be in control right now, I sure as shit was gonna let him. "We can change things up here, you know. You can take me this time, 'stead o' always bein' on the bottom." Yup. I said them words and I meant 'em too.

Cory's smile was almost wicked. "I like it on the bottom."

Okay, then. I nodded, happy with that fact.

After flingin' my towel to the floor, I slid my boy's boxers down his legs and then kicked 'em right offa the edge. Needin' to be overwhelmed by my boy's taste and smell, I flopped back on the bed, yankin' Cory by his hips right down so's his knees was on each side of my face. Without even thinkin' 'bout it none, I lifted my head up enough so's my mouth could get to work on them treasures before me.

While I was busy doin' my thing, Cory spoke. In a shaky voice, he said, "I l-like it when you're in m-me, Brett, and I *want* you to be in me tonight, b-but I wanna be in charge."

Slidin' my face from his groin, I uttered, "Whatever ya want, baby, you're the boss here this evenin'." And them words came from my heart. I made an attempt to get back to the business that I'd only just started, but Cory spoke up again.

"Let go of me now and… and just lie down flat on the bed."

As Cory climbed offa me, I straightened my knees and stretched out flat on my back, like the kid'd said to do. And I watched with wide open eyes as Cory kneeled down beside me on the bed, reached into the drawer, pulled out the lube, and began preparin' himself for me. Gotta say, that there was about the most hottest thing I ever saw, my boy all twisted around, concentratin' real deep, makin' himself ready to please me. When he was done, he dropped the lube onto the floor and climbed right on.

And the kid wasn't jokin' when he said that he wanted to be in charge of our lovemakin'. He lowered himself onto me real super slow, and every time I pushed up to get inside a little more, well, my boy came to a stop. And I'm talkin' about a complete fuckin' standstill; maybe even pulled offa me a measure, he did. (Taught me a lesson 'bout who was the boss in that there bed right then, that's for sure.) So's I took what he gave me, without tryin' to get myself even a little bit more, ya see?

Then he started movin': risin' up and fallin' down, as if my manhood was his to use however he wanted it. At first my boy was ridin' tall, but soon he bent right down so's his little teeth could find my ears and my neck. And right about then it dawned on me that it was real clearly *himself* that Cory aimed to please tonight, which, in turn, pleased the hell outta me. Couldn't barely fuckin' breathe, it was so good.

For a while, he kept this nice gentle rhythm goin', but it didn't take long for his steady movin' to turn into furious pumpin'. Sure as the sun rises in the east, my baby took what he wanted from my body.

When his buckin' reached its fiercest, he lifted one of my hands from where it rested on his hip, and pushed it right onto his part, which was by now more'n a little bit needy for my attentions. "Rub me," he demanded. "Rub me hard and fast." That there was an order, and I pretty much jumped to obey it.

And at the very moment he was spendin' and I was spendin', both of us findin' heaven together, I heard him kinda murmur in my ear, "Never leave me alone again…."

Never leave me alone again. That there's just exactly what Cory said at our peak of ecstasy. Not "I love you," not "this here feels like heaven," and not even "please love me forever." Nope. My boy'd begged me to never leave him *alone* again.

And then I knew what I'd suspected was right on the money: Cory was scared shitless o' somethin'. And even though I didn't have a clear idea 'bout what exactly he was fearin', I was gonna do what I could to fix him. Not by shelterin' him from everythin' evil in this dog-eat-dog world no more, 'cause that'd stopped workin', hadn't it? This time, I'd get the job done by helpin' Cory to find his own power again.

December 4, 2007
Cory

"You're acting so weird, Cory. Not like your usual self at all." Ally wasn't thrilled with me right now, to put it mildly. "You used to *always* want to go for a run after history class."

"Will you give me a break, Ally? I told you ten times that I have a headache." I rubbed my temples for effect. "Last I heard, having a migraine wasn't a crime in this state."

"Well, lying through your teeth is a crime against our friendship." Ally jutted out her left hip and raised her hand to point at me. "I know you, and you don't have a headache, boyfriend."

Shrugging nonchalantly, I closed up my laptop and slid it into my backpack. "Are you still gonna walk back to my apartment with me?"

She slugged my arm playfully and allowed a good-humored grin. "You know I will."

I hated hiding the truth from my friends, not to mention from my father and Brett. But at this point, although I had desperately racked my brain over it, I just couldn't see any other way to handle this situation. Anyone I told would be put at risk.

Yes, my abrupt withdrawal from certain aspects of my life had already made those who knew me best somewhat suspicious, but it was better than what would happen if I completely freaked out. Because if I showed too much agitation, it would simply drive Brett right over the edge, and not in the fun way. None of the limited options that I could come up with of how to react to the threats would make Steven leave me alone, but I had to do *something*. And hiding out in my apartment seemed to be the least of the evils.

"So, are you gonna fill me in on what's got your panties in a knot?"

"Panties in a knot? That sounds eerily close to something Ian would say."

"Yeah, I stole that line from him. Don't tell him, though. He's strangely possessive over his dry wit." Ally shifted her heavy backpack to the other shoulder. "Anyways, what's up? You're acting... *different.*"

"Okay, you got me there! It *is* my panties—they *are* in a knot! How did you know?" I jumped around a bit, pulling at my jeans, as if I did indeed have the mother of all wedgies.

Ally slugged me again, and I stopped hopping. "You're a goofball. But don't try to change the subject, Cory. I'm worried about you. This is the second time in a row you've had a 'headache' on a day we usually jog."

"Haven't you ever heard 'not tonight, dear, I have a headache'? Well, sometimes it really *is* a headache." I was doing everything I possibly could to put her off the scent of just why I was becoming increasingly, well, I guess you could call it reclusive.

Pulling me up against her side and giving me a squeeze, she said, "It's because I love you that I'm worried, honey. Did you get more of those freaky e-mails or something?"

A spike of heat shot up my neck and prickled the skin on my cheeks. "Oh—oh no, Ally, it's nothing like that...."

"So there is an 'it'; I knew it!"

"Give me a break, Ally. Can't you just drop it?" Oh my gosh, I'd just yelled at her.

Ally looked at me with a strange, sort of injured, expression.

"I'm sorry... really, Ally. I didn't mean to snap at you. Listen, I'll talk about it when I'm ready, okay?"

She blinked, satisfied that she'd made at least minimal progress. "You promise?"

"Of course I do, sweetie. Just give me a little bit of time… please." I had to change the direction of this conversation. "So when we get to my place, do you want to come in and make nachos? Brett picked up all the stuff we need." No subject distracted Ally more efficiently than food. Cheese and chocolate were two separate but equal pathways to her heart. (A strong mocha latte would go pretty far in that direction, as well.)

"Do you have a bag of that Mexican-flavored shredded cheese that we used last time?"

I knew she was coming inside even before I answered. "Two bags."

"That's it, honey, we're cooking!" We broke into a trot as we crossed the street in front of my place. "By the way, what happened to your headache?"

I had to scramble to find an answer. "I think it's a hunger headache. I need nachos—and fast!"

"Don't think you're off the hook about that little talk, either. I'll give you a couple of days to spill the beans, but no more."

We climbed the stairs in my apartment building and before we reached the second floor, Ally said, "I think we should invite Brett to our talk too."

Even if I wanted to, I couldn't do that, but I played along. "Sure."

The kitchen was warm when we entered; the usual evening heat explosion had already begun in our apartment. We dropped our backpacks by the door, and I went to the refrigerator to pull out the ingredients.

"Did Brett mention that the Women's Empowerment Club is sponsoring a self-defense course tomorrow night?"

Ally was already munching away at the tortilla chips, so I swiped the bag out of her hands so we wouldn't have to make our nachos on toast. "Yeah, he wants me to go to it. How embarrassing would that be—me and twenty-five *young ladies* all learning how to protect our precious virtue together?"

"Well, I'm gonna go, I think. Ben told me about it, and he really wants me to attend. I thought maybe you and I could go together." She looked at me, very hopeful. As a matter of fact, she had the same look on her face as Brett did when he'd told me about the self-defense course last night. "And just because it's sponsored by the Women's Empowerment Club, doesn't mean it is only for girls, you know."

"Yeah... I guess." I laid out a cookie sheet on the counter. "Let's make a lot so Brett can have some when he gets home."

"Listen, Cory, guys need to know how to protect themselves too." She was really being pushy. "So, will you go with me?"

"Well...."

"I really don't want to go alone."

It might just make sense for me to go. I'd never be able to take on Steven in a fight and win, but maybe I could learn how to do *something* to at least slow him down.

"So? Will you be my date tomorrow night? I'll need someone to practice my moves on, and I want that someone to be you." Those dark eyes of hers were pleading. And in my mind's eye, it was last night again, and I was back in our dark bedroom, Brett's green eyes imploring: would I please, please take the self-defense course?

"Sure, honey. I'll go. But I'm not gonna take it easy on you, so you'd better get ready."

Attending the self-defense course really couldn't hurt anything, I decided. And speaking of *hurt*, today's less-than-friendly e-mail from Steven was still fresh in my mind: "I'M GONNA HURT YOU BAD."

Maybe there was something more I could do about this situation than to make sure that I was the only one to get hurt.

"I'LL HAVE MY VIRGIN SOON."

Ally had left, and Brett had yet to come home from work. Even though I'd cracked a few windows to let some of the excess heat escape, our apartment still smelled like an All Saints' Day fiesta in Mexico City. And the menacing e-mails continued to roll right on in.

I sat at the kitchen table, head in hands, staring at my laptop and trying to make sense of the situation.

Steven's just messing with my mind; he's not gonna actually do anything to me.

Torturing someone psychologically could be rewarding all by itself, couldn't it? I surely wished I could buy fully into that sentiment, but I knew that Steven Percy's attempt at revenge would ultimately be physical. This mental torture part was just a precursor. An appetizer before the main course: my rape.

I quickly reviewed the reasons that I couldn't tell anyone about "the situation." Brett was truly happy for the first time in his life. He had finally acquired the simple things that make life sweet: a home, some friends, a fulfilling job, a life partner. Self-respect. I would be hard-pressed to rob him of those things by spilling out my story of woe. Oh, and then there was also that *tiny* detail that Steven Percy would probably kill Brett if I opened my big mouth.

Oh my God—and then there was my father! Roderick had been sober for just seventeen and a half precarious weeks, not that I was counting or anything. A phone call home informing him that his son's attacker from last summer was sniffing around again, clearly hoping for round two (yes, Roderick, with sonny-boy as the punching bag), would most certainly drive my dad directly to the Downtown Pub's bar for a couple of shots.

I might as well push him off the wagon with my very own bare hands!

Could I tell Ally? Not unless I wanted Ben and Brett to know.

What about Ian? No, I didn't trust that Steven wouldn't go after him the same way he'd go after Brett.

I have to protect them.

It was actually a rather easy decision for me to make because I loved these people so much. And now I had a spark of hope in my heart that I'd survive whatever was coming, because I was going to the self-defense course tomorrow night.

Time to get real, Cory.

Could one evening's instruction in self-defense actually help *me*, a small, skinny, submissive type of guy, to survive an attack? The rational part of my brain was far from convinced of the likeliness of that. I could actually feel my heart sink when I admitted my doubts. But stranger things had happened, I reminded myself, and I really didn't have anything to lose by trying.

Oh God... another one. "VERY SOON." This last e-mail served as a cruel "good night, sleep tight" from the man who wanted to destroy me.

December 5, 2007
Brett

ME AND Ben got to the Sports Complex early, 'bout fifteen minutes before eleven o'clock, seein' as it sure was dark and late, and we didn't want Ally and Cory to have to try out their new self-defense skills tonight. I'd pretty much kept my fingers crossed all day, hopin' that this here course'd be what it took to give Cory the confidence he'd lost since that motherfucker'd tortured him last summer. Figured that maybe it'd give me a boost of faith too, knowin' that Cory had got himself a grasp on some tactics for how to survive if the worst was to ever happen... again. After dwellin' on it (a helluva lot) today, I figured that it was *just possible* that the way I guarded him so painstakin'ly, like Ian always said, took away from Cory's own sense of power. Still, me and Ben got there early to pick them two up.

A coupla minutes after eleven, Ally and Cory, and a whole flood of females, includin' about five young ladies on the B&G's servin' staff, exited from outta the yoga room in the back of the buildin'. Cory's face and neck was all flushed; he had that energy-filled look like he did right after me and him made love—the real *rough and tumbly* kind of makin' love, y'know? Yeah.

I leaned down and kissed him light on his cheek, but he surprised me and turned his head toward my lips, and then he dished out what I'd call a super-enthusiastic kiss in return.

Just to get it straight, I ain't complainin' none.

Ben was the first to speak. "How did it go in there tonight, guys? Learn some ways to beat the bad guy to smithereens?" Now, in my humble opinion, that there was a tall order for what we oughta be expectin' from outta a single four-hour class. But seein' as how he was nuts over Ally, I'd got the picture that he'd kept his own fingers crossed all day too.

"All I can say is, don't sneak up on me in the hallway at night, baby. I can take you down!" Ally leaned in to Ben, nuzzlin' her nose into his neck a bit so's he knew she was just yankin' his chain.

"Thanks for the fair warning, Ally." Ben smiled big, likin' what he heard. "So, really, what fighting tactics did you learn?"

Ally took a step back from Ben as she tugged on her coat. "It's not all about fighting, Ben. It's about surviving. Which means doing what is necessary to get out of someone's grasp so you can run like hell!"

Cory hadn't said nothin' yet, but he'd stuck out his hands in front of him and was kinda gazin' at em.

"What're ya thinkin' 'bout, kid? Huh?"

"My hands... my knees... even my head... and other stuff too, but mostly my brain. I can use any of them to end an attack on me." He seemed almost shell-shocked with that realization. This was turnin' out better'n I'd hoped for.

We started walkin' toward me and Cory's place, seein' as earlier in the day, I'd invited Ally and Ben back for hot chocolate after the class was done with. I was starin' at Cory, gotta say, 'cause he was actin' weird and not in the scared way he'd been actin' so much lately. He was more like dazed, I s'pose.

"Our goal is survival; we are not there to fight. But there are times when we'll need to use our own built-in weapons, which are our heads, elbows, knees, fists, and feet to get the time we need to get the hell out, right, Cory?"

Cory nodded.

"You see, the attacker knows he's bigger and stronger than us, and he expects us to fight back in a certain way. We learned most important not to panic, and then they showed us ways to surprise our attacker, to catch him off guard so he'll release his grasp and we can get away."

Finally Cory broke outta his daze and spoke up. "Brett, turn around and face me."

We all stopped walkin', and I did as he said.

"Go ahead, try to grab me by the wrist."

I reached out with one hand and grabbed a hold on his wrist, and before I knew it Cory'd squatted down a measure, leaned forward, pulled his elbow down 'til it touched my forearm, and rotated his wrist so's I had to let him go. "Not bad."

Cory's face was glowin' like a harvest moon. "And I know how to get out of a choke hold, a bear hug, and a mount position too."

Ally and Cory kinda glanced shyly at each other and smiled. Ally added, "We practiced on each other."

"Did you learn *any* ways to fight?" Ben and his friggin' one-track mind.

Cory was in talkin' mode now. "We learned that our best bet is to do something to get away before the bad guy has full control of us—so we can *avoid* the fight, Ben. We have to use the element of surprise, and we should never stay still, but if we have to strike, we know what parts of our body to use and what sensitive parts of the bad guy's body to aim for… for maximum damage."

"Yer whole body's a lethal weapon, huh, baby?"

"I wouldn't say that, but now I'll have a fighting chance to get away when—I mean, *if* someone was to attack me."

All three of us stopped and gawked at Cory for a long second, but he kept right on strollin' along. He glanced back over his shoulder at me and winked. "But I'm gonna need somebody to practice on."

That there could be helpful to Cory and fun at the same time. I raised up my hand like a kid in a classroom. "Can I volunteer to be that there *somebody*?"

December 6, 2007
Cory

THIS time I just scanned it briefly and then quickly deleted it (though my fingers shook so violently I nearly missed the delete button). I didn't need to pore over it. The general idea behind this latest message kind of popped out at me: Steven was very much looking forward to our near future meeting, so much so, in fact, that some salivation was involved. Yes, those were more or less *my words* for his latest disgusting little love note.

I didn't reciprocate his feelings.

But even though my fingers still shook at the notion of meeting up with Steven Percy, on the brighter side, I wasn't feeling quite as helpless about it as I had been the day before yesterday. So at this point there had been at least ten *uplifting* messages e-mailed to me, but I wasn't about to go searching through my deleted files to confirm my numeric estimate. However, I really didn't *need* to go back and look at them one by one to realize that the e-mails had started off rather scattered and benign, and had gradually escalated to the point they were at now, arriving regularly, complete with vulgarity and intimidation tactics. Enough so that I was constantly looking over my shoulder for the man himself.

Tonight I had almost forgotten about "the situation" because I was caught up in what had become a weekly calculus tutoring session with my oversized students. I'll admit, I jumped at the chance to stay home and play teacher in my own apartment rather than facing the dark of a December night to go study at the library. Hadn't the guys who'd taught the self-defense course said prevention was the best way to stay safe? Well, I realized that I couldn't hide at home forever, but maybe I'd avoid trouble until I'd practiced my newly gained moves on Brett a few more times. And Ben, Hunter, and Christian were so thankful for the help; it made me feel stronger. Like *I* was somebody's hero.

Brett had come home from the B&G early, and instead of brooding silently in a corner, waiting for the guys to leave, he sat on the puffy arm of the recliner, listening in to our math-talk, and making an occasional "this stuff is so far over my head I'd need me a ladder to even touch it" kind of comment.

Still stranger, when Brett wasn't hovering over our study group, he was sitting on the futon with Ian, deep in conversation over the only thing I was aware of that they had in common (other than me): their love of the band Nirvana, and the world without Kurt Cobain. It was almost like... like they were friends. As I said, strange.

Luckily, the e-mail had arrived after the guys had left and Brett had headed for the shower, so I got to do my shaky-fingered-button-pressing when he wasn't looking over my shoulder. But if Brett had seen the e-mail he'd know for sure what I was convinced he already strongly suspected: something was wrong in my world.

Face it, Cory, he knows you nearly as well as *you know yourself.*

"Hey, baby, I'm gonna hit the hay. You done with yer studyin'?" Brett stepped over to the bed and slid beneath the covers. "I wouldn't mind me some company." Those bedroom eyes promised complete gratification if I joined him.

"Sorry, I have to finish a letter-writing project for my business class. But I won't be long." I snapped off the bedside lamp, moved from the recliner to the kitchen table, and opened my laptop.

"Okay, but wake me up when you come to bed, 'kay?"

"Sure, Brett." I wasn't certain if that answer was the truth or a lie. Sleep was pretty much my only complete escape from being afraid, but I had to admit, sex with Brett came in as a close second. When he was holding me in those strong arms, loving me with all of his heart and body, it was difficult for me to think at all, let alone to remember to be afraid.

For some reason, though, instead of working on my business letter, I opened my assignment notebook, turned to the note pages in the back, and I started to write. I just needed to expel the worrisome thoughts from my mind, and since I really couldn't talk to anyone about "the situation," I decided to put down my thoughts on paper.

"Fear is changing me: knowing that pain and humiliation could be right up the road, around the next bend, is turning me into someone I don't know. And what's worse is hiding the truth from Brett. Despite how well-intentioned the reasons, I am still lying to him."

I lay my head down on the table beside the computer and fought my exhaustion. But although I was certainly emotionally drained from all of the worry and the mental preparations for my self-defense, the simple act of writing had relieved me. So I dragged my head up and put my pen back to the paper and continued to scribble out my thoughts.

"Steven Percy will go for what he wants; he is that type of guy. He thinks that someone needs to pay for his frustration. All I am certain of: that someone will not be Brett."

I was actually able to breathe easier after I'd put those particular thoughts down on paper. Those words reminded me why I was keeping "the situation" all to myself: to keep Brett safe.

"I can survive this. Even if he gets to me, I will talk to him, or de-escalate the bad situation, as I learned in class, and I will change his mind about hurting me. And if that doesn't work, I will use my new physical skills to get away from him."

After reading it over, I realized that my last entry, although I really wanted to believe I could defend myself in the real world, was potentially complete rubbish, so I drew a single line through it. Instead, I wrote:

"I can prevent this if I try. I'll still never walk anywhere alone, but I will no longer avoid the library and going jogging with Ally. I must remember that in public places, I will be safe even without Brett as long as I am not alone. I'll stay in well-lit areas when I'm out at night, and I will carry my apartment keys between my fingers when I jog. Time and time again, I will frustrate his efforts to get to me. Eventually, he will give up on his plans for revenge."

When I'd finished writing, I perused the text of my "survival statement" and immediately considered ripping up the paper into tiny pieces. But right then I heard Brett sigh deeply and mutter something about how lonely the bed was without me, so I just closed up my assignment notebook and returned it to my backpack.

Feeling better once again, I slid into bed beside my husband, hooking my ice-cold feet around his toasty ankles, and then waiting for what would come next.

I seemed to be doing a lot of that lately.

December 10, 2007
Cory

I'D MADE good on my promise to myself that I was not going to hide away from the world in my apartment any longer, so here I was, in my third-floor study spot near the stairs in the L.U. library, trying to get caught up on my Women in American History reading that I'd neglected over the past few weeks. And I'd made progress, but as I'd read, I'd indulged in one too many crème brûlée lattes. Feeling jittery, I decided I'd go back downstairs to the little cafe on the main floor to buy a muffin or a bagel that would hopefully absorb some of the excess caffeine rushing through my veins.

Before I got up, I texted Brett to see if he could come at quarter past eleven to pick me up tonight, as I was convinced that I could finish the rest of Isadora Duncan's *My Life* with a few extra minutes. And like always, Brett texted me right back with, "Your wish is my command, Prince Cory," an inside joke that we'd shared since high school. The students who studied around me were also regulars who I was sure recognized me, as well, so I decided I could safely leave my backpack, and they wouldn't let anyone touch it while I was gone. I folded the top down on my computer and slid it into the bag, and then checked that my phone was on vibrate and slid it in the pack's front pocket. Before I left I placed my backpack on my chair and pushed it under the table.

As I descended the first flight of stairs, the skin under my arms started to prickle, and by the time I reached the next flight the tips of my fingers and toes were tingling, as well. And though I can't really explain why, it felt like someone was watching me.

Get a grip, Cory.

Glancing around the stairwell, I reassured myself that it was the same as always—dusty, a bit dark, mostly empty of people. But I also came to the speedy conclusion that I felt much safer back in my chair upstairs and that I didn't actually *need* to buy anything to eat; I was pretty sure Brett had stuck a granola bar in my backpack this morning. So, I turned around quickly to head back up the stairs.

Clearly the man right behind me on the stairs, the only other person in the stairwell with me, wasn't expecting my sudden change of heart. When I spun around, he nearly rammed into my chest; then he lowered his head and pretty much turned in unison with me. What were the chances that the only other person in the staircase, who just happened to be walking closely on my heels, would experience a need for a direction change at precisely the same moment that I did? Not very good.

I am in danger. Or I'm completely paranoid.

The very second I felt the duct tape being wrapped around my wrist, I knew that the former was the case.

Duct tape? They didn't tell us about how to deal with duct tape at the self-defense course!

Cold, callused hands grabbed my hands, which were now tethered behind me, and yanked my body roughly against his. Knocked off balance, I fell into the man, noticing, when I did, his massive size and bulk, which for some reason called to mind those World Wrestling Federation guys my dad used to watch on television when I was a kid. And he smelled dirty: a combination of stale cigarettes and unwashed skin.

"Just keep your mouth shut and I won't have to hurt you," the giant rumbled, his breath hot and wet in my ear. An oversized sweatshirt, as unclean as the man, himself, was then draped over my shoulders to hide my restrained hands, and I felt sharp metal, far colder than the hands that had grabbed me, thrust against the skin of my lower back.

Your brain does the unexpected when taken off guard in such a brutal manner. In my mind, over and over again, a single, rather stunned, concept replayed: "this is not Steven Percy… this is not Steven Percy… this is not Steven Percy…." As we walked, I stumbled once, and meaty fists boxed my side a couple of times, a clear warning. He was so much bigger than me; he didn't need to go for my vulnerable eyes or throat or groin to achieve "maximum damage," did he? I was already fully under his control.

"Wh-who are y-you?"

"I told you to keep your motherfucking mouth closed!" And then I felt a stinging prick on my hip and I knew for sure that the sharp metal object pressed against my back was a knife.

This isn't the body I've been watching out for; this isn't the voice I expected.

A white flash of panic set in. My breaths came faster and harder, and I knew I was losing control. Every part of my body started shaking, a response to extreme fear that I recognized; I'd experienced genuine terror before, a time or two.

More questions invaded my stupefied brain: what was happening? Who was this man gripping my wrists and holding a knife to my back?

"This shaking thing you're doing ain't gonna work too well, boy. You gotta cool your jets. We have to go through that lobby, and you're gonna be still or else…." The point of the knife made a return visit to my hip and pierced my skin just enough to catch my attention quite effectively. "Now, cool your jets!"

I think I nodded, but it might have just been my head shaking so violently.

Rule number one: do not panic. (A very tall order. But still I'd try.)

One and two and breathe… one and two and breathe…. Slow it down, Cory.

"A single sound, buddy, and you're a dead man—believe me, I ain't got nothing to lose here." He lowered his unshaven face and looked right into my eyes without revealing even an ounce of regret. And again, a prick to my skin.

I believed him.

With one burly shoulder, the man shoved open the heavy door that led into the lobby. And all of a sudden he was hanging on me, the hand that wasn't holding the knife to my back draped over my shoulder, as if he knew me intimately. "What do you say we get some dinner and catch a movie? You'd like that, wouldn't you?" Nuzzling my neck as if he were my lover, he kept up the meaningless banter until we'd crossed the lobby and exited the building through the huge front doors. And everyone looked away from us because they didn't want to witness a queer couple's PDA. No one took note of how completely disconcerted I was.

"Well done, boy. Now we're gonna go for a little ride." Side-by-side we staggered awkwardly across the parking lot toward an old dark-colored sedan. "Are you gonna play nice?"

I nodded numbly. I had "played nice" so far, but what choice did I have with a knife pressed against me? Plus, the other night, I had learned that I should conserve my energy for a moment when I actually had a chance to get away. *Be smart, Cory.*

Before I knew it, he was opening the back door to his oversized car and was pushing me in face-first. After glancing around to check the parking lot for any nosy observers, he pulled out the same roll of duct tape that he'd used on my hands and secured my feet together. My chances of getting away were looking slimmer and slimmer every second. Almost everything I'd learned the other night had involved using my hands and my feet and my balance. At that shattering realization, my violent shaking rekindled.

"Don't sit up." He slammed the door and circled around the car.

But I still had my brain, didn't I? (Not that it was functioning at full efficiency right now.) So I forced myself to keep my breathing even, just the way Brett had showed me last summer, and I took in my surroundings like I'd learned in class: torn black vinyl seats… unfortunately, that was pretty much the extent of it. So I tucked my body into a fetal ball and concentrated on surviving as he began to drive.

De-escalate the bad situation.

Talk to him, Cory. Change his mind.

"My name is Cory, sir… did you know that? Well, I'm nineteen, and I'm a student at L.U. and… and I'm gonna get married this summer... and my dad, well, he's tryin to get sober and... he really needs me, sir."

Silence.

"And I'm sure you've got really good reasons for thinking you have to do this, but, uh... don't you think there's a better way to go about it? If it's money you need, my fiancé has a good job... and I'm sure he'd give you anything you want, if you let me go...."

"Your fiancé ain't got the kind of money the guy I'm doing this for has, I'll tell you that much, boy."

So someone had hired him. This guy was just the muscle. *Breathe, Cory.*

"You don't have to do this—you know you could get in big trouble if something happens to me. Just drop me off on the side of the road and we can forget that this whole thing ever happened."

Nothing.

"I swear it, sir—I won't go to the police...."

"You're wasting your breath, boy. I'm getting paid really good for this job. I'm gonna take the cash and get the hell out of town." He chuckled. "You ain't gonna talk me out of this, so stop wasting your breath."

I'm not going to give up.

Maybe at least I could get some information from him. "S-so you're d-doing this for s-somebody else?" My suddenly shaky voice wasn't cooperating as well as I'd wished.

"I sure ain't got no taste for dudes myself, boy. I'll take round boobs and a plump ass any day." So he was doing this for someone rich and probably gay. "This ain't nothing but a job to me."

After taking a very sharp corner that sent me sliding uncontrollably across the cool vinyl, the man spoke again. "But this guy wants you bad, let me tell you. He's forking out a fucking fortune to get you delivered to him." Then, in his raspy smoker's voice, the man belted out the refrain of a Dirty Laundry number-one hit, "No Way Out," all the while drilling his fingertips on the steering wheel as if he were rocking out on a drum set. Finally, he turned around and presented me with a lopsided, toothless leer. "I'd say you two are gonna have some fun tonight."

I think I have my information… and the name Steven Percy sums it up quite well.

As the car whipped around yet another corner and flew over countless bumps in the road, I was starting to feel dizzy and lightheaded in the big backseat. All I could do now was try to survive the crazy ride while searching the sky for clues as to where we were going.

And there was one more thing I could do to fight off the panic that hovered on the edges of my consciousness, threatening to encroach. So I conjured up an image of Brett, focusing on details, letting them distract me. His blond tangles—they were so much softer than they looked, and not just on his head… and his lips— when we'd met years ago they'd usually been frozen in a cynical smirk, but now it seemed like tiny invisible strings were constantly tugging the corners upward, especially when he caught my eye… and his shoulders—as capable in love as they would be in destruction.

Brett… deep breath… oh, Brett….

It seemed as if we were heading southeast toward Winter Lake.

Brett

I SORTA dawdled my way up them never-swept stairs of the L.U. library, one reluctant foot stuck in front of another. I wasn't exactly in no big rush; Cory'd asked for a coupla extra minutes to finish that there book he was readin' 'bout that lady who in Cory's words was "the mother of modern dance." (Whatever the hell that was.) The kid seemed to like the book, so's I'd figured Isadora Duncan must've been a better mother to modern dance than Sheila Taylor'd ever been to me.

But the real actual reason I wasn't in no hurry to get to Cory was 'cause I'd made me a decision, it hadn't been no easy one, and I was dreadin' what I hadta do next. See, I was pretty sure Cory wasn't gonna like what I was gonna say too well at all. But tough shit for him, huh?

Soul mates share everythin' and we is soul mates.

I woulda much rathered that Cory'd come to me by his own free will to spill out what the fuck it was that'd been eatin' away at him lately, seein' as us two was s'posed to be, as Cory'd said, "kindred spirits," huh? But that there hadn't happened, and yeah, that fact stung my heart more'n a little, but it wasn't no deal-breaker 'tween us two. Cory most prob'ly had a whole bunch of fucked-up reasons for keepin' his shit private, but his closed trap was gonna open up tonight.

Yup, Cory's mouth'd been shut up tight as a nun's bedroom door at midnight for the past coupla weeks, but tonight we was gonna have ourselves a nice little heart-to-heart. Loved the boy enough that I wasn't gonna let him keep on sufferin' alone, I did.

No more secrets 'tween us. 'Cause them secret-keepin' days are long gone.

Uh-huh. If I hadta drag it outta him, the truth was gonna get spilled tonight.

By the time I got to the place where Cory usually studied, I'd worked up a nervous sweat and my belly was rollin'.

Then—*What the fuck?*

The kid wasn't in the place he *always* planted his ass to hit the books, the place I'd fuckin' *put* him four hours or so ago. Nope, there wasn't a friggin' soul in the room; the only thing left sittin' there was Cory's backpack on his chair, his shit all stuffed inside like he was waitin' for me to come get him. But there wasn't no *him* to get! I picked up the bag by a shoulder strap and it felt heavy, and it looked full, so's I knew his computer and his heavy sweatshirt was both stuck in there. And that was pretty fucked-up all by itself. My boy didn't normally leave his shit lyin' around where it could get swiped.

And I'll admit it: when I caught me a glance of that there empty chair, a bolt of lightenin' fuckin' shot from my gut straight to my heart and back again. Hadta bend over a measure and clutch my belly so's I wouldn't drop right on down to my knees.

Talk about over-fuckin'-reactin'!

I shook my head a coupla times, took me a deep breath for steadiness, and trotted right back to them stairs. The kid'd prob'ly had to take a leak—musta overdone it in the coffee-drinkin' department. *Yeah, that's it.*

The men's room on the second floor was one of them single-stallers, so's I knocked soft on the door, then turned the knob and cracked open the door when nobody answered. "Cory, you in there, baby?" When there still wasn't no answer I pushed the door open wide and sure as shit, the bathroom was empty as Fenway Park on a rainout.

So's I headed down to that there lobby on the main floor, seein' as it had a little snack bar there, and knowin' my boy was mostly always hungry, he'd prob'ly stopped by for a snack. These two gals was loungin' on a couch right near the café, sippin' on cups o' tea or somethin', so's I stumbled up to 'em, real awkward-like.

"Uh, 'scuse me, ladies...."

The brown-haired girl spoke up first. "I'm very sorry; I just can't do that. Because there's no excuse for you." She winked, all sly-like. The flirtin' had begun straight off—no big fuckin' surprise there.

"Oh, yeah... right." I tried to fake a smile, but I don't think it worked too good. "Can I... I need to, um, to ask you two somethin'." *I ain't never been particularly smooth with the ladies.*

The second girl with the blondish hair stuck her cup on the side table, got up offa the couch, and kinda slinked over to me. Right insida my fuckin' personal space, she got, and I didn't like it none. "You, honey, can feel free to ask me *anything*."

"Me too." Girl number one was on her feet super fast, like she'd just realized that she was sittin' on a pincushion.

"Thanks... uh... You girls been here long?" They shrugged, seemin' sorta spellbound. And I wasn't fuckin' stupid; I knew what kinda effect my face had on some girls, but right now I didn't give a flyin' fuck what they thought of me. "You guys seen a kinda small, dark-haired dude comin' in or outta the café?"

Them two ladies looked at each other and then back at me, and shrugged again.

"Maybe ya know him, name's Cory Butana... he's a business major...."

Them girls exchanged glances one more time. Number two said, "You're looking for a *guy*?"

"Yeah...." Now I was startin' to get impatient. "So's, have you seen him?"

That there girl number two already looked bored, like she'd got herself the picture that I wasn't never gonna hold no interest in her or her friend. She shook her blondish head as if she couldn't give a shit. But the other girl was kinda sweet. "You want us to help you find him?"

"I... uh...."

"Did you check the men's room on this floor? It's near the end of the hall, you'll see it down there on the left." She pointed.

"Thanks." I don't know if she heard me say that, though, 'cause I was already halfway down the hall.

BY THE time I got back upstairs to Cory's usual spot, my belly wasn't feelin' too good. Coulda made ice cream, it was churnin' so fierce.

I must be the world's biggest fuckin' dumbass! In my blind panic, scramblin' all over the library like a kid chasin' a runaway balloon, I'd forgot to do the most obvious thing possible—I forgot to call Cory's fuckin' cell phone!

Why didn't I do that when I first got here? Coulda saved myself a near fuckin' nervous breakdown! Prob'ly took five years offa my life span, it did. So's I pulled my phone from outta my sweatshirt and called Cory on speed dial, now breathin' a measure easier. But when I heard the soft vibration of Cory's phone comin' from outta his backpack, well, that there nervous breakdown I mentioned before, it came right on back for round two.

Why don't Cory have his fuckin' phone on him? If he was goin' somewhere, he woulda took his cell phone, huh?

So's I put his pack on the table and parked my ass in Cory's chair, my bugged-out eyes locked on that there door, prayin' like hell that the next face I saw comin' from outta the stairway'd be my boy's.

No such goddamned fuckin' luck!

That there damned door didn't never even swing open once in the next ten minutes.

This here is so fucked-up! Cory wouldn't never pull a stunt like this on me.

I reached insida Cory's pack, found me his assignment notebook, turned 'til I got past a coupla pages of Cory's notes, scribbled much messier than usual, and tore a single sheet out. Findin' a pen, I scribbled down a note for him in case he came back, tellin' him to borrow somebody's cell phone and give me a goddamned call ASAP (before I friggin' keeled over from a case o' heart failure), and I'd come and get him. I stuck it on the table and weighed it down with a coupla his pens.

Grabbin' Cory's backpack, I slung it over one shoulder and made for the stairs, my brain all filled up to the brim with *what-the-fuck* and *where-the-fuck* and *why-the-fuck*.

Cory

After a thirty-minute ride that left me ready to vomit on those ugly vinyl seats, the car came to an abrupt halt. I sincerely wanted to feel relief that the torturous ride was over, but I just felt growing despair because I knew that I was getting closer to my fate. The WWF guy got out of the car, and I was left alone. But he'd be back; somehow I knew that my misadventure was far from over.

When the man returned, he opened the back door and unceremoniously grabbed my feet and yanked, sweeping me up into his arms and carrying me, as if I weighed no more than a toothpick, down a long, pebbled path to a cottage, that under different circumstances I may have considered quaint. Although there were no outside lights on, I could see that the front door already stood open, and then he paused for a minute, as if he was trying to remember what he was supposed to do next. In that brief moment, I found the strength to follow the instructions from the course—I took in my surroundings. Yes, it was very cold, and it was certainly quite dark, but I could somehow tell that we were in a low-lying, moist-feeling, forested area, and I could distinctly hear the sound of waves breaking on a shore on the other side of the house. There was a long path that led to the street and woods on either side of us. I was almost positive that this cottage was somewhere along the shore of Winter Lake.

Once he got me inside, the giant dropped me to the floor with a thud and took a second to close and lock the door behind him. Then he turned around in front of me, grasped me from beneath my arms, and dragged me down the hall. It appeared that my ultimate resting place was going to be a tiny bathroom. My hysteria got a third wind at that point, and I nearly started to hyperventilate, but then I bit my lip so hard I think it actually bled a little bit, just to give myself something else to focus on other than my likely very undesirable fate.

"Wh-what are you g-gonna do to me?" I didn't mean to speak; the words just escaped somehow.

"Well, since you asked, I'm gonna start things off by shutting you the fuck up!" He ripped off yet another strip from the roll of tape he'd conveniently been wearing around his wrist, and slapped it over my mouth.

That was the final straw! All of the chaos that was swirling around haphazardly inside my brain, which I'd tried so hard to keep under control, washed right over me. I just didn't have enough calm left in my mind to concentrate on slowly breathing from my nose. In no time I was wheezing and gagging, and my eyes felt like they were bulging out of their sockets.

"This sure ain't gonna work—the boss ain't gonna pay me shit for a dead body." He leaned over and ripped the duct tape off of my mouth with a single painful tug.

All I could do was pant, and I felt tears streaming from my eyes. I wasn't exactly crying; my body was just reacting to the fear and the lack of oxygen, I guess. But the free flow of air was the best thing I'd ever experienced in my life, except for Brett's arms around me.

Then the guy looked down at me where I lay crumpled on the cold tile floor. And I could swear that I saw a trace of guilt in his beady little eyes. "I don't see no reason why I have to tape your mouth shut. Nobody'll be able to hear you screaming out here this time of year, anyways. But I'm sure that this'll cost me big time...." When he pulled out a box cutter, I saw my life flash before my eyes, but very efficiently, as if he was well-practiced in the art of slice-and-strip, the man bent and cut off my jeans and pulled off my sneakers, then tossed them all into the shower stall leaving me in my T-shirt and boxers. "And I ain't gonna leave you stark naked like the sick pervert told me to either, there ain't no reason for that. It's fucking freezing in here... plus, I'm sure he'll have you naked in no time flat. He can do that part his self."

I shivered, but it was from his words, not the cold. However, the little room was quite frigid, as if the heat hadn't been turned on for the winter. I felt goose bumps rise on my arms and chest, at the same time realizing that freezing to death was the least of my worries right now.

Finally he yanked me toward the towel rack and pulled my wrists up in front of me. After he taped them to the metal bar, he turned around, studied his handiwork for a brief moment, and then said, "I'm gone."

I watched silently as the door closed with a click.

Now what?

I'd like to say that I immediately started practicing my deep breathing for calmness and that I began sizing up my surroundings, but that would be a lie. Left alone with my raging thoughts, I simply panicked.

I should've told Brett all of it.... My latest mistake is probably unfixable.... I'm gonna get beat up and raped, and I'll die here alone.... Brett will never smile again.... He'll blame himself.... My father will fall off the wagon.... This is all my fault.... I'm so cold....

I'm so scared....

I honestly didn't know if I could survive this time—and I also didn't know if Brett could survive without me.

Brett

Well, I hadn't sent my ass outside in the cold for a nighttime jog for longer than I could even recall, but I still did my damn fuckin' best to sprint back to our studio. On the way, my sweaty palm somehow managed to cling on to my lifeline: my godamned cell phone. I'd only be able to breathe again once I heard my baby's voice on the line, so's I ran like a bat outta hell, all the while listenin' for a ring. But that there phone stayed as silent as a hayfield on a snowy night.

Once I got to our buildin', I took the stairs in prob'ly three steps and started knockin' even as I stuck the key into the lock in our door. Pushin' the door open I heard my voice screamin', all shrill-like, "Cory? You here? You in bed, baby?"

Looked like I was screamin' to myself. Our place was all fuckin' dark and empty. Hadta bend right on over, the pain in my gut and my chest and my brain hurt so bad right then.

You don't have no fuckin' time to lose it, Brett.

That there love nest of me and Cory's real suddenly'd turned into a cage; I was stuck inside it without a hope or a clue. Paced its borders like a caged-up tiger, I did, past the bed, the can, the kitchen table, the recliner, and back again. Pretty much fuckin' frantic, is what I was.

Gotta do somethin'!

That's when my brain kinda clicked back on. I lifted my shakin' hand and dialed my phone.

"Yeah?" Ian's voice was all crackly from sleep.

"Tell me he's with ya…."

"*What?* Brett, is that you?"

"Cory—is he with ya?" I didn't have no patience at all. Just none.

"Nah, man, he went to the library tonight." Ian yawned. "I thought you kept tabs on your boy. Slacking off on the job, big guy?"

"Fuck me! Just fuck me!"

I'd almost hung up when I heard Ian's voice again, but all wide awake now. "What's the matter, Brett?"

"It's Cory. He ain't there… at the library. He ain't at home, neither."

"Did you try to call him?" Ian spoke slowly. I could tell he was tryin' to act all reasonable.

"He left his phone and his backpack on his chair at the library…. Fuck this shit!"

I heard some rufflin' around and shiftin' on the other side of the line. "Okay, Brett. You need to calm down and answer me. Did you call Ally or Ben or the other guys? Maybe he went to help them study."

"No… no, man, I didn't have no chance yet. Could ya wake them guys up and see if they got a clue where Cory is? And could ya call Ally too? I gotta get my ass back to the library. Let me know what they say, 'kay?"

"Okay, will do. Be listening for your phone… and Brett, the library is gonna close soon. You'd better get moving."

"Huh? What'd ya say?" I'd completely lost my train of thought as I'd rifled through my pockets in search of my truck keys. Then I decided it'd be quicker to run than to go get my truck at the B&G. "Huh?"

Ian hesitated for a minute, and finally he said, "Brett, you gonna be okay?"

I glanced over at our puffy purple cloud of a bed. "I don't know."

Cory

SO MAYBE I'd be lucky, and I *would* freeze to death before Steven got here.

I was so cold; I hadn't ever been this cold before. My hands were numb and tingling, but I was pretty sure that was from the way they were suspended up by my shoulders rather than from the icy air. Leaning heavily against the cold tile wall, I wiggled my fingers every few minutes to keep some feeling in them, which seemed to be working, at least for now.

In addition to dwelling on the tempting prospect of freezing to death, the time I'd spent in this icebox of a bathroom had offered me a chance to gather my wits. I tried to remember everything that I'd learned at the self-defense course. I reviewed each hold that they'd taught us in my head, and what I was supposed to do to get loose. I pictured the cottage from the outside, its proximity to the trees, and the long walkway to the road. Then I tried to remember how long the hallway was and which way the door opened.

Then I thought about my husband. The reason I had to survive this night.

And I reviewed everything I'd learned one more time.

Brett

SURE as shit, that there library was closed when I got my ass back there. Panting like some kinda overheated dog, I stormed up them steps that led to the library's huge-ass doors, yanked on each oversized handle, but them things was locked up tight. That wasn't no matter; I knew Cory wasn't in there anyhow.

So's where the fuck is he, then?

Okay, now I was what most people'd call fuckin' desperate. A basket case with a capital *B*. I stomped down them concrete stairs so's I could start a frenzied search of the library's grounds. Stuck my arms into each and every shrub that lined the buildin', parted the branches of all the trees and bushes I could find me, and then I started pullin' at the door handles of each o' the coupla cars that was left in the parkin' lot. I got down on my belly so's I could check under them cars, and peered like a peeper insida their windows. And I done all that for fuckin' nothin'. There wasn't no sign of my baby nowhere.

I can't deal with this fuckin' shit no more!

And I dropped down hard onto my knees 'cause I couldn't very well just *stand* there and do nothin', now, could I?

Wasn't a very far ways down from my knees to my ass, then, was it? And once I'd planted my ass on the frozen ground, I couldn't hold it back no more. I turned my head just slightly, hunched over a measure, and lost every fuckin' morsel o' food that'd touched my lips all day. When I couldn't hurl no more, I lay flat on my back, right beside, maybe even on top of that there nasty mess I'd just made. Stared into that frigid sky, prayin' to who-the-fuck-knows, 'til the spasms in my belly had me curlin' up in a dead spider ball again.

And I was glad for them friggin' belly spasms; they was a fuckin' godsend to me. Them things hurt so bad that they took away all o' my control and left me just a writhin' mass of puke-smellin', sweat-covered, good-fer-nothin' madman. And that was fuckin' perfect; wouldna had it no other way.

Don't want control no more. Don't have no use for control, now that Cory's gone and nothin' fuckin' matters.

Then I lost my cool in a super-big way. I'm talkin' King Kong kinda big. 'Cause once I couldn't barf no more, well, let's say alls I had left to do was cry, and them tears started fallin' in bucketfuls. But the fuckin' worst part came after the sobbin' had slowed down a measure: the thinkin'. Seemed my brain was set on torturin' me now.

Where's my baby gone to?

Will I ever get to feel his sweet little body all tucked up in my arms again?

Is he hurtin' right now?

How'd I manage to let him down so fuckin' bad?

And all of a sudden it hit me harder than I'd ever got hit before: ain't nobody home no more. Prob'ly never gonna be neither.

I don't have no home now. Don't have no reason neither.

Closed my eyes, I did, right then. Closed my eyes and wished for a fuckin' ginormous boulder to drop outta the sky and crush me like a bug so's it'd all be over.

Sorry to say it, but I gone and gave up.

"PULL yourself together, Brett." That sounded like Ian Webster. With a voice that wasn't none too kind neither. "Get your head out of your ass, and get the fuck up off the ground."

Next thing I knew I was gettin' dragged up offa my back by a pair o' strong hands. "He's gone. He's gone, Webster. An' I ain't gonna keep on goin' without him."

But Ian wasn't hearin' me. "I'm not gonna let you abandon him. Cory needs you, so it's time to get your head the hell out of your ass and earn the right to call a guy like Cory yours!"

"But what if he's sufferin'? Huh? He can't go through that hell again!" I started to curl into a ball again; it felt safer that way, somehow. And then I reached my hands up to clutch my head so as to cover it all up and make the world go away. "I can't think no more on this. It's too fuckin' much. Don't go makin' me think."

But instead of the world goin' away, I got Ian's face stuck right in front o' mine. "You are going to get up off of your sorry ass and get yourself a grip." He spoke quiet, but still I heard him better'n good. Angry claw-like hands hooked into my own and pulled me up onto my feet. I tried to focus my drippin' wet eyes on Ian's face, but focusin' on anythin' wasn't too fuckin' easy, seein' as I was seriously fucked-up. "You've got to get a grip, now, brother. You're not going to be any help to Cory like this!"

"But Ian," I said, real sure of my words, "I ain't never been no help to Cory... fuckin' lost him, I did...."

He grabbed me by my collar and pulled me right back into his face for a stare-down. "You, my friend, are *everything* that Cory wants and needs. Don't let him down now when he needs you most!"

"But... but I don't think he can survive it again." I wasn't yankin' his chain about that. "And I can't breathe without Cory." Them last words came out real quiet but firm 'cause I surely meant 'em. See, the truth was, I didn't *wanna* breathe without Cory.

Ian pulled me into his arms and held me tight, which was real super-surprisin', seein' as we'd just barely started toleratin' each other's presence on the planet Earth. "Listen, let's not even go there, buddy. Cory's only been missing for a few hours, right? We don't even know that he's not back at your place, right now, as we speak."

The voice of reason—*the voice of bullshit.*

"Come on, I called everybody, and we're all meeting at your place in a couple of minutes. We're going to figure this thing out." It seemed that Ian'd taken control, and I was damn glad for it, seein' as I'd been bawlin' like a helpless newborn up until about two minutes ago. Lost all the wind in my sails, I had. Got me a sharp nudge in my ribs right then. "Brett, don't give up on him now."

He took off runnin' in the direction of me and Cory's place, and so's I followed along.

Cory

OVER the past hour or so of lying crumpled against a bathroom wall, cold, stiff, and maybe a little bit numb in places, I'd managed to completely change my tune: from guiltily blaming myself for getting into my current predicament, to assigning the culpability to the person who truly owned it. Steven Percy was the only person responsible for this situation.

I did not ask for this to happen to me. This is not my fault.

At this point, hindsight would make me inclined to admit that honesty really *was* the best policy in most situations, but I hadn't been withholding information from Brett and my friends to cause harm to anyone. Quite the opposite, in fact. I had been holding back the truth in an effort to protect people I loved, and I had even developed strategies to keep myself safe; they simply hadn't been effective. Maybe I had exercised poor judgment, but I didn't deserve to be punished for that.

And yes, I was scared. In fact, *scared* was far too weak of a word to describe my current emotional state, but still I hadn't lost my head. I had come up with what you might call a very general plan. I was going to continue to analyze and reanalyze my situation as it escalated (as I was certain it would), and I'd *do* whatever or *say* whatever I determined necessary in my struggle to survive.

To keep myself calm, I reached into my memory and pulled out a cherished image of Brett. Dwelling on the tiny details articulated the image; I almost believed he was there beside me, stretched out on his side, observing my every move. And now, just like all of the other times when I woke up in the morning and turned to regard his face, his thoughts, themselves, were truly vociferous; I was somehow fully aware of what was going on in his mind just by looking into his eyes.

I heard utterances of love and longing, adoration even.

I can't breathe without you, Cory. It was like he spoke those words right into my ear.

And then my beautiful reverie was shattered. The sound I'd been dreading since the moment I'd been so unceremoniously dumped on this floor drove into my ears, although, in reality, it was probably close to noiseless.

A key in a lock. A door swinging open. Footsteps on the hallway floor.

Stay with me, Brett.

Brett

ALLY was fuckin' stunned. She slammed her cell phone down on the kitchen table and stomped over to stand beside the bed, where I sat with Ian and Ben. "The campus police said that college kids are constantly 'disappearing' like this, and they always pop up the next day with a hell of a hangover."

"That's bullshit!" Ian was pissed. "Cory doesn't even drink at all!"

At this point, I was strugglin' not to lose all hope. I mean, it was like somethin' had snapped insida me when I'd broke down in the parkin' lot, and alls I could do was just hang, real desperate-like, onto a shredded strand of sanity. Yup. Apparently, my huge emotional outburst earlier had taken me down more'n a few notches, so to speak, so's now I just sat there, miserable as hell. Not sulkin', just thinkin', really. And I was thinkin' so hard my head hurt, tryin' to figure out what the hell'd happened to Cory and gettin' nowhere real super fast.

"They said to call back tomorrow afternoon, and if he hasn't shown up, they'll look into it."

"Cory could be de—" I was about to say "dead by then," but I managed to cut off them words in time. Didn't seem to matter; Ian got the jist of what I was thinkin', anyhow.

"Jesus Christ, Brett, you can't be thinking that way. Cory needs you, and part of that is to stay positive." Ian's fist found my shirt collar for about the fifth time in the past thirty minutes, and he shook me hard. "Get your head outta your ass and help us, damn it!"

Just then Christian and Hunter barged through the doorway.

"You guys find him yet?" Christian sounded frazzled. He'd really taken a shine to Cory since them two'd been studyin' calculus together.

"No, he's still gone, and the campus police won't help." Ally once again shook her head in disbelief. "But we aren't gonna wait until tomorrow, are we, boys?"

All of us guys shook our heads. And right then I felt a little bit of my super-heavy depression lift up at the prospect that I had me some company in this little slice of hell I'd got stuck in.

"Could the guy from last summer who assaulted Cory have come back and taken him?" Ian's dark eyes was searchin' my face, tryin' to make sense of this whole fuckin' shitstorm.

I still wasn't sure I was ready to face the strong chance that what he'd just said might real likely've been true, but I couldn't afford to deny it no longer, could I? Felt all o' the blood drain right the hell outta my face when I forced my mouth to say the words. "Yup, that there's a strong possibility, I'm 'fraid." Bile rose up my throat, but I swallowed it back. "Yes, sir."

Once again, Ian got right in my face. "We need to hear *all* of the details about what happened to Cory last summer, and maybe then we can figure out if it's the same asshole, back for more."

My head pretty much spinnin', I just sat there for a minute, thinkin' that Ian was right. I needed to spill out all o' the facts, which was gonna suck, seein' as I was truly ashamed of the role I'd played in Cory's bad treatment last summer. But truth was, I'd do anything to help my boy. I was just froze up by the fear that whatever we did wouldn't work and we couldn't save him and Cory'd be hurt, or worse, and.... It'd be so much easier for me to just jump off a fuckin' bridge, huh?

"Well? What the fuck happened last summer?" Ian's sharp voice knocked me outta my downhearted thinkin'. The dude was 100 percent right about me needin' to spill the details and even more so about me needin' to get my head outta my ass. But I was findin' it mostly impossible to climb up outta my current state of gloom and darkness high enough to see the light.

"Okay... so's last summer, me and Cory's friendship, which was actually much more'n just friendship, broke up on account of I was an asshole, and then Steven Percy came into the bar we worked at—"

I got interrupted by a coupla them at the same time, Ben and Chris, if I hadta guess. "Steven Percy—Dirty Laundry's drummer?"

"No way!"

"A famous guy beat up on Cory?"

"The one and only—Steven the Motherfucker Percy." Uh-huh. That there was my less-than-sweet nickname for the asswipe.

"So *what happened?*" Ian clearly wanted to get down to the details.

"Percy put the moves onto Cory real strong, and I didn't do nothin' to discourage him, seein' as me and Cory wasn't gettin' along too well right then." I stopped for a minute to take a coupla breaths and to steel myself for what I hadta say next. "As it turns out, Cory went out with the asshole one night, it was kinda a favor to his dad, and Percy fuckin' attacked him. Beat him 'til ya couldn't barely recognize him. Nearly raped him too, but Cory's dad came home and stopped that part. And accordin' to what Cory's dad told me, Percy was pretty pissed off at bein' interrupted halfway through the act." I was pretty much squeezin' the stuffin' right outta Cory's pillow at this point.

Hunter looked at me like I'd bitch-slapped his grandma. "So, tell me, Taylor, why is that asshole Percy still alive? Because I don't know about you guys, but I'd have fucking killed him if he did that to somebody I cared about."

Ally put her hand on my shoulder, 'cause she knew that Hunter's words'd been way worse to me than a kick in the gut coulda ever been. "Brett told Ben that Cory had begged him not to do anything to Percy—and I'm sure Cory had his reasons for that. We're not gonna get anywhere if we just sit here playing the blame game, though."

"No, Hunter's right—I shouldna let that asshole walk…."

"So, Brett, has Cory heard from Steven Percy since that night?" Ian was on some kinda fact-findin' mission, it seemed, and I was glad of it. Somebody had to be on task, and I sure as hell hadn't rised up to the challenge, had I?

"Not that he told me 'bout."

"Oh my God!"

All five of us guys snapped our heads around to stare at Ally.

"Oh my God!" This time her hands flew up over her mouth, and she dropped her ass down onto the bed, sorta like her knees'd collapsed. "E-mails... the e-mails...."

Well, gotta say, the look on her face, like a good swift kick in the ass, worked to break me outta the slump I'd got stuck in. As a matter of fact, it had me pretty much flyin' up offa my spot on the bed and divin' over Ben to get to Ally. I knelt beside her on the bed without even a single inch between us. "What e-mails, Ally? Huh?"

Ally's face'd changed from concerned to sickened. "Like, I'd say, maybe back at the end of October or so, Cory asked me if I'd sent him any prank-ish e-mails, you know, trying to be funny...."

"And?" Ian and me barked out together.

"I told him I hadn't sent them, but we talked about the e-mails. I made him tell me what they said. It sounded like he had some kind of a secret admirer."

"What did the e-mails say?"

"Who sent 'em?"

Ben got up offa the bed and went to get Ally a soda; she looked real shocked, almost like she was gonna faint or somethin'. "Cory didn't recognize the sender. But one of them said something like, 'I found you,' and there was one that said that Cory was still so pretty, and the third one said that—oh my God...."

Now, I hadn't never laid my hands on a woman, not outta love or outta anger, but I sure wanted to grab Ally and shake her hard so's the details'd all fall outta her mouth. "What did the third one say? Come on, Ally...."

Ally was kinda shiverin' now. "The third one said that they had some unfinished business to take care of."

"Holy fuckin' shit."

"Where's Cory's computer?"

"I'm good with computers. Is it okay if I search his e-mails and his trashed e-mails too? There are probably more e-mails from the asshole."

"Can we look through all of Cory's stuff to see if he left any clues?"

Seemed that everybody was all talkin' at once. 'Cept for me, that is. I'd gone spiralin' right on back to my downhearted thinkin', uh-huh.

Unfinished business, right…. Cory'll be lucky if alls he gets is raped.

Cory

THE bathroom door swung open.

"Ronny didn't follow my instructions." Steven Percy shook his head slowly, his disappointment obvious. "You're supposed to be awaiting my arrival bound, gagged, and naked." He shook his head one more time. "It's just so hard to find good help these days."

I looked up at him, completely unsympathetic to his plight, but facing my worst nightmare, I nonetheless felt myself begin to shatter. *How on earth am I supposed to make my brain function now?*

"Well, it'll cost him, but that surely isn't any concern of yours, is it?" His eyes and hair were darker than I'd remembered, but his features were just as pointy. And he was bigger, stockier, I guess. But all of that paled when I caught a glimpse of the knife he clutched in his hand. I wasn't sure what kind of knife it was—hunting, fishing, or survival, maybe. Brett would know; he knew all kinds of stuff like that. But it didn't really matter what that knife was supposed to be used for or that Brett could recite an outdoorsman's perspective of its purpose with encyclopedic detail, did it? Because its purpose tonight was sufficiently clear to the two people in the room, and that's all that mattered. Steven thrust it forward and sliced the tape that held my wrists to the towel rack but left them bound together. "We'll be so much more comfortable in the bedroom, don't you think?"

He lifted me like a sack of flour, easily tossing the top of my body over his shoulder. When my arms finally hung down in front of me, I started wiggling my fingers, trying to bring some blood back into them. And I told my back to relax and to conform to the odd angle at which it was bent, which turned out to be much easier to say to myself than it was to do. I wasn't supposed to waste my energy struggling until, or much more likely, *if,* I had a chance of getting away.

"No fighting? No begging or tears?" He sounded disappointed. "Well, we'll have plenty of time for that later. And patience *is* a virtue. Thanks for the little reminder, Cory."

The mattress on the bed I was dropped onto was covered by a stark white sheet, complete with fold marks and that new from-the-package smell. And in no time at all, Steven towered above me. "See this here?" He brandished the knife as if it were a sword. As both a drummer *and* a criminal, he possessed a flair for the dramatic, I thought frantically. "Now, if you stay still and cooperate with me, I'll *only* cut the rest of your clothes off. If you struggle, well, Cory, sometimes accidents *do* happen." He bent down, and the look of intent in his eyes made me shudder; the dull side of the cold blade slid down my chest, as he sliced the entire length of my T-shirt. He pulled it apart, his eyes now rolling back in what looked like ecstasy. Then he stabbed several times into the fabric of my boxers, which compliantly fell to the bed.

Being naked before Steven's probing eyes set off feelings of vulnerability in me that I hadn't expected to be quite so potent. My extremities shriveled just a bit, trying desperately to be smaller, to escape his attentions. But I knew that if I let myself succumb to my fear and humiliation now, I had absolutely no chance of surviving this night. So, I bit down on my lip, again seeking that life-affirming pain, and took a deep breath.

Brett, are you still with me?

Strong fingers found my nipples and twisted cruelly, ignoring my whimpers. "You are so beautiful, just like I remembered...."

I couldn't help it; I raised my bound hands to push his fingers off me. "Now that's what I want to see… finally a little spirit." The torture to my chest continued until he had me exactly where he wanted me, despite my best intentions. I was trying to fight back, twisting and turning in an effort to get away from him, and exhausting myself in the process. But surprisingly, even that wasn't enough for him. "You know, I was so fucking *pissed off* that we got interrupted last time… yeah…." He pulled the knife out from wherever he'd stuck it in his belt or pants and started slicing the duct tape that bound my hands together. "I liked it better in July when your hands were involved… yeah, that was way more fun…."

Once my wrists were free, I tried to fold my arms across my chest to stop the torture, but Steven just reached down and dragged them out to my sides. "Now, remember the rules? I can hit, I can scratch, and if you try to push me off of you, then I can bite. And you? Well, your part is much easier: you can lie there and take it." He pulled the remains of my T-shirt off of my chest. "Any questions, Cory?"

After swallowing back a groan, I looked into his eyes, feeling simultaneously panicked and perplexed. "Why? Why are y-you doing this t-to me?"

Judging by the way his pointy chin tilted to the side and he looked off toward the ceiling as if the right answer was written up there, I was convinced that Steven was genuinely puzzled by my question, even rendered momentarily speechless. But he quickly recovered his haughty demeanor, and replied, "Oh, Cory, that's easy—I detest unfinished business."

Brett

"OKAY, I think I found all of them. Do you guys… um, do you want me to read them *out loud*?" Hunter, it seemed, was some kind of computer genius, and he'd managed to break into Cory's computer, access his trashed e-mails, and find all of the fucked-up ones.

"Well, yeah. I think we need to hear them. Maybe they'll give us a clue or something." Ian seemed much more ready to hear them things than I was. But I knew it hadta be done.

"Some of them aren't too... too *nice*, you know?"

But Ian was insistent. "Hunter, just fucking read them to us."

The dude looked kinda sickened just as Ally had a little while ago, and prob'ly like I had since last night at eleven fifteen, when I discovered that Cory was missin' from his chair at the library, but after taking a quick nervous glance at me, the kid got his ass in gear and read. "Number one: 'There you are. Found you.' Two: 'Still so pretty.' Three: 'We have some unfinished business.' Four: 'I always get what I want.'" Hunter stood up from his seat at the kitchen table and stretched his neck around a bit, then he blew off some steam by sorta punchin' the air a coupla times and sat back down to read. "Uh, this one's... well, Five: 'If you like your pretty busboy keep him out of this. I'd hate to have to hurt him too. Enjoy your turkey.'"

"He's a fucking bastard—he sent one on Thanksgiving Day," Christian groaned.

And I was sorta mumblin' to myself, at the same time. "That's why my boy didn't talk, 'cause Percy threatened to hurt *me* if he told me anythin'." That there realization just pissed me off more.

"Keep going, Hunter."

"Okay, number six: 'You made me wait for it. Nobody makes me wait for it.' Seven: 'Nobody can stop this.'"

"*I* coulda." Everybody looked at me. I just blinked and then mumbled some curse words.

"This sucks, Ian. I don't want to read the rest. Here, you read them." Lookin' uneasily over at me, he got up, and then Ian slid into his seat. Hunter pointed to a place on the computer screen.

"Eight: 'I'm gonna hurt you bad.'"

My belly wasn't gonna be able to handle too much more o' this shit.

"Nine: 'I'll have my virgin soon.' And ten: 'Very soon.'"

Even Ian was apparently having some trouble spittin' out the next one. He looked at me, his eyes all filled with "I'm sorry." "Eleven: 'I want to fuck you so bad I'm drooling.'"

Yup. I barely made it to the can before them dry heaves hit me fuckin' hard. And I could still hear the rest of 'em murmurin' real quiet while my head was stuck in the goddamned bowl. Sounded like they was talkin' about the last e-mail, number twelve, the one that Cory hadn't never even opened.

"It says, 'On my way.'" Ian's voice broke and the whole room went silent.

Cory

"DID you ever really doubt that I'd be back for you?" He dragged four fingernails down my chest again. I was gritting my teeth as hard as I could and counting the strokes to distract myself from the pain. At this point, I knew only two things for certain: it was the twenty-second time he'd scratched me, and counting wasn't working very well to get my mind off of the bitter sting. "This is like tracing—I can just follow the little white lines that I made last time, you know?" He hadn't bitten me yet, but then again, I hadn't fought back.

I shrugged as if I was indifferent to the physical torture, as well as his punishing questions, but the scratches were burning with a fire I thought I had forgotten, until tonight's painful reminder. I didn't think I was gonna be able to follow the guidelines that I'd learned in my self-defense class. It just hurt too much.

Frustrated by my lack of response, he backhanded me across the face. The whole world blurred up for a few seconds while my brain settled back in my head. "I told you I always get what I want, and then I reiterated it in a little e-mail, remember? Just so you wouldn't forget." His hand flew across my face in the opposite direction. I tasted blood and tried to reach up to touch my mouth, but Steven whacked my hand away, and then, again, he appeared puzzled. "I just don't understand faggots like you. You coulda had some fun with me last summer, but instead you had to turn it into a big scene."

The moment his hands moved to his belt was the moment when I lost any restraint I'd shown thus far. I tried to scratch him in the face and batted savagely at his hands and bared my teeth; in other words, I fought like an animal to get out of his grasp. And God, did I ever beg.

"Please... no, not that... please, Steven, I can't do that with you!"

A satisfied sneer replaced any traces of puzzlement on the man's face.

He's enjoying my struggles.

I was providing him with exactly what he wanted: physical proof of my pain and fear and anguish. I had to get a grip on myself.

Okay, Brett. I'm going to count backward, just like we always do when one of us needs to calm down....

And I knew that Brett was still with me; I could swear I heard his voice counting.

Ten... nine... eight....

I struggled a bit more, but now I was more acting than fighting with my whole heart. Steven scratched me again. And again. And again.

Seven... six... five....

I allowed myself to breathe heavily, to let him see my exhaustion. Was my panting a mere act or the full truth? I didn't know. But I did know that pure instinct told me not to hide my utter weariness. Steven slapped me once, twice—but both times were with less force than before.

Four… three… two….

I did what I swore I wouldn't. And I think I did it on purpose, but I can't be sure.

Yes, I cried. Steven laughed.

One….

I lay still, trying to curl my body in on itself.

Steven went back to unbuckling his belt.

Brett

WHEN I came outta the can, everybody was starin' at me like I was the thing that'd just stepped outta a spaceship. And all I could think of to say was, "Steven's gonna fuckin' kill him."

That there served real nice to snap them all outta their gawkin'-at-Brett-Taylor-like-he's-an-alien daze. Them dudes and Ally gasped together like they was all part of a big gaspin' choir.

"Where would Steven Percy take Cory?" Ian asked the obvious question.

"Well, Webster, if I fuckin' knew that, I'd fuckin' be there, now, wouldn't I?"

Ally ignored my smart-ass reply. "Brett, just stop and think about it for a minute. When Steven Percy was in Belton last summer, where did he hang out? Who was he with? Where did he stay?"

Felt like somebody'd dumped a big bucket of icy cold water over my head, it did. "That's it! I just thought of somethin'— where's my cell phone?" Yup. I was wide awake now, my adrenaline back to runnin' on full throttle.

Ally scrambled over to me with my cell phone in her hand, but nobody dared to ask me nothin' right then 'cause they could tell I was on a roll. I snatched it and pressed speed dial for the Downtown Pub.

Brian picked up. "Downtown Pub."

"Brian, it's Brett." My voice broke so's I tried again. "Got us an emergency situation up here."

"Is it Cory? Is the kid okay?"

I cleared my throat. "Don't know, man. He's missing… pretty damned sure it's Percy again."

"Jesus Christ!"

"I know, I know. Now listen up, man, I need your help."

"Anything, Brett. Just ask."

"Remember last summer when you had to go and pick up one of our waitresses at the place where Percy and his crew was stayin'?"

Brian hesitated. "Um, yeah, I think I remember that."

"Do you have a rough idea of the address?"

"Uh… yeah, yeah. Not the exact street number, but the place was down towards the end of Windsor Drive in Ashton. You know, near Ellis Beach."

"I know that area. I can find it, at least. Which house?"

"Well, it was a cottage, down on the left before the docks, definitely waterfront. Dark paint, I'd say, maybe green or gray. Long rocky path to the front door."

"Okay, thanks, man. Thanks."

"No problem. Should I call the police?"

"I don't know. The L.U. campus police wouldn't even do nothin' 'til tomorrow, so's…." Ian started pulling on my arm and trying to ask me questions. "I gotta go."

"Look, I'll grab Jon and Roderick, and we'll head up to your apartment. Now get your ass to that cottage and find Cory."

"Will do. I'll be in touch." I hung up my cell phone and made tracks to the door.

Ben blocked my path, which was easy for him, with his brick wall of a body. "Where the hell do you think you're going?"

"I think I know where Cory is."

Everybody stood up at once. Christian said, "We're coming with you."

"I'm gonna need to run over to the B&G and pick up my truck, but I can do it myself."

"Fuck that, man. I borrowed my brother's Jeep for the weekend, and I still have it. It's right outside," Ben offered. "I'll drive."

"You guys, you gotta know, this ain't gonna be no walk in the park. This dude is sick." I had to make 'em understand. "Look, it could be dangerous, see?"

"Fuck you, man. You know how I feel about Cory! I'm comin'! I want to be there. I want to help!" Ian'd pretty much blurted out his love for Cory right in front of the whole gang, but that didn't matter none. Ian was gonna come with me to save my baby.

"We all love Cory, Taylor! We're *all* going, so let's hit the road, alright?" Chris and Hunter headed for the door.

I pulled Ally aside. "Ally, will you stay here and wait for our family from Belton? It'd sure mean a lot to me if you'd welcome them guys and help 'em not to have no nervous breakdowns, 'specially Cory's dad."

She looked up at me with scared dark eyes. "Of course, Brett. Whatever you need."

"Thanks."

"You'd better get going… and be careful."

"Sure, we'll be real careful." I turned around to leave, but then I felt this soft little tug on the back of my sweatshirt. So's I turned to face Ally again.

"And Brett… bring Cory home, okay?"

"I'm gonna try."

Cory

"STEVEN... l-let's talk about this... m-maybe we can work something out."

He had easily maneuvered me into what the teachers at my course had referred to as "the mount position," which was pretty much exactly what the name said. Steven had mounted me, missionary-style, and I was on my back, pinned to the floor. And he was gonna rape me now. That's what he'd wanted all along, right?

"That's what I'm doing, I'm *working out* all of my frustrations... on you."

I shook my head in denial; my mind refused to accept that this was gonna happen to me. My body wasn't Steven's. *My body is Brett's.*

Just prior to pinning me, though, Steven had realized that he wasn't going to get very far, in terms of the sex act, if I couldn't spread my legs apart. So he'd sliced the duct tape around my ankles and without too much trouble he'd managed to position me beneath him, just the way he wanted me.

"No!" I fought him off some more, but my energy was seriously waning. "Don't do this to me—I'm not even a virgin anymore, so—"

Steven froze. "He fucking took it?" Murderous was the only word I could use to describe his expression. "That fucking busboy, he fucking stole—That bastard got what was supposed to be mine last summer!"

Somewhere deep inside my very core, a fresh spark of fear spiked out in all directions, sending what seemed like electrical jolts to my fingertips and toes. Informing Steven that I was no longer a virgin had been a serious miscalculation on my part. Yeah, it had felt good to crush his depraved hopes the split second I'd said it, but it hadn't made him want to let me go. It had only served to put me in more danger.

And wasn't I supposed to be calming him right now, not riling him up? I knew what was coming next.

"Doll, you're going to seriously regret that."

In my opinion, the beating that commenced was an expression of Steven Percy's complete narcissism. I had insulted his pride by not wanting him in the first place, and I had rubbed his face in it by giving my virginity to another man. And in his twisted brain, a far lesser man. Believe me, I paid a high price for my stupid mistake. Steven no longer used his flat palm, or even the back of it. Now he pounded on my face, my neck, my ears, with his fists tightly clenched.

"I don't want some loser's leftovers!"

I took a vicious blow to my jaw. It hurt to speak, but I nonetheless blurted, "I was lying... I was lying to get you mad... me and Brett, we haven't—"

"*Now*, you're lying... *now* you are!"

My jaws... my ears... my neck.... I could barely breathe. "Please, dear Jesus, please God, help me... make him stop...." Then something told me to draw my head back and try my best to smash my forehead into Steven's face. So I tried. Not effective.

"Still so spunky. I love your spirit."

It's time to stop fighting. Stop fighting, Cory.

When I found myself searching my hazy brain for that cherished image of Brett to take with me into unconsciousness, I accepted that it was a useless struggle. I let my head fall back in submission.

Steven looked down at me, his expression smug; he knew he had me beaten. And if I was going to be honest with you, I'd admit that I agreed with him. I was almost completely exhausted and was fast losing my grip on the tattered shreds of hope that I could escape.

Between rasping breaths, I began to coach myself again. I didn't have too much left to lose, did I?

Cory, your ankles and wrists aren't bound any longer.

I'd suffered a severe beating, but I was actually in a better position than I'd been in all night. Although that may have been true, however, my arms and legs were still stuck underneath Steven.

I was well and truly trapped. And when I realized that, I knew the time had come that I try to escape.

When you have no other options, it is time for the false surrender.

"Okay, okay, I give up... I give up. I'll do whatever you want, just please don't hurt me anymore." Somehow, and it must've been something of a miracle because I didn't have much left in me to work with, I found it within myself to follow the verbal script I'd learned on Wednesday night. "I give up, Steven."

Steven hesitated, but he didn't loosen his grasp; he wasn't yet convinced. So I completely relaxed all of my straining muscles so my body language matched my words; I became soft and compliant beneath him. Patting his shoulders gently, I repeated my well-learned lines, "Listen, Steven, I'll do whatever you want. Just please, please don't hurt me anymore."

When our eyes met gravely, I knew that he finally believed that he was in full control of me. And I admit again, he wasn't alone in his belief. I felt trampled on, crushed, defeated.

"You mean it?" I nodded, assuring him that my submission was absolute. "Well, it's about time you figured out who's in charge here." Knowing that he could do whatever he wanted to me now, he loosened his hold, and his head dipped down to my neck, where he went to work nipping and sucking and murmuring in my ear.

"Kid, I think you're gonna really like it with me."

And I knew that this was my chance; I'd have only one try at it. If I didn't manage to get away right now, he'd beat me to a pulp, rape me, and maybe even....

Well, it just has to work.

I have to get back to Brett.

"And I haven't ever had a lover yet who hasn't come back to me begging for more."

What I had to do now was to behave like a preprogrammed robot. I had to somehow sift through all of the quaking agitation inside my head and find one small corner of dead calm. It wasn't easy, but I did my best.

"You liking this, sweetheart? We're good together, so good...." And what was even more difficult was to make myself wait for the right moment, biding my time as he violated my body with eager lips and teeth, and my mind with his panted intentions.

"And you taste as good as you smell... yeah...."

When I was as certain as I could be that he was fully engrossed, evidenced by his mouth, which was painfully busy on my throat, I switched into autopilot and did what I'd been taught and had practiced over and over with Ally and Brett. In some sort of a mechanical daze, I simply hooked a hand on his right wrist and used my other hand to grab behind the same elbow, and I trapped his right foot with my left one. Then I lifted my hips, which threw us off balance, and let gravity do its job, rolling us right over. The split second I was on top, I jumped to my knees and then up to my feet.

Standing there and looking down at my tormentor, I felt a sudden rush of giddiness; in fact, I think I came inexplicably close to laughing.

"You little shit." Steven was as stunned as I was; he lay there staring up at me in a haze of bewilderment. "You little fucking shit." He pulled himself up until he was seated.

Now don't go thinking I was cool-as-a-cucumber Cory, because I wasn't. The entire time I was busy executing that little "hook and roll" maneuver, my heart was pumping so hard and fast, I was half expecting to be the first "robot" in history to have heart failure. And when I was finally standing over him (after that brief moment of mirth), I took a split second to absorb Steven's bemused expression and shocked muttering, and I decided that one swift kick to his nose (achieve maximum damage) would be a prudent use of my precious time before I ran like hell. Not that I was living out some sort of a revenge fantasy, I really wasn't; I just wanted to do what was necessary to slow him down, to buy myself time, in what was surely going to be a chase.

So I drew my knee up and back, and then let my foot fly.

It wasn't the world's most devastating kick, in fact, it was rather lame, but it served its purpose. Steven bent right over, clutching his nose, and that gave me the chance to get the hell out of there.

Brett

"YEAH, I'd say this is the right road. I think the house is down near the end on the left." It was darker than a pocket outside tonight, and seein' as this here area along Winter Lake was a summer vacationin' community, there wasn't no lights on in no houses and no headlights from oncomin' cars. Just pitch blackness, made even blacker by the shadows of lots of trees. And that was all.

Our Jeep's headlights flashed down the street, and I saw a dark-colored Hummer parked at an angle near the place where the cottage was s'posed to be. "That there Hummer's the kinda truck the asshole drove last summer. The house has gotta be right down there!" I pointed toward the shorefront side of the road. Thankfully, Ben used his brain and turned the headlights off, so's Percy wouldn't have a clue that we was comin'. Then he stopped the Jeep on the shoulder, up the road a ways from the cottage, and we all stepped out onto the cold dirt, but so as to be real quiet, we didn't slam them car doors.

Ian stepped forward. "Me and Brett will go down there in the woods toward the house; you guys stagger yourselves along the road and catch Percy if he makes a break for it. Ben, you stay near the car in case we need to get away fast."

Alls I cared about was the part where I could go into the cottage and get Cory, so's that there plan was fine by me. Me and Ian trampled along the side of the road 'til we found a place where we could break into the woods and cut over toward the cottage. But as we was trudgin' through them cracklin' leaves on the forest floor and pushin' aside them frozen branches that was in our way, me and Ian caught each other's eyes. 'Cause sure as shit, we both heard it— these pantin', raspin' sorts of noises comin' from outta the woods just below us. When I looked out in front of me to scan them dark woods, somethin' kinda white-skinned and human—*fuck, it looked like Cory*—was runnin' toward me at full speed, his arms and legs flailin' in every which way, prob'ly losin' strips o' skin to them pointy branches but not even seemin' to notice. In the shadowy night, mostly alls I could see was them whites of his eyes, which was real wide with fear, and it was also clear that my boy was stark fuckin' naked 'cept for some dark patches of somethin' stuck onto his ankles and wrists. So's I started runnin' for him and rippin' my sweatshirt offa me at the very same time, so that by the time I got him insida my arms, I'd have me somethin' to wrap him up in.

Felt so fuckin' amazin' when that there skinny frozen body barreled into my shakin' arms. Like every good feelin' I'd ever had with Cory all put together, bound up like a ginormous ball of yarn, had got stuck insida my heart, makin' it almost *need* to explode. Or maybe, like if the real God up in heaven came right down onto earth in the middle of the night in Ashton, New Hampshire, and handed Brett Taylor the best gift anybody coulda ever asked Him for. That there shiverin', clutchin', shriekin' man I loved with my whole entire heart was back insida my arms where he'd fuckin' always belonged.

"Brett! Help me! *Please…* Brett!"

"Christ, baby." I felt my heart poundin' in rhythm with the throbbin' pulse in Cory's temple, which was pushed right up against the side o' my face. And my hands wanted to just hold on and squeeze him, but instead they roamed up and down his slim body, just makin' sure the kid was really all there. "I thought I'd lost you!"

Cory's only reply was this little squeak of agreement, which slipped right outta the corner of his mouth, seemin' to indicate that he mighta thought that very same thing. Then, breathlessly, he begged me again, "Don't let me go… *please, Brett…* and be careful… Steven has a knife…."

"Is Cory alright?" Ian was suddenly beside me, peekin' over my shoulder at the boy in my arms with my sweatshirt wrapped 'round his middle.

"He's alive and kickin', Webster, that there's all I know." Wanted to pry Cory offa my chest just a measure, seein' as he was clingin' to me hard and fast, so's I could check on what his face was doin' just then, but he wouldn't let me. So's both of us just kept on huggin' and makin' moanin' noises, but mine had words mixed into 'em. "Baby... baby, I was so fuckin' scared... couldn't hardly think... couldn't hardly breathe, neither...." And finally, when we was both quiet, Cory kinda pulled his face and neck offa me, and them big blue eyes gazed up at me, kinda shocked-lookin' and real swelled-up from apparently takin' more'n a few knockout sorts o' punches. "How'd ya get away from the asshole? Baby, how?"

That there shocked look sorta fizzled a bit and then drifted outta his eyes altogether, and Cory said, his voice still raspy and quiverin' but also a tiny bit proud, "I used self-defense."

Well, that there reply filled up my soul with so much joy that I grabbed my boy and yanked him right back into my arms, but then I noticed him wincin' in pain, and I knew that he hadn't escaped this evenin' scot-free. Nope, not even close. But it didn't look to be quite as bad as last summer.

"Here, Cory, put on my coat." Ian was now cautiously tuggin' at Cory's duct tape-covered arms and slidin' 'em, one by one, into his bomber jacket. And it looked like that super-cool Goth dude was cryin', it did.

Wanna know what the next thing my baby said to me was? He fuckin' said he was sorry.

"I-I'm so sorry, Brett. I... I didn't really... *mean* to lie to you, b-but...." And then he started bawlin', lettin' out all of his hurt and fear and anger along with his tears. But I already knew that Cory hadn't told me the whole truth about the e-mails on account of how deep he loved me; he'd gone and faced his biggest fear outta his need to protect his husband.

Know what happened next? I went and did the very same thing as Cory and Ian was doin'. I bawled like a tiny baby with a friggin' huge set of lungs, outta happiness and sadness and relief and pissed-off-ness and so many other feelin's that I couldn't possibly name 'em all if ya gave me a fuckin' week to do it. And I had so many more questions that needed answerin', but seein' as we heard Christian yellin', "We got him! We got the asshole!" from up by the street, I knew that it wasn't the right time or place.

Nonetheless, real quick, I leaned down and said to my boy, "Did ya get away *in time*?"

I think he knew what I was askin', 'cause he nodded and said, "He just hit me and scratched me, nothing else."

That there answer sure pissed me off 'cause it was clear Cory was one hurtin' unit, but it put my mind to rest a bit, 'cause I was pretty sure that him bein' beat on was gonna be easier to recover from, in his body (less complications as far as the medical shit goes) and in his mind, than gettin' raped woulda been.

We climbed the gravelly slope back up to the street, and I used my cell phone as a flashlight to figure out where the hell we was. I heard voices back over by the car, so's me and Ian each stuck an arm under Cory and helped him in that there direction.

"I don't wanna see him, Brett… please don't make me see him…." Cory's tears'd started up again, but they was more quiet now. "It hurts so bad and… I just can't see him."

"I promise, you ain't gonna hafta look at that loser no more, baby." I led the kid around the opposite side of the car from where the guys was standin' and stuck Cory in, and then I ripped off my T-shirt and tucked it around him. "I'll be right back."

When I got over to the other side of the car where Ben and Hunter had that motherfucker standin', one giant on either side of him holdin' his arms behind his back, with Ian and Christian hoverin' real close by for backup, I didn't hesitate none. No, sir, I walked right on over to the asshole, my bared chested all puffed up like Tarzan or somethin', and looked him square in them goddamned beady eyes. My head was filled up to the brim with all o' these super violent intentions that I coulda prob'ly got myself arrested for. And the asshole had the nerve to smirk and say to me, "I had a good time with your boyfriend, and did you pick out those blue silky boxers he was wearing with me in mind? I really have to thank you, busboy, that was a nice touch."

And right then I knew that I was gonna fuckin' kill him.

"Let go of him." Even under these fucked-up circumstances, I was up for a fair fight.

"Brett, he had a knife, we aren't gonna let him go. Who knows what else he has?" Hunter said, clingin' onto the asshole tight.

"Then stay right the fuck beside him, if it makes you feel better, but let him go."

So's Ben and Hunter dropped his arms, just as I'd asked.

"Put 'em up, Percy, we got us some major fuckin' *unfinished business* to take care of." And I went at him. Prob'ly only smacked the dude ten times in all, which was prob'ly two thousand smacks less than he deserved. At first, he made a halfhearted effort at protectin' himself, but soon he just fell down onto the frozen ground. "I guess you should go and take a self-defense class like my *fiancé* done, huh?" And that goddamned motherfucker had the balls to smirk at me again.

That there was when I lost my marbles, I s'pose you could say. In fact, I hadn't never been more riled up in my entire life than I was right then. My hands seemed to act without even no thought whatsoever from my brains, they did.

You didn't never show Cory no mercy; I ain't gonna show you none neither.

I grabbed onto that shithead's throat and started to squeeze. Gotta say, at that point my thinkin' was all fucked-up; the whole world was kinda a blur to me. Them other dudes tried like hell to pull me offa him, and they was yellin' and shoutin' about how they'd called the cops, and I had to let the asshole go. But time seemed to stand still, and I just squeezed.

"Stop it, Brett!" That there was my husband's voice, huh? "Don't ruin our future together because of *him*!"

Without lettin' go of the asshole, I turned toward the car. Cory'd opened up the door wide, and he was lookin' at me, them bashed-up, but still beautiful eyes pleadin' for me to let the motherfucker loose. And seein' as I couldn't never deny my boy even one single thing in the past, well, I figured that I wasn't gonna start denyin' him nothin' right now neither. I dropped that loser to the ground like the load o' shit that he was and made my way over to my baby. Then I slid my ass right onto the car seat beside my boy, pulled him up onto my lap, and said, "Ben, could you start up the car? Cory's here's gonna freeze his ass off."

Ben'd returned to the car too, so's he turned on the ignition the very second I asked. "We wouldn't want that, now, would we?" He turned to us with a kinda nervous smile. "I'm really glad you're okay, Cory. I mean, I know you're not in perfect shape or anything, but… well, Ally's gonna be so relieved."

Cory was doin' his real super-scared shakin' thing, but he managed to chatter out a coupla words. "Sh-she knew something was wrong, and I wouldn't t-tell her either. I'm really s-sorry."

"Don't worry about it, Cory. She'll understand." Ben caught my eye for one meanin'ful second, sorta like he was checkin' in on me to make sure I still had my shit together, and when I nodded he stepped outsida the car where them other dudes was glued to the asshole.

It was my turn to say somethin', and I was damned well gonna do this here little speech up right. "Look at me, Cory, and listen up real good, y'hear?" Them banged-up eyes looked guilty as a thief's as they shifted from somewhere near my chin up to my eyes. "I ain't mad at you for keepin' them e-mails from me; none of us are. I know that you done it to protect me. But Cory, from now on there ain't gonna be no more secrets 'tween us. There just ain't."

A coupla teardrops rolled down over all of them bruises and cuts that marked up Cory's pretty face. "I put you all at risk by not telling you guys, but all I was trying to do was handle it on my own."

Shakin' my head, I replied, "But baby, I need to know that from now on you's gonna trust me in everythin'. Good or bad, if it affects you, it's mine to try an' fix. And even if I can't fix it for ya, well, seein' as you and me share ev'rythin', it's mine to know about." I took a peek under Ian's coat at them fire-red scratch marks that striped up Cory's chest. They was so fuckin' nasty that I felt the stirrin's of anger buildin' up in me, but somehow I managed to suck it all back in. "I need to get me a promise that you ain't never gonna hold back nothin' from me ever again."

Cory nodded, all super solemn-like.

"Now, we're gonna get you to a doctor so's he can check you out real good."

Again, Cory nodded, remindin' me of the obedient child that I never was. Then he asked me, "And what happens after that?" As he waited for my answer, them swollen eyes just stared outta the window where the lights of a coupla cop cars was flashin' in the distance. Seemed so fragile and worried, he did, and I knew he was thinkin' 'bout all of the legal crap and media shit we was prob'ly gonna hafta face.

"What comes next?" Repeatin' his question, I pulled the only person I'd ever loved in this whole damned universe tight against my chest and then leaned down to kiss his battered cheek, but real super light, for good measure. "What happens next is that you get better, Steven Percy gets what's comin' to him, and then me and you get ourselves married, y'know, we make it official. How's that there sound?"

"Sounds good." He leaned his head against mine like he was tired, which he prob'ly was. For good reason too.

"And after the whole weddin' thing, well, I'm thinkin' that us two deserve one hell of a rockin' honeymoon, huh? It's gonna be Disney World, it is…." Yeah, I wanted to see the kid's face when he was starin' up at Cinderella's Castle for the first time in a fierce kinda way.

Most prob'ly thinkin' about Disney World, Cory nearly shot up offa my lap, in that happy, excited way he had that I'd always fuckin' loved, but then the pain from his sudden movement made him slump back down again. I reached under my sweatshirt that was coverin' his privates and rubbed his bare legs to comfort him, happy to see that they was finally warmin' up beneath my hands. "So's, does that there sound like a plan?"

"Yeah, that sounds like a plan."

EPILOGUE
July 26, 2008
Cory

"AND he still walks me to all of my classes, even though… well, even though Steven Percy has been serving his time since early in the spring." I glanced up at Brett, who was, as usual, hovering right over my shoulder, one hand set firmly on my waist.

"What can I say? Old habits die hard, huh?" He didn't appear to be even slightly apologetic about his choice. He leaned in very close and whispered in my ear, "I *like* walkin' ya to class, baby. Ain't never gonna stop doin' it, neither."

And when I glanced up at him, I couldn't help but lose my breath for a split second. Brett looked… well, how can I phrase it tactfully? Even in the dull light of the Downtown Pub, my lawfully wedded husband of less than sixty minutes looked absolutely stunning in his black tuxedo. The contrast between his long golden hair, tumbling in its usual unruly fashion over the collar of his crisp black jacket, those piercing green eyes that seemed to see right into my soul, and the soft expression of unmitigated satisfaction (he wore *that* as well as the tuxedo), I must admit, formed an image in my mind that I knew I'd never forget. And so maybe it *was* a touch less than tasteful, but I'd chosen to wear a smaller version of the exact same tuxedo in white. And maybe it was true that my shoulders didn't stretch the material across the jacket's back to the same degree Brett's did, but we were a matched set, nonetheless.

The pub looked better, and far brighter, than I'd ever seen it before. I thought it would be fitting that our wedding had a rainbow theme, seeing as it wasn't every day that two men were united in matrimony up here in the Lakes Region of New Hampshire. I'd mentioned my vision to my father who was giving us the reception as a wedding gift. And Roderick totally went to town. He'd even extended my "rainbow vision" to be more of a "tie-dye rainbow vision," hence, the tables were all draped in what would have made excellent Grateful Dead T-shirts. Balloons of all colors were tied to every chair, and no shortage of rainbow streamers "decked the halls," I guess you could say. Even my wedding cake, made with tie-dyed batter as well as rainbow frosting, would have satisfied the dessert needs of many a seventies hippie. All it needed was a peace sign on top.

Maura, my best friend from high school, grabbed the hand of her "University of Connecticut first-string soccer player" boyfriend who stood beside her (I'm sure he had a name, but that was how Maura referred to him) and dragged him right up against her side. After purring in his ear for a few seconds, she turned back to me and asked, "So that jerk Steven Percy took a plea deal instead of taking his chances at trial?"

Without hesitation Brett stepped forward, pushing me back toward the vibrant head table behind us, protective as always. "We decided that it'd be better for Cory, here"—he glanced back at me soberly—"to avoid the media circus that'd sure as fuck come with a public trial. But the asshole got himself a year in the pen, so's... so's we feel he's payin' a price. And... and he can't come 'round Cory; if he tries to, he'll find himself in deep shit." After a brief pause, he added, "Yes, sir."

"I don't know how you guys managed it," Maura continued, completely oblivious to Brett's growing discomfort with the subject, "but it really hasn't been *too* widely publicized. I mean, yeah, I read about it online and saw it on the entertainment channels and maybe even in a couple of magazines at the grocery store—" She stopped talking to rearrange the way her carrot-orange curls fell over her bare shoulders. "—but there weren't any pictures of 'the victim', and it faded away pretty quickly... really, it could've been *so much* worse."

Maura may have been unaware of Brett's increasing agitation, but I wasn't. Time for our graceful exit from this little conversation, before Brett came unglued. But I had to admit that Maura had made some legitimate points: Steven Percy *had* successfully avoided a trial, major publicity, and a sizeable prison sentence, which didn't sit too well with my husband. On the other hand, he *had* gotten punished, and more importantly, if he wanted to salvage his career, he'd be forced to stay far away from Central/Northern New Hampshire.

It was my turn to step out in front of Brett; I was capable of protecting *him* too. "Well, Maura, you guys have fun. Have you hit the buffet yet?" I nodded toward the long (flamboyantly colorful) buffet table. "My father went all out with the food service, that's for sure. I'd suggest you two try the stuffed shells, those things are tasty!" In an effort to encourage Brett to start walking away from Maura and toward our more tactful friends from college, I lightly pushed on his chest, which I could actually feel heating up under his shirt, despite the air conditioning in the Downtown Pub's restaurant. "Don't let what she said get to you, Brett. Especially not today. I'm fine and you're fine and he's in jail, so it all worked out." And now the redirection. "Let's see if Ben and Ally want to dance, okay?"

Brett's twisted expression relaxed a bit, and then he took my hand and led me across the room to our friends' table.

"This is an awesome party, you guys!" Christian was clearly enjoying the buffet. He sat at a table draped in lime green and hot pink-hued tie-dye, two plates, overflowing with food, in front of him. "I might need sunglasses to look at the décor, but the food is amazing. Glad I didn't bring a date; I couldn't chow down like this with a girl around!"

Ian, it just so happened, was wearing shades, but more for the image they projected than for actual eye protection from excessive decorative brightness. He snorted. "I thought I was your date, Chrissy, and I have to say, I like a man who can eat like a man!" He placed both palms boldly on the sides of Christian's face and got himself a kick in the combat boots for his efforts. "Ouch, that fucking hurt!"

"I'm banning all violence at my wedding." I looked at Christian, then Ian, and then back again, a warning in my eyes.

"Well, I'll try to hold back, but only if you save me a dance, Mr. Taylor." He linked his arm through mine and then leaned in with a smile. I thought it was a serious request, but it was hard to be certain since I couldn't see Ian's eyes.

"You'll have to check with my husband, the other Mr. Taylor, but it sounds doable."

"I might let ya dance with my husband," Brett teased Ian, "when I'm all tired out and need to take a break from the action. But no funny business, ya hear me?"

"Of course not." Ian leaned in toward Brett and kissed his cheek with a loud smacking sound. "I want you to save me a dance too, Brett-y."

"Oh, yeah… right." And even though it was fairly dim in the restaurant, so I couldn't see the proof, I knew that Brett was blushing.

"Let's hit the dance floor. I want us to show Missy, here, how real men move." Hunter, it appeared, had taken more than a passing interest in Barry Janek's little sister, who had come to the wedding as her big brother's date. Apparently, his interest in the young lady even trumped his interest in the buffet; he practically swept her off to dance with him.

On our way to the dance floor, Ally pulled me aside. "This is a beautiful wedding, Cory, and you and Brett are certainly handsome grooms."

"Thanks, sweetie, and I agree. My dad definitely got the details right today." I couldn't hold back a grin as I stepped beneath the huge rainbow balloon arch that you had to walk under to get onto the little dance floor that had been set up near the entrance to the kitchen. Between the decorations that he'd obviously contemplated quite carefully, the long buffet table, jam-packed with Italian food that was pushed against the far wall, and the music, my father had certainly made up for lost time in terms of spoiling his son.

I glanced over to where Roderick stood behind the microphone with his ramshackle band. They actually sounded great, but I wouldn't have cared if they'd totally sucked, because my father had done all of this for me. He'd invited everyone I loved, all of whom I considered to be my family, had given me away with a father's share of tears, and he'd even written a few "I'm sorry/forgive me/I love you/let me make it up to you" types of songs, which he'd dedicated to me, and sang with a penitent voice. And a contrite expression.

When Dad saw my husband and I approach the dance floor, he spoke quietly to his band, sent a wink over to Brett, and began to sing his a cappella rendition of Lifehouse's "Everything," which was perfect and romantic, especially once Brett took me in his arms.

Brett

DIDN'T never think a day could be fuckin' perfect, that is, not 'til today happened.

Me and Cory's weddin' day was blue-skied and breezy, just like how I knew it'd be. We got hitched out in the back parkin' lot of the Downtown Pub, right near the place where us two met. *(Maybe a dumpster backdrop don't seem romantic to you, but we had us our reasons.)*

The first thing I'd noticed when my baby stepped outta the back door of the pub, his dad grippin' onto his arm like Cory was *his* anchor, was them gorgeous eyes. So fuckin' brilliant, sparklin' just like them sapphires in our wedding bands—we went and got me one to match Cory's—and them eyes was shinin' at me. *Just for me.* That sight nearly brought me to my knees, and I ain't fuckin' with ya. In that there white tux, well, Cory was an angel. Didn't say *like* an angel, so's please don't get me wrong on this; that boy *was* an angel to me. It was a fact he was beautiful, that dark silky hair swishin' around his perfect face in the breeze, and he looked slim and fragile, but not frail, standin' beside his father.

About twenty of our friends (who me and Cory secretly considered to be our put-together family) stood outside with us as we tied the knot, all official-like. Gotta say, we had us some classy groomsmen and a coupla nice-lookin' groomswomen too, who'd stood beside us when we done the deed, all of them as important to us as any fathers, brothers, and sisters coulda been: Brian, Jon, Barry, Ian, Maura, and Ally. The food at the party wasn't too shabby, neither, mostly Italian with a sorta down-home flare, and the music—well, some of them tunes Roderick wrote for Cory woulda broke my heart in two if I'd let 'em.

Bubbles flew and cameras flashed and people danced.

But none of that there is what's makin' my day fuckin' perfect.

On the dance floor, I reached down to take ahold of the *real* reason that today was fuckin' perfect, and just like I knew he'd do, Cory raised his arms, and then them beautiful eyes, to me. And I hadta smile right then for another reason too; 'cause outta the corner of my eye, I caught me a glimpse of Roderick over there where the band was sittin', wavin' and winkin' at me before he started singin' that tune called "Everything." (Okay, so's maybe I mentioned to my father-in-law-to-be a coupla times how much that there song meant to me, 'cause Cory surely was *my* everything.) Uh-huh. Cory *was* my strength and my hope and my light. Just sayin'. And Cory liked the song too. When he smiled up into my face I felt more alive, like God had just breathed insida me.

Us two sure didn't need no piece of paper to know that we was forever partners, but somethin' kinda old-fashioned that lived deep down insida my heart felt warm and satisfied 'cause we now had it.

Time to call a spade a spade, huh? I was fuckin' thrilled down to my very bones to have a piece of paper that said Cory and me was legally married. Was most prob'ly gonna find me a purple frame and hang it up over our bed.

"This day… it's perfect, Brett."

"You, that's what's perfect."

And on that there dance floor we clung tight together, kinda the same way as we had since we was just a coupla broken and lonely teenagers. Sure, me and Cory was now bonded together on account of the love in our hearts that'd growed like a wild grape vine over the past five years, but now we was also bound in the eyes of our family and friends and the law and God, so's neither of us needed one thing more.

Roderick sang them words of my heart, and I slow danced underneath a gigantic balloon rainbow, holdin' my own personal pot of gold in my arms.

There wasn't no more unfinished business in our lives; me and Cory was complete.

MIA KERICK is the mother of four exceptional children—all named after saints—and five nonpedigreed cats—all named after the next best thing to saints, Boston Red Sox players. Her husband of twenty years has been told by many that he has the patience of Job, but don't ask Mia about that, as it is a sensitive subject.

Mia focuses her stories on the emotional growth of troubled men and their relationships, and she believes that sex has a place in a love story, but not until it is firmly established as a love story. As a teen, Mia filled spiral-bound notebooks with romantic tales of tortured heroes (most of whom happened to strongly resemble lead vocalists of 1980s big-hair bands) and stuffed them under her mattress for safekeeping. She is thankful to Dreamspinner Press for providing her with an alternate place to stash her stories.

Mia is proud of her involvement with the Human Rights Campaign and cheers for each and every victory made in the name of marital equality. Her only major regret: never having taken typing or computer class in school, destining her to a life consumed with two-fingered pecking and constant prayer to the Gods of Technology.

Contact Mia at miakerick@gmail.com.

Also from MIA KERICK

Beggars and Choosers

Mia Kerick

http://www.dreamspinnerpress.com

www.ingramcontent.com/pod-product-compliance
Lightning Source LLC
Chambersburg PA
CBHW071006280626
47160CB00015B/1425